THE BROKEN BUBBLE

Books by Philip K. Dick

THE
BROKEN
BUBBLE

PHILIP K. DICK

ARBOR HOUSE | William Morrow

NEW YORK

Library of Congress Cataloging-in-Publication Data

Dick, Philip K.
  The broken bubble.

  I. Title.
PS3554.I3B76   1988   813'.54   88-914
ISBN 1-55710-037-3

Printed in the United States of America

First Edition

1 2 3 4 5 6 7 8 9 10

THE
BROKEN
BUBBLE

1

Luke trades big. Summer is here and Luke is mighty ready to make a deal with you, mighty ready, at three big lots, all of them busting with cars—cars—cars. What d'you think your old car's worth? Maybe it's worth more than you think on a brand-new Plymouth or Chevrolet four-door sedan or a Ford custom deluxe Ranch Wagon. Luke is trading big these days, buying big and selling big. Luke thinks big. Luke is *big!*

Before Luke came, this wasn't much of a town. Now it's a really big car town. Now everybody drives a brand-new DeSoto with power windows, power seat. Come see Luke. Luke was born in Oklahoma before he moved out here to great old sunny California. Luke moved out here in 1946 after we beat the Japs. Listen to that sound truck that's going up and down the streets. Listen to it go; it goes all the time. It pulls that big red signboard along, and all the time it's playing the "Too Fat Polka" and saying "Regardless of the make or condition of your old car . . ." Hear that? It don't matter what kind of old heap you got. Luke'll give you two hundred dollars for it if you can drag walk tow push it into the lot.

Luke wears a straw hat. He wears a double-breasted gray suit and he wears crepe-soled shoes. In his coat pocket he carries three fountain pens and two ballpoint pens. Inside his coat is an official *Blue-Book.* Luke takes it out and tells you what your heap is worth. Look at that hot California sun pouring over Luke. Look at his big face sweat. Look at him grin. When Luke grins, he slips twenty bucks into your pocket. Luke gives away money.

This is Automobile Row; this is the street of cars, Van Ness Ave-

1

nue, San Francisco. Windows on all sides, all along and up and down, glass with words written in red-and-white poster paint; banners are pasted up high, and flags flutter, and over some lots are wads of colored aluminum strung on wire. And there are balloons and, in the evening, lights. At night the chains go up, the cars are locked, but lights come on, fine spotlights, fine big beams of color frying the bugs. And Luke has his clowns, his painted lady and gent clowns; they stand on top of the building and wave their arms. Luke has his microphones, and the salesmen call to people. Free quart of oil! Free dish! Free candy and cap gun for the kids. The steel guitar sings, and how Luke likes that. It sings like home.

Bob Posin, holding his initialed briefcase, wondered if he had been recognized as a salesman, which in fact he was. He put out his hand, saying, "I'm Bob Posin. From radio station KOIF. Station manager." He was now at Looney Luke's Used Car Lot, trying to sell air time.

"Yeah," Sharpstein said, picking his teeth with a silver toothpick. He wore gray slacks and a lemon yellow shirt. Like all the West Coast used car dealers, his skin was baked red and dry, flaky around his nose. "We were wondering when we'd hear from you."

They meandered among the cars.

"Nice-looking cars you have here," Posin said.

"All clean," Sharpstein said. "Every one a clean car."

"Are you Luke?"

"Yeah, I'm Luke."

"You thinking of doing anything over the air?" That was the big question.

Rubbing his cheekbone, Sharpstein said, "What sort of coverage your station got?"

He gave an estimate twice the actual size; in these times he was willing to say anything. Television was getting the accounts, and nothing was left now but Regal Pale beer and L & M filter cigarettes. The independent AM stations were in a bad fix.

"We've been having a few spots on TV," Sharpstein said. "Works out pretty good, but they sure cost."

"And why pay for coverage of the whole Northern California area when your customers are right here in San Francisco?" He had a talking point there. Station KOIF with its thousand watts of operating

2

power reached as many people in San Francisco as did the network AM and TV stations, and at a fraction of the cost.

They strolled to the car lot office. At the desk Posin scratched figures on a pad of paper.

"Sounds good to me," Sharpstein said, his arms behind his head, his foot up on the desk. "Now tell me something. I have to admit I never got around to hearing your station. You got some kind of schedule I can see?"

KOIF went on the air at five forty-five A.M. with news and weather and Sons of the Pioneers records.

"Yup," Sharpstein said.

Then five hours of popular music. Then noon news. Then two hours of popular music from records and transcriptions. Then "Club 17," the kids' rock and roll show, until five. Then an hour of Spanish-language light opera and talk and accordion music. Then dinner music from six until eight. Then—

"In other words," Sharpstein said, "the usual stuff."

"Balanced programming." Music, news, sports, and religious. Plus spot plugs. That was what kept the station alive.

"What about this?" Sharpstein said. "How about a plug every half hour between eight A.M. and eleven P.M.? Thirty one-minute spots a day, seven days a week."

Posin's mouth fell open. Jesus Christ!

"I'm serious," Sharpstein said.

Sweat fell from Posin's arms into his nylon shirt. "Let's see what that would run." He wrote figures. What a bundle. Sweat stung his eyes.

Sharpstein examined the figures. "Looks okay. It'll be tentative, of course. We'll try it a month and see what kind of response there is. We haven't been satisfied with the *Examiner* ads."

"Nobody reads that," Posin said hoarsely. Wait, he thought, until Ted Haynes, the owner of KOIF, was informed. "I'll do your material myself. I'll handle the material personally."

"You mean write it?"

"Yes," he said. Anything, everything.

Sharpstein said, "We'll supply the material. It comes from Kansas City, from the big boys. We're part of a chain. You just put it on the air."

3

***

Radio station KOIF was located on narrow, steep Geary Street, in downtown San Francisco, on the top floor of the McLaughlen Building. The McLaughlen Building was a drafty, antiquated wooden office building, with a couch in the lobby. There was an elevator, an iron cage, but the station employees usually went up by the stairs.

The door from the stairs opened onto a hallway. To the left was the front office of KOIF, with one desk, a mimeograph machine, typewriter, telephone, and two wooden chairs. To the right was the glass window of the control room. The wide-board floor was unpainted. The ceilings, high above, were yellowed plaster, cobwebbed. Several offices were used as storerooms. Toward the back, away from the traffic noises, were the studios; the smaller of the two was the recording studio and the other, with more adequate soundproof doors and walls, was for broadcasting. In the broadcast studio was a grand piano. A corridor divided the station into two sections. The corridor cut off, from the main offices, a large room in which was an oak table on which were piles of folded and unfolded mail-outs, envelopes, cartons, like the workroom of a campaign headquarters. And, next to that, the room in which the transmitter controls were located, the board itself, a swinging mike, two Presto turntables, upright record cabinets, a supply cabinet on the door of which was tacked a photograph of Eartha Kitt. And, of course, there was a bathroom, and a carpeted lounge for visitors. And a closet in which to hang coats or hats, and to store brooms.

A door at the back of the studio corridor opened onto the roof. A catwalk led past chimneys and skylights, to a flight of shaky wooden stairs that connected with the fire escape. The roof door was unlocked. Occasionally station employees stepped out onto the catwalk for a smoke.

The time was one-thirty in the afternoon, and KOIF was transmitting songs by the Crewcuts. Bob Posin had brought in the signed contract with Looney Luke Automotive Sales and had gone out again. At her desk in the front office, Patricia Gray typed bills from the accounts receivable file. In the control room Frank Hubble, one of the station announcers, leaned back in his chair and talked on the telephone. The music of the Crewcuts, from the PM speaker boxed in the upper corner of the wall, filled the office.

4

The stairs door opened, and another announcer entered: a tall, thin, rather worried-looking man wearing a loose-fitting coat. Under his arm was a load of records.

"Hi," he said.

Patricia stopped typing and said, "Have you been listening to the station?"

"No." Preoccupied, Jim Briskin searched for a place to put down his records.

"Some Looney Luke material arrived. Hubble and Flannery have been giving it off and on. Some of it's recorded and some isn't."

A slow smile spread across his face. He had a long, horselike face, and the overgrown jaw that many announcers seem to have. His eyes were pale, mild; his hair was brownish gray and beginning to recede. "What's that?"

"The used car lot up on Van Ness."

His mind was on the afternoon programming. He was planning out "Club 17," his program, his three hours of tunes and talk for the kids. "How is it?" he said.

"It's just awful." She put a page of material before him. Balancing his records against his hip, he read the typed pages. "Will you call Haynes and *read* this stuff to him? Bob called him and slurred over; he just talked about the income."

"Be quiet," he said, reading.

> 1A: The car you buy TODAY from Looney Luke will be a CLEAN car! And it will STAY CLEAN! Looney Luke GUARANTEES IT!
> 2A (Echo): CLEAN! CLEAN! CLEAN!
> 1A: A CLEAN car . . . CLEAN upholstering . . . a CLEAN DEAL from Looney Luke, the volume car dealer who OUT-SELLS in big-volume sales ALL OTHER car dealers in the Bay Area.
> 2A (Echo): SELLS! SELLS! SELLS!

Instructions on the script called for the announcer to record the echo parts in advance; the counterpoint was his own voice, knocking against itself.

"So?" he said. It seemed routine to him, the usual used car pitch.

Pat said, "But that's yours. For the dinner music stretch. Between the *Romeo and Juliet Overture*"—she looked at the evening programming—"and *Till Eulenspiegel.* "

Picking up the phone, Jim dialed Ted Haynes's home number. Presently Haynes's measured voice was heard saying, "Who is calling?"

"This is Jim Briskin," he said.

"On your phone or the station phone?"

"Tell him about the laugh," Pat said.

"What?" he said, putting his hand over the mouthpiece of the phone. And then he remembered the laugh.

The laugh was Looney Luke's trademark. The sound truck carried it about town, and the loudspeakers in the illuminated towers of the car lot blasted it at the cars and pedestrians. It was a crazed laugh, a fun-house laugh; it went around and around, rising and falling, getting down into the belly in a slowed-down manner and then shooting up into the sinuses, all at once a sharp laugh, very shrill, a giggle. The laugh bubbled and simpered; something was wrong with it, something terrible and basic. The laugh became hysterical. Now it could not contain itself; it burst frothily, fragmenting itself. Collapsing, the laugh sank down, winded, gasping, exhausted by the ordeal. And then, dragging in deep breaths, it started over. On and on it went, fifteen hours without letup, rolling out above the shiny Fords and Plymouths, over the Negro in knee boots who washed the cars, over the salesmen in their pastel suits, over the flat lots, the office buildings, the downtown business district of San Francisco, and ultimately over the residential sections, over the apartment houses with their single walls joining them in rows, over the new concrete houses near the Beach, over all the houses and all the stores, all the people in the town.

"Mr. Haynes," he said, "I have some Looney Luke material here for the dinner music program. This stuff isn't going to go over, not with the kind of audience I have. The old ladies out by the Park don't buy used cars. And they turn this stuff off as fast as they can get to the radio. And—"

"I see your point," Haynes said, "but it's my understanding that

Posin agreed to air Sharpstein's material straight across the board each half hour. And anyhow, Jim, this is in the nature of an experiment."

"Okay," he said. "But when we're through, we won't have any old ladies or any other sponsors. And by that time Luke will have dumped his ninety carloads of '55 Hudsons or whatever it is he's pushing, and then what? You suppose he's going to keep this stuff up after he breaks the back of the other lots? This is just to knock them off."

"You have a point," Haynes said.

"Darn right I have."

"I suppose Posin bit on this."

"Afraid so."

Haynes said, "Well, we've signed the contract. Let's go ahead and finish out our commitment to Sharpstein, and then in the future we'll be more wary of this sort of thing."

"But," Jim said, "you mean you want me to go ahead and give this on the dinner music? Listen to this." He reached for the script; Pat handed it to him.

"I know how it reads," Haynes said. "I've caught it on the other independents. But I feel, considering the signed contract, we're really obliged to go ahead with it. It would be bad business to back out."

Jim said, "Mr. Haynes, this will kill us." It would kill sponsorship of the classical music, anyhow. The little restaurants who supported classical music would back off, would vanish.

"Let's give it a try and see," Haynes said, with the tone of judgment. "Okay, boy? Maybe it'll work out to the good. After all, this is currently our heaviest advertising account. You must take the long-term view. Now perhaps a few of those little fancy restaurants will act huffy for a while . . . but they'll be back. Right, boy?"

They argued a little longer, but in the end Jim gave up and said goodbye.

"Thanks for calling me," Haynes said. "I'm glad you feel you want to discuss this sort of problem with me, out in the open where we can talk about it."

Putting the phone down, Jim said, "Luke's cars are *clean* cars."

"It's on, then?" Patricia said.

***

7

He took the script into the recording studio and began putting the "2A (Echo)" part onto tape. Then he switched on the other Ampex and taped "1A" also, and combined both so that at program time he had only to start the transport going. When he had finished, he rewound the tape and played it back. From the speakers his own professional announcer's voice said: "The car you buy *today* from Looney Luke . . ."

While it played, he read over his mail. The first cards were requests from kids for current pop tunes, which he clipped to his continuity for the afternoon. Then a complaint from a businessman, a practical outgoing individual protesting that too much chamber music was being played on the dinner music program. Then a sweet note from a very gentle little old lady named Edith Holcum, who lived out in Stonestown, saying how much she enjoyed the lovely music and how glad she was that the station was keeping it alive.

Blood for his veins, he thought, putting her letter where he could refer to it. Something to show the advertisers. On went the struggle . . . five years of work, keeping up the pretense that this was his interest in life. He was devoting himself to this, to his music and programs. His cause.

From the doorway, Pat said, "You going to play the *Fantastic Symphony* tonight?"

"I thought so."

She entered the room and seated herself across from him, in the comfortable armchair. Light flashed, a spark of yellow, as she lit a cigarette with her lighter. A present from him, given three years ago. Her legs rustled as she crossed them, smoothed her skirt. At one time she had been his wife. A few trivialities still connected them; the Berlioz symphony was one. An old favorite, and when he heard it, the whole background swam up: smells, tastes, and the rustle, as now, of her skirt. She liked long heavy colorful skirts and wide belts and the kind of sleeveless blouse that reminded him of the chemises of the girls on the covers of historical novels. Her hair, too, was that flowing uncombed mass, dark, soft, and always amiably in her way. Actually she was not large; she weighed exactly 111 pounds. Her bones were small. Hollow, she had once informed him. Like a flying squirrel's.

There had been a number of such similes tying them together; when he remembered, he was vaguely embarrassed.

Their tastes did not basically differ, and it was not on that account that the marriage had collapsed. The inside story he kept to himself, hoping that she had done the same; as office gossip it would have yielded indefinite harvest. They had wanted kids, right away and plenty of them, and when no kids appeared they had consulted specialists and discovered—lo!—that he, of the two of them, was sterile. But that had not been as bad as the next part, which involved Pat's desire to locate what was ingenuously called a donor. The bickering over that had split them up. In all seriousness—but with overtones of self-contempt and rage—he had suggested that she get herself a lover; an affair, with emotional involvement, had seemed more acceptable to him than the science fiction device of artificial insemination. Or, he had suggested, why not simple adoption? But the donor idea intrigued her. His theory—and it had not gone over well with Pat—was that she yearned for parthenogenesis. And so they had gradually lost any real understanding of each other.

Now, glancing up at her, he saw this attractive woman (she was still not over twenty-seven or twenty-eight) and made out, as easily as ever, the qualities that had excited him in the first place. She had a genuine feminineness about her, not merely a daintiness, or a diminutiveness, or even a gracefulness; those were present, but in addition he recognized in her a basically active spirit.

Across from him, Pat said in a low voice, "Do you know what this Looney Luke business means? It means the end of your classical music. He'll want Okie music, steel guitars, Roy Acuff. You'll be squeezed out. The old ladies won't listen . . . the restaurants won't keep on with us. And you—"

"I know," he said.

"And you're not going to do anything?"

"I did what I could," he said. "I made my gesture."

She arose and put out her cigarette. "The phone," she said.

In a sweep, a flow of color, she passed him. The brightness of her blouse brushed by. Buttons, too, at the center.

How odd, he thought. Once, with his love for her, he had been on the proper track, a good husband. Now, if the idea came to him, it was a sin, and the act itself was unthinkable. Time and intimacy, the incongruity of life. He watched her go, feeling lonely, feeling that perhaps he did not have the answers even yet. The principle of expectation . . . in him yet was this model, this standard of judgment. They had been divorced for two years, and in that time he had not seen anyone who could equal her.

I hang around her, he thought. I still have to be somewhere nearby.

Returning to his records and letters, he prepared notes for his dinner music program.

2

At five in the afternoon his program of popular music and talk for teenagers ended. Usually he went across the street and ate dinner in a booth in the back of the café, with his script beside him, his notes and ideas for the dinner music program.

On this July afternoon, as he finished "Club 17," he noticed before the glass window of the studio a group of teenage kids standing, peering at him. Lifting his hand, he made a motion of recognition. The kids had been in before. The boy with glasses, wearing a sweater and brown pants and carrying a binder and school books, was Ferde Heinke, president of a science fiction fan club called The Beings from Earth. Next to him stood Joe Mantila, very dark and squat, like a troll. Joe's shiny black hair oozed oil down his cheeks and neck, down his bumpy flesh to the cultivated fur of his mustache. Beside Joe was Art Emmanual, wearing a white cotton shirt and jeans; he was a good-looking blond kid, with a sturdy face, blue eyes, and great laborer's arms. The first two were still in school, at Galileo High, and Art Emmanual, a year older, was out of school and apprenticed—he had told Jim—to a printer, an old man named Mr. Larsen, who had a shop on Eddy Street and who did wedding announcements and business cards and, occasionally, tracts for fundamentalist Negro religious sects. He was a bright, fast-voiced kid who, when excited, talked with a stammer. Jim liked all three of them. Now, as he left the studio and walked toward them, he thought how important this was to him, this contact with the kids.

"H-h-hey," Art said, "that was a cool show, you know?"

"Thanks," he said.

11

The three kids shuffled shyly. "We gotta go," Joe Mantila said. "We gotta get home."

"How about playing not so much of that sentimental big-band stuff?" Ferde said. "More combo, maybe."

"You coming?" Joe Mantila said to him. "I'll drive you."

Two of them, Ferde and Joe, went off. Art remained. He seemed unusually keyed-up; he stood first on one foot and then the other. "R-r-remember that time," he said, "wh-wh-when you let us sit in the control r-r-room when you were doing the show?" His face lit up. "That was cool."

Jim said, "I'm going across the street and eat. You want to come along and have a cup of coffee with me?" Sometimes kids trailed along with him, asking him questions about radio and music, this and that. He enjoyed their company at dinner; they kept him from feeling lonely.

Glancing around, Art said, "My wife's with me; she wants to meet you. She always listens to your show."

"Your what?"

"My wife," Art said.

"I didn't know you had a wife," Jim said. It had never occurred to him that this eighteen-year-old boy, just out of high school, earning fifty dollars a month, might be married; he had taken it for granted that Art lived with his family in an upstairs room with model airplanes and school pennants stuck up on the walls. "Sure," he said, "I'd like to meet her."

Art's wife was in the station's carpeted lounge.

"This is my w-w-wife," Art said, blushing and, with his hand, touching the girl on the shoulder.

The girl wore a maternity dress. Except at her waist, she was exceptionally thin. Her hair was clipped short, ragged. She wore neither makeup nor stockings. On her feet were flat slippers. She drooped as she waited, and her face was expressionless. She had a narrow, somewhat small nose. Her eyes were striking. The pupils were quite dark, and she gazed in an absorbed, preoccupied way, seeing off into space. She was a rather undernourished-looking girl, but he could not get over her eyes; they certainly were majestic.

"Hi," he said.

"Her name is R-r-rachael," Art said.

The girl was still staring down at the floor. On her forehead was a frown. Then she glanced up at him solemnly. She reminded him of Patricia. Both of them were small-boned. Both had an unkempt animallike toughness. Of course, he realized, this girl was no more than seventeen.

Art said, "R-r-rachael here listens to your show all the time; she's home in the afternoon after she works, fixing dinner. She wanted to come up and meet you."

To the girl Jim said, "Can I buy you a cup of coffee?"

"Oh no," she said. "Thanks."

"Come on," he said. "Across the street with me while I eat dinner. It's on me."

After a glance at each other, they followed. Neither of them had much to say; they were docile but withdrawn, as if a part of their minds was uncommitted.

In the booth, he faced them across his plate of veal chops, his coffee cup, his salad and silverware. Neither Art nor Rachael wanted anything; they sat close together with their hands out of sight. The café was noisy and active; the counter was jammed with diners, and all the booths were filled.

"When's the baby due?" he asked Rachael.

"In January."

"You have room?" he asked. "You've got a place for it?"

"We have this apartment out on Fillmore," Rachael said. "Down in the basement."

"How many bedrooms?"

"One," she said. "And a kitchen and living room."

"How long have you been married?" he asked her.

"Since April 14," Rachael said. "We got married up in Santa Rosa . . . we sort of ran off. You know? I was still in high school, and they didn't think we should get married. We told the license woman we were older. I said I was eighteen, and I wrote a note—I said he's twenty-one." She smiled.

Art said, "She signed the note with my mother's name."

"We used to get out of school that way," Rachael said. "And then we'd walk around town or just sit in the Park. Golden Gate Park. My handwriting looks good." She put her hands on the table, and he was

13

conscious of the long, bony fingers; mature fingers, he thought. Grownup hands.

"A-a-and," Art said, "the sheriff, he was the best man."

"He even had a gun on," Rachael said. "I sort of thought maybe he might do something to us. Take us back. Afterward he came over and shook hands with Art."

"A-a-and the judge said—"

"If we didn't have five dollars to pay him," Rachael said, "we didn't have to. But we did. We hitchhiked up. We stayed there that night with a girl I knew, at her house. We told her family we were camping or something. I don't remember. And then we came back here."

"What happened when they caught up with you?"

"Oh, they threatened us with a lot of different things."

"They said they'd put me in j-j-jail," Art said.

Rachael said, "I told them I was going to have a baby. I wasn't then. So they let us alone." She was pensive a moment, and then she said, "One night we were walking home; we were walking back from a show. And a police car stopped us and made Art stand up against the wall. And they asked us a lot of questions. And they pushed him around."

"There's the curfew," Art said. "We were out after the curfew."

For some reason it had never occurred to him that there was a curfew for kids. "You mean they can pick you up if you're on the street at night?"

"Any kids," Art said. He and his wife nodded somberly.

"And they didn't believe we were married," Rachael said. "We had to go with them in the police car to our place, and show them the license. And while they were inside, in the apartment, they looked all around; you know? They sort of poked into things. I don't know what they were looking for, just looking I guess."

"Well, what did they say?"

"Nothing. They just asked us questions."

"Th-th-they asked what I did for a living," Art said.

"I'll be darned," he said. It was macabre.

"There's a lot of places we can't go," Rachael said. "I mean, even though we're married. They think we're going to bust something or steal something. Because we're kids. Like one time we went into this restaurant, when we were just married. I got my job, this job with the airline I have. I figure out how much tickets cost."

"She's real good at math," Art said.

"And we wanted to go out and have a good time. Go to dinner and everything. And they asked us to leave. That was at this real nice-looking restaurant."

"We didn't have the right clothes," Art said.

"No," she said, "I don't think that was it."

"If we'd had the right clothes, they wouldn't have thrown us out." He nodded vigorously.

"No, it was because we were kids."

Jim Briskin said, "Didn't anybody do anything? Protest or anything?"

"When the police car stopped us that night," Rachael said, "a bunch of people—they were coming out of bars, I guess—stood around and watched. There was these old women, these fat old women in ratty-looking furs. They were yelling something at us. I didn't hear what it was."

"And," Art said, "they're always telling us what to do. Like Mr. Larsen, this old guy I work for, this printer; he's always got some sort of a-a-advice. Like one day he said to me, d-d-don't never give any credit to Negroes. He really hates Negroes. And he does business with them all the time. But he doesn't give them any credit; they have to pay cash."

Rachael said, "I used to know this Negro boy, and my mother and father almost went crazy; they were afraid I might—you know—start going around with him."

"Delinquents," Jim Briskin said, following her account and finding in it no humor, whether in her attitude or in the account itself.

Art said, "That's what one of those old dames was yelling. Delinquents. I heard what she said."

Rachael looked up at him. "Is that what they were saying? I couldn't hear. So much was happening."

"It seems as if there ought to be something you can do," Jim said. "Curfews for kids . . . they could extend that to men in their twenties or whatever they wanted. Why not forty-year-old men with red hair?" Anybody, he thought. Whatever they wanted.

Now, he thought, he was saying "they." He was thinking as Art and Rachael were thinking: in terms of the unyielding "they." But to him the "they" would not be adults; they would be—what? He pondered, drawn into this in spite of himself. Looney Luke, perhaps. Or Ted Haynes. Or, for that matter, anyone and everyone.

But nobody was keeping him out of restaurants. Nobody had halted him at night and shoved him against a wall. So it was in his mind; it was not real. For these kids it was real enough. Civil rights, he thought. The good people talk about civil rights, the protection of minority groups. And then they passed a curfew.

"No children and dogs," he said.

"What?" Art said. "Oh yeah, r-r-restaurants."

He had not expected either of them to understand. But they had. The sign in the restaurant windows in the South: no niggers or dogs. But here it was not Negroes. Not exclusively, anyhow.

Art said, "H-h-hey, how'd you get to be a disc jock?"

"It must make you feel strange," Rachael said, "to know when you say something everybody's listening. I mean, anything you say, like you always say to drive carefully, it's not as if you were just talking to one person."

"It's a living," he said.

"Don't you enjoy it?" The girl's eyes, the immense dark eyes, fixed themselves on him. "It must be very strange. I mean, you must feel funny."

She did not seem able to make herself any clearer than that. Both of them were agitated, trying to put something across to him; the tension reached him but not the meaning.

"No," he said, "you get used to it. You mean if I fluff a line or something? Get a word backwards?"

Rachael shook her head. "No," she said, and she seemed then to drop into a mood; she no longer was trying to talk to him.

Art said, "We better get going. We have to get home."

"Excuse me," Rachael said. She slid to the edge of the seat and stood up. "I'll be right back."

As she went off among the patrons, Jim and Art watched her.

Jim said, "I never realized you were married."

"Just for three months."

"She's very pretty."

"Y-y-yeah," Art said, scratching with his nail at the table.

"How'd you meet her?"

"Bowling. We used to bowl. I mean, I knew her in school. And then we were in this bowling alley, me and Joe Mantila, you know? A-a-and I saw her and I recognized her."

Rachael returned. She carried a small white paper bag, which she placed in front of Jim. "For you."

Opening the bag, he found she had bought him a roll, a sweet Danish pastry roll.

"She likes to do that," Art said, standing up beside his wife. He put his arm around her. "She buys people stuff."

Rachael said, "Would you like to come over sometime and have dinner with us? Maybe some Sunday. We don't know an awful lot of people."

"Sure," he said, also getting up. Automatically he began closing up the white paper bag. Nobody had given him a roll before. He did not know how to react. He was deeply distressed, and he wondered what he could do for them. He grasped the fact that he owed them something.

Pushing back his sleeve to uncover his watch, he said, "You have a car to get home in? Maybe I could—"

"We're not going home," Rachael said. "We thought maybe we'd go to a show."

"Thanks," Art said.

"Maybe some other time," he said. Casting about for something more to offer them, he said, "How would that be?"

"Okay," Art said.

Rachael said, "I'm very glad to have met you." It was a formal little set of words, but she gave the words an energetic push; she twisted them and squeezed them and put them forward in a carefully worked fashion. And then she said, "Did you really mean that, about coming by sometime?"

"Absolutely," he said. And he did.

He watched the two of them go out of the café. Art walked ahead, leading her, holding on to her hand. Her movement was slow. The weight, he thought. Already she was beginning to bulge; the dress lifted out before her, and she walked with her head down, as if she were meditating. At the sidewalk they halted. They did not give the impression of going anywhere in particular, and he had a vision, an image of them wandering along the sidewalk, not noticing anybody, not aware of where they were, drifting on and on until they became tired and went home.

His meal was cold, and he did not feel much like finishing. He paid his check and walked outside, across Geary Street, and back to the station. The impression of Art and Rachael persisted, and he stopped in the front office, marking time before he returned to his job. Over the past years it had been his custom to bring his preoccupations to Pat: he now approached her desk. But all the small objects on her desk were away in the drawers. Her desk was neat and barren. Pat had left the station and gone home.

Was it that late? he wondered.

Going into one of the back rooms, he spread out his records. He continued putting them in order for the evening program. With the records was the Looney Luke copy, and clipped to the copy were sixteen-inch transcription discs which the Looney Luke people had sent over. The discs were canned commercials. He put one of them on a turntable and started the first band playing.

The speaker beneath the turntable said, "Ho-ho-ho-ha-ha-ha-haw-hee-hee-hee-*ho-ho-ho-hawwwwwwwww!*"

Jim put his hands to his ears.

"Yes sir, friends," the speaker declared, "I'm telling you one and all to *come down to Looney Luke's,* where you'll get yourself not only one square deal like you never heard of before, but, my friends, you'll be getting yourself a real all-around clean car you can take out on the highway, friends, and you can drive that car, my friends, all the way to Chi-cawgo. . . ."

In his mind he saw the Kansas City announcer with his wide empty smile, the witless smile with its hanging chin and loose lips. The tone of sincerity . . . faith in the overblown nonsense, in the rotgut. The giggling, vacant, fun-house face that drooled and believed, drooled and believed. He reached to lift the tone arm from the disc.

"Ha-ha-ha, folks," the speaker blubbered, "yes, that's right, ha-ha, Looney Luke'll take that old ho-ho in and give you hee-hee on the line, ha-ha!"

Ha-ha, he thought, stopping the disc. His fingers slipped, and the tone arm swept across the soft plastic surface; the diamond stylus cut a path from the outer rim to the label. Now he had done it. The disc was ruined. Occupational hazard, he thought, listening to the fierce racket as the stylus scored and rescored the label. The label disintegrated and bits of it shredded away and were tossed at him, white particles that were flung out in all directions.

3

That night Bob Posin celebrated the Looney Luke account by giving away a valuable phonograph record from the record library of station KOIF. He had it at home, at his apartment.

"I'll be happy to pay you ten bucks for it," Tony Vacuhhi said, comparing the number on the record label with the slip of paper he had brought with him. "I mean, you know it isn't for me anyhow; what would I want with classical stuff like this? It's for a client. So I'm just going to sell it anyhow; I mean, that isn't right."

Tony, an agent, solicitor, man about town, wore a respectable pin-stripe suit; the night hours were his business hours. His hair was greased back and combed in place. His chin was blue with talcum powder, and the glint of his chitinlike eyes had faded and mellowed at this fine acquisition.

Bob Posin said, "It didn't cost me anything. Take it." He put the record in a sleeve and then into a bag. The record was dusty and worn; it was played every week or so on the Italian-language program Sunday night. The record was Gigli's "Che Gelida Manina," an ancient Victor pressing.

"Just so it's the right one," Vacuhhi said.

"It's the right one." He was in a good humor. "How's Thisbe?"

"Now there's a girl," Tony said.

Bob Posin was tempted to expand his celebration to include Thisbe. "Is she doing anything tonight, to your knowledge?"

"Well, she's down at the Peachbowl, singing. You want to drop down? We could drop by. But I got business; I'll have to let you off. I mean, ʃ can't stick around."

"Wait'll I change my shirt." He took off his shirt and got a clean one from the dresser drawer, a brand-new pink shirt that he had never worn. This was a special occasion.

While he was changing, he turned on the Magnavox combination in the living room. Symphonic music came from the twin speakers; the dinner music program was in progress.

Tony Vacuhhi, reading a magazine he had picked up from the coffee table, said, "You know Thisbe cut a couple of records for Sundial, that outfit over on Columbus. Snappy tunes but nothing right out that might start trouble, if you get my point. How about if I bring them around, you maybe using them on that disc jockey show?"

"Ask Briskin," he said, fixing his tie.

"Maybe she could personally appear," Tony Vacuhhi said. "You ever do things like that? Where she ought to be is on television. Boy, that's no lie, you know?"

"That's where we all ought to be," Posin said energetically. "That's where the money's going; if you wonder why people aren't sitting in bars listening to song stylists, it's the same thing as we're up against with an independent AM radio station. What do people do? They turn on "I Love Lucy," the mass morons. Sometimes eighty million people at once watch that kind of escapist trash. I wouldn't have a TV set around."

The music from the radio ended. Jim Briskin's professional announcer's voice took its place. "The *Romeo and Juliet Overture,* played by Edward van Beinum and the London Philharmonic." For an interval the radio was silent.

"I know what you mean," Tony Vacuhhi said. "All them people at once—"

"Shut up a second," Posin said, smoothing his hair.

Now, from the radio, Jim Briskin's voice continued, "The car you buy today from Looney Luke will be a clean car. And it will stay clean."

Good, Bob Posin thought. He's doing it good.

"Looney Luke guarantees it," Briskin went on, in a firm, clipped voice, a spirited delivery. "Clean! Clean! Clean!" he said. And then, in a reflective voice, he said, "No, I can't give this. I gave it during the afternoon, and that's enough." As if he was speaking to himself.

He said, "And now we'll hear Richard Strauss's tone poem *Till Eulenspiegel.*"

Tony Vacuhhi laughed nervously. "That's funny."

Symphonic music began again. Posin felt the back of his head heat by degrees until it was scorching red. He felt as if his scalp was shriveling under waves of blasting intensity. And all the time he went on fixing his tie, smoothing his hair. He could not believe it.

"I can't believe it," he said. "What did he say—did he say he wasn't going to give it?"

"I don't know," Vacuhhi said uneasily, sensing that something was wrong.

"Of course you know; you heard it, didn't you? What did you hear him say? Did he say he wasn't going to give it, isn't that what he said?"

"Something like that," Vacuhhi muttered.

Posin put on his coat. "I have to go."

"You don't want to go over to the Peachbowl and—"

"No, I don't want to go over to the Peachbowl." He pushed Tony Vacuhhi and his record out of the apartment and slammed the door. "How do you like that?" he said. As the two of them went down the hall, Tony several steps behind, he repeated, "How do you like that? What do you think of a thing like that?"

At the sidewalk he left Tony Vacuhhi and began walking aimlessly. "I can't believe it," he said to himself. "What do you think of a thing like that? Can a man openly do a thing like that?"

To his right was a drugstore. He entered the public phone booth in the rear and dialed the station. Naturally there was no answer. At night the announcer was alone; he worked the board himself, without an engineer. It was hopeless trying to get Briskin at night.

He thought of getting his car from the garage under the apartment building and driving to the station. Leaving the drugstore, he started back up the sidewalk.

A small grocery store was open. Inside, a radio played. The owner and his wife were at the counter listening to Marimba music. Bob Posin stopped at the doorway and yelled, "Hey, can I get something on your radio? I have to hear something; it's important."

The owner and his wife, old people, stared at him.

"This is an emergency," he said, going inside, past the sausages and bins of peas, to the counter. The radio was a tiny wooden Emerson with a trailing antenna. He rotated the knob until he had found KOIF. The owner and his wife, both of them dressed in wool coats, withdrew in an injured fashion, leaving him alone with the radio. They pretended to be doing something else. They did not care what he did.

Still music, he thought. The goddamn music.

"Thanks," he said, hurrying past them, out of the grocery store, and onto the sidewalk. Then he ran back to his own apartment. Panting, he reached his floor and searched in his pockets for his key.

His Magnavox remained on. He paced back and forth as the music finished itself out. During the final coda his impatience became a frenzy. He went into the kitchen for a drink of water; his throat was dry, burned by his agitation. He thought of all the people he could ring up: Sharpstein; Ted Haynes; Patricia Gray; the station's attorney, who was on vacation in Santa Barbara.

The music ceased. He ran back into the living room.

Jim Briskin's cultivated voice came on. "Artur Rodzinski and the Cleveland Orchestra, in Richard Strauss's *Till Eulenspiegel.* From a Columbia Masterworks long-playing record."

Then a pause, a mind-wracking pause.

"I guess," Jim Briskin said, "most of you have been over at Domingo's lately. You've seen the new arrangement of the tables so you can look out over the Golden Gate while you're eating. But I can't help mentioning . . ." He went on, describing, in his usual manner, the restaurant.

Bob Posin picked up the telephone and called Patricia Gray. "Listen," he said. "Did you hear Briskin tonight? Do you have your radio on?" Now the music had returned.

Patricia said, "Yes, I was listening."

"Well?"

"I—listened."

"Did you hear anything?"

Her tone was obscure: he could not pin it down. "I guess I heard."

"The Looney Luke commercial!" he shouted into the phone; his voice bounced back at him, deafening him.

"Oh," she said.

"Did you hear it? What the hell was he doing? Is it my imagination?

23

That's what he said, isn't it? He said he was fed up and he wasn't going to read it, he was tired of reading it."

He got nothing out of her. Disgusted, he slammed down the phone and went back to pacing in front of the radio.

But still the music continued, and still he had to phone somebody. He tried the station again, without results. In his mind he pictured Jim Briskin at the microphone, in the green swivel chair, with the records, turntables, scripts, and tape transport before him, showing no emotion as the red light that indicated the phone blinked on and off.

Standing before his Magnavox radio, Posin realized that he was never going to find out, never going to be sure; he would never get hold of Briskin if he phoned and waited a thousand years. The radio would continue playing music, and he would never hear Looney Luke mentioned again, and it would be nothing but a conjecture of his memory. Already he was losing the sense of conviction.

"Goddamn," he said.

The telephone at station KOIF was still ringing as Jim Briskin shut the equipment down for the night. The time was twelve midnight. The street outside was less active; many of the neon signs were off.

The stairs were dismal as he descended floor by floor to the lobby of the McLaughlen Building. Under his arm was his regular packet of records; they had been borrowed from record shops, and tomorrow they went back into stock.

The night air was thin and cold. He took a full breath.

On the sidewalk he started in the direction of the station's parking lot. But a car at the curb honked. The door opened, and a woman's voice said from far off, "Jim—over here."

He walked toward the car. Drops of night mist gleamed on the fenders and hood. "Hello," he said to her.

Patricia switched on the headlights and started up the engine. "I'll drive you," she said. She had her heavy cloth coat bundled around her, buttoned and tucked under her legs. In the cold, her face was pinched.

"I have my own car. It's in the lot." He did not feel like company.

"We can just drive around, then."

"Why?" But he got in. The upholstery was icy as he adjusted his packet of records beside him.

She drove the car out into traffic among the other cars. Neon signs and headlights sparkled, colors in a variety of sizes. Words flashing on and off. "I phoned the station," she said presently. "But you didn't answer."

"Why should I answer? It's either somebody complaining or somebody with a request. I only have the records I brought; I have to play what I planned to play."

She listened to his short burst of resentment without visible reaction; he saw no response. What a bleak expression, he thought. How set her face was.

"What's with you?" he said. "Why this?"

"I listened," she said. Now her eyes were fixed on him, unwinking, wet. "I heard what you said about the Looney Luke commercial. You must have practiced a long time to say it like that."

"I didn't practice. I started to read it, and then I gave up."

She said, "I see."

"It's the only way I know," he said. "These guys who work in factories throw their shoes into the machinery."

"Is that what you're doing?"

"I guess it's lousy."

"I wouldn't say lousy. Dangerous is what I would say. Fatal, if you want to know what I think."

He said, "You were the one who didn't want me to read the thing."

"I—" She closed her eyes for a moment.

"Watch the traffic," he said.

"That's not what I wanted you to do. I wanted you to make some sort of rational protest. Well, it doesn't matter now."

"No," he said. "I guess it doesn't."

"What are you going to do?"

"I can get a job easily enough. I know people in the area. If I have to, I can go to the East Coast."

"You don't think this will follow you."

"There's an announcer," Jim said, "who today has a half-hour TV show coast to coast, who once on a network radio show told his listeners to pour Jergens' lotion in their hair. He was so crocked he could barely stagger through the show. And it was only a fifteen-minute show."

"What are your plans? Do you have anything worked out?"

"I just want to go home and go to bed."

She made a right turn and brought the car around in front of the McLaughlen Building once more. "Look, go get your car and follow me. And we'll both go have a drink at your place or my place."

"You think I'm going to go berserk?" he said.

"And maybe listen to old Mengelberg records," she went on, as if he had not spoken.

"What old Mengelberg records? Those old worn-out clunks we built our marriage on?" Broodingly, he said, "I guess you did get most of them."

"You kept *Les Préludes,*" she said, "which was the only one either of us really wanted."

And he had kept the *Leonore No. 3,* but she didn't know about that. During the vindictive days of dividing up their possessions—under the California Joint-Property Settlement Act—he had told her fables, and one of the fables was that the records in the album were broken. Sat on, he had said; one night, at a party, she had done the sitting on a whole chairful of albums.

"Sure," he said, "why not?"

He went to his car, started it up, and in it followed Pat's cream-and-blue Dodge up Geary Street, past Van Ness, and then up the hill on the far side.

Ahead of him the taillights of the Dodge blinked red, massive coils like the turrets in a pinball machine. He could not see her; he followed the taillights of her car. Here and there, he thought. Wherever she went. Uphill and down. Like a child's fantasy of faith. And so, he thought, they lived happily ever after, the two of them in their cottage on the side of the hill, the two of them in their candy-bar home where nobody could find them. The Dodge stopped—its brake lights blazed warningly—and he wondered where he was; he had lost track of the streets. The Dodge's turn signal blinked, and the car turned left. He followed.

The Dodge was at the curb, and he almost went on past; he heard the sound of her horn at the instant he realized she had stopped. How few times, he thought, he had been here to this apartment. The location, the address were shut out of his mind, as if the place did not exist. Twisting his neck, he began to back the car against traffic. The Dodge was directly beside his car, and now he was pulling behind it,

26

parking parallel to it. The red taillights dazzled him. A variety of lights, turn lights, brake lights, white backup lights; they made his head hurt. The gaudy bedroom-and-chrome cars, he thought. Carpets and record players. He shut off his headlights, rolled up his windows, and stepped out onto the sidewalk.

Pat stood shivering, her arms folded, as he locked his doors.

"It's the fog," she said, as they walked up the broad concrete steps of the apartment building. The door was bronze and glass, locked. They had to wait while she found her key. The hall inside was soundless. On each side of them the doors were shut. Everyone here, he thought, believed in the good solid things of life. To bed at eleven, up at six.

Trustingly, he went along after her, letting her find the right door. She seemed to know; her long dark hair bounced at the collar of her coat as she trotted over the carpet. Her heels made no sound. Like a long vault, he thought, a passage into the side of the mountain.

The door was open, and she was inside the apartment, switching on lights. As she reached to pull down the window shades, he said, "These big apartment houses—they're clammy."

"Oh no," she said matter-of-factly.

"It would bother me, each person retiring to his sealed chamber."

Still in her coat, she bent to light the heater. "You're just full of morbid images." Going to the closet, she took off her coat and hung it on a hanger. "You know, in some ways you're rational and in other ways you're erratic and nobody can tell what you're going to do; you just stand there with a blank look, and nobody can reach you or get across to you, and then finally, when we've all exhausted ourselves talking and waving our hands in front of your face—" She closed the door to the hall; the door banged. "Then you suddenly come to life and start charging everything in sight."

He went into the tiny clean-sparkling kitchen to see about drinks. In the refrigerator was a bowl of potato salad. When Pat came in, she found him eating the potato salad from the bowl with a soupspoon he had pulled out of the sink.

"Oh god," she said. Lines formed about her eyes and spread like minute cracks to her lips and chin. "You make me feel like crying."

"Old times?" he said.

"No. I don't know." She blew her nose. "I hope for your sake you can survive this. I'll do what I can to smooth it over, at the station. I think I can talk to Haynes better than you or Bob Posin."

"You're a great one to smooth," he said.

She said, "All right, and you might consider this: you talk about going to another station. Do you think you'll get away from Looney Luke? That stuff is on all the independents and on the network AM stations and on TV; I heard it the other night late, on TV, after the movie. So what good will it do? Are you going to quit when they give you Looney Luke commercials? And are you going to confine it to Looney Luke? Why just Looney Luke? What about the bread commercials and the beer commercials? Why be arbitrary? Don't read any of them. Isn't that so? Aren't you being arbitrary? And you pretend I wanted you to do something like this, I'm somehow responsible." She was yelling at him in a little high-pitched shrill whistle of a voice, her old domestic-argument voice. "Isn't that right? Aren't you trying to pretend it's my fault? I put you up to this or something—God knows what. You know this wasn't what I meant. I wanted you to do something rational, show Haynes it wouldn't go on the dinner music program. You say you started to read it, and then you just gave up. Why did you give up? Why did you have to say that over the air? Why couldn't you just—not have started it? You can't say things like that over the air; you can't say you won't read it, you're tired of reading it."

"Take it easy," he said.

"This finishes you," she said. "God, I had such high hopes for you—and you're winding up nowhere, nowhere at all. Just because you couldn't go out and meet this rationally, and go to Haynes and discuss it before you went on the air; no, you had to wait until you had the script in your hands and you were alone in the station, and maybe then you felt safe, you could get away with it, and then you opened your mouth and fucked up the script so that god knows what sort of grief we're in for, maybe a lawsuit, maybe a fine by the FCC. And what about your music? What about the five years you worked fixing it up with them so you could play classical music, whatever you liked; they even let you pick it out and call it your show, like "Club 17." Are you just going to junk that? Isn't that what this is all about? Weren't you trying to protect that in the first place? Isn't that why you didn't want to read the commercial? You didn't want to offend the old ladies, and now you just throw away the whole program, much more than reading it would have. I don't understand you. I can't make any sense out of it."

"Okay," he said.

"Five years," she said. "Wasted. Thrown away."

As he figured it, he had put at least ten years into the hopper getting this far. First there were the four years at Cal, getting his B.A. in the music department under Elkus, the counterpoint and composing. Then the two postgraduate years, doing a little conducting, singing (a so-so baritone) in their own group, the Marin Choral Singers, writing a moribund cantata dealing with peace among nations and the like. Then his fine job at the NBC music library: the Big Move to San Francisco, away from the university. Eleven years, he decided. Lord, it was almost twelve. He had first gone on the air as a private record collector—a discophile, as the term had it—and his easy delivery, his lack of snobbishness and pedagoguery, had put his program over long after the notion of inviting collectors had withered. He had a natural radio personality; he talked spontaneously, directly, without the customary rhetoric of the classical music fancier. And most important of all, he liked all kinds of music—classical and pop and moldly-fig jazz and progressive Los Angeles jump.

He said, "No, I didn't do it to get away from Luke."

"What then?" she said.

"To get away from you. Or maybe to get closer to you. Probably both. It's intolerable as it stands. Seeing you every day at the station. Do you realize, a couple of years ago you and I were married? Remember that?"

"I remember," she said.

"What a diabolical business."

She said, "Like—who was it?"

"Somebody. Somebody in a myth. Separated by the winds of Hell."

"It's your own fault."

"It is?" he said.

"It's this same kind of thing, this purposeless wandering activity."

"Plus," he said, "the slides in Doctor—what was his name, McIntosh?"

29

"Yes," she said, "McIntosh. Plus what you couldn't see letting happen because it might wound your vanity; it might have made you feel superfluous."

"There's no point in arguing it out now," he said.

"No," she agreed.

He said, "The only thing I don't understand is the picture I get, probably inaccurate. But I see you sitting around the place that Saturday afternoon by yourself, meditating everything over rationally in your mind, and then, click, you had it worked out. As calm and cold-blooded as—" He lifted his hands.

"I thought it over for months," she said.

"But you came to your conclusion like an IBM machine." And then, he thought, after that there was no talking to her. No arguing, no discussing. Not after her mind was made up. Their marriage had been a mistake, and the next question had to do with how to divide up the joint possessions and how to get the thing through court as cheaply and simply as possible.

The hiring of mutual friends, he thought; that was the really evil part. Sending them down—picking them up in the car and driving them down—to the courthouse, to testify to the travesty he and she had invented. What a pitiless time that had been.

Across from him, Pat said, "The phone's ringing."

"What?" he said. It was, but he had not even heard it. Still ringing, even here, at her apartment. "So it is," he said, glancing around.

"I'll get it." She disappeared into the living room. "Hello?" he heard her say.

He opened the refrigerator and examined the unopened fifth of Gilby's gin, excellent stuff, and a cheap vermouth, and a pint of vodka, and wine of every description. The Gothic script on the label of a Mai Wein bottle attracted him, and he began to translate the German.

Pat appeared in the kitchen doorway. "It's Ted Haynes."

He went stiff-legged into the living room. "Does he want me?"

"He wants to know if you're here." She had her hand over the receiver, but he had never believed in that; he knew that the other person could still hear. They got the sound through the Bakelite, as the deaf person got sound through the bones of his skull.

"Sure I'm here," he said.

Pat said, "He's so mad he can hardly talk."

"Well," he said, still holding the bottle of German wine, "I guess Posin must have called him."

"Don't blame Bob," she said. The phone dipped, and he took it from her. "Don't blame him or me."

When he took the phone, Haynes's voice said hoarsely in his ear, "Jim, a man named Sharpstein called me just now here at my home and said they're canceling, and if they ever see our sales representative near their lots they'll call the police and have him thrown into the street."

"Sharpstein," he said. "He must represent them or something. What's his first name? Luke?"

"I'd like to see you in the next half hour, preferably at the station, or if you feel you can't make it down there again on your own time I'll meet you where you are now. You're at Pat's apartment; that's not very far from where I am. If you're going to be there for a while, I'll drop over and we can settle this on the spot."

His brain was too fuzzy; he could not follow what Haynes was saying. "If you want," he said.

"I want you to call Bob Posin and ask him to come over so he can be present. It isn't essential, but he's more familiar with the union rulings than I am; I have no time to memorize that sort of business. I have too many other important things on my mind to waste my time with that. All right then, I'll see you where you are now in about fifteen minutes."

"Goodbye," Jim said.

The phone clicked first, before he was able to get the receiver down. He felt childishly defeated.

"Did they hear?" Pat said. "Did the Luke people hear?"

He said, "I have to call Bob Posin."

As he reached to take up the telephone book, Pat said, "It's on the cover. By the corner."

"Oh?" he said, with rage. "You keep it handy?"

"Yes, I keep it handy."

"What's this?" he demanded.

"What do you mean, what's this? Oh my god." She walked out of the living room: a door slammed, probably the bathroom door. He stood a moment, and then he dialed Bob Posin's number. There was only the one brief buzz and then Posin's voice saying, "Hello?"

"This is Jim Briskin," he said.

"Oh, did Haynes get hold of you?"

"Yes."

"He wanted to get hold of you." Posin's voice had a muted quality, as if his own rancor had been punctured; as if, Jim thought, now that Haynes had come onto the scene Bob Posin was bowing out. "Say," Posin said, "that was quite a stunt you pulled tonight."

"Tell me," Jim said, "how did the Luke people get into it? Were they listening?"

"Yes, as a matter of fact they were. Just a minute." A long minute and then Posin was back. "I had a cigarette going. Say, well, apparently they were gathered around the radio. Can't hear enough of their own bilge, I suppose. Something on that order. He must really have hit the roof. I got this all secondhand, of course. He—Luke Sharpstein, I mean—called Haynes, and Haynes got hold of me; he was looking for you. By that time you had left the station."

Jim said, "I'm over at Pat's."

"I see," Posin said. "Well, how about that."

"Haynes told me to call you," Jim said. "You're supposed to be here. He's coming over in fifteen minutes or so."

"What's he want me around for? To hold the bowl, I guess. You know, the bowl under the neck, after they make the cut."

"I'll see you, then," Jim said and hung up. This time he was the first to get the phone onto the hook.

Pat had come back out of the bathroom. She was in the process of fixing her hair, putting it up for the night. "Did you tell him to come here?" She seemed to have settled down a trifle; her voice was less uneven. "It's almost one o'clock."

"Not my idea," he said. "Haynes is coming too. Both of them."

"Now I'll tell you exactly what to say," she said. "I was working it out while you were talking."

"More smoothing," he said.

"You tell them, yes, of course, you stopped in the middle of the commercial; you admit they heard you. But here's why you did it; you decided a lot of entertainers like Arthur Godfrey and Steve Allen and all those have been more successful with an—"

"Okay," he said. "I'll tell Sharpstein and Haynes and Posin that. I'll tell them I wanted to be another Henry Morgan. Remember him?"

"Yes," she said.

"It's hard to," he said. "It really takes you back."

She said, "Henry Morgan is on television; he's on the 'Garry Moore Show.' Every week."

Shrugging, Jim said, "It doesn't matter. I have nothing to tell them. Let's just get it over. I'm sorry it has to be here in your apartment. That wasn't my idea."

She stood considering, meditating. Then she returned to the bathroom and resumed what she was doing to her hair. He remembered the nightly setting. The metal clips, the cloth, the smell of shampoo and wave lotion, the bottles and cotton pads. Her back to him, she said, "Can I ask you something?"

"Okay," he said.

Her hands worked methodically at the base of her skull, lifting her hair, sorting, massaging, putting the hair in place. "Do you want me to quit my job? Would you feel easier if I left the station?"

"Too late for that now."

"I could." She turned toward him. "I've been giving a great deal of thought to that. I might anyhow, no matter how this turns out."

He had no answer for that. Sitting down on the couch, he waited for Bob Posin and Haynes.

"Do you understand what I'm talking about?" she said.

"Sure I understand; you want to get married. Don't they all want to get married? But this time make sure. Get him up to Doctor McIntosh and get the slides going." It was the meanest thing he could think of, the bitterest remark.

Pat said, "I'm fairly sure."

33

4

Haynes entered the apartment several minutes ahead of Bob Posin. He was a small, rather delicately built gentleman, in his sixties, with luminous white hair and a thin, celluloidlike nose, a nose without bone. The veins on the backs of his hands stood out, blue and distended. His skin was mottled by liver spots, and his walk was the half-shuffle of the elderly professional man.

"Good evening," he said to Patricia. His voice was shaded with elegance. Jim thought of a conductor on a Southern railroad, a rigid old conductor with pocket watch and shiny, black, narrow-pointed shoes.

"Where's Bob?" Pat asked. A heavy damp towel was wrapped around her head, elongating her skull, obscuring her hair; she supported the towel with one hand.

"Parking his car," Haynes said. To Jim he said, "The first thing to get settled is, do you want to continue working for KOIF? Or was this a method of telling us that you intend to leave?"

The question bowled him over. "It sounds as if it's up to me," he said.

"Do you want to leave the station?"

He said, "No."

"What is it then? The summer? Thinking about fishing in the mountains?"

At the door Bob Posin knocked, pushed the door open to look in. "Hard to park," he said, entering. He had on a yellow Aloha sports shirt, hanging out at his waist, and dacron slacks. His hair was uncombed, and he looked seedy and harried.

"Then that's settled," Haynes continued. "As far as I'm concerned, you're a fair enough announcer. We've never had any complaints about you up to now."

"I'll resign," Jim said, "if you want."

"No, we don't want you to resign," Haynes said. His hands behind his back, he went over to the corner of the room and looked at something hanging from the ceiling. "What's this?" He touched it circumspectly. "Is this what they call a mobile? The first one I ever saw made out of—what is this? Eggshells?"

"You want the truth?" Pat said.

"I'll be darned," Haynes said, scrutinizing the mobile. "You made this yourself? Very clever."

Pat said, "I'm going to have to go to bed. I have to be at the station at eight A.M. tomorrow morning. Excuse me." She disappeared into the bedroom. At the door, she stopped momentarily. "You—didn't want to ask me anything about all this, did you?" she said to Mr. Haynes.

"No. I guess not. Thanks. We'll try to keep the voices down."

"Good night," she said. The bedroom door closed after her.

Ted Haynes threw himself down on the couch and faced Jim Briskin and Bob Posin, his hands on his knees. After an interval, Posin also seated himself. Jim did so too.

"You know," Haynes said, "I've been thinking, maybe TV would be the thing you ought to go into." He was addressing Jim. His tone was considerate, the Southerner's tone. The voice of a gentleman. "Ever give any thought to that?"

Jim shook his head.

"I've heard one of the network TV stations is looking for a disc jockey to put up against Don Sherwood. Same sort of thing, talk and spot plugs, interviewing singers and entertainers . . . no records, just live talent from the Bay Area. People appearing at the different spots."

"Sherwood's too good," Jim said shortly.

That settled that.

Scratching the side of his nose, Haynes said, "How about a more secluded job that would get you away from the bustle and pressure of the city, long enough for you to think things over and straighten out your mind. You might like it. The reason I say that is that somebody the other day told me that one of the valley stations—

Fresno or Dixon, some place like that—is looking for a combination man."

"Then you do want me to resign," Jim said.

"No, I don't want you to resign; I just want to find out what's the matter with you."

"Nothing," he said.

"How does this sound, then?" Haynes said. "I'm going to put you on one month's suspension, without pay, subject to the approval of the union. At the end of that time you come into the station and tell us if you want to keep working for us, or if you want to call it quits, and we'll part friends and you can go on to something else, whatever you want."

Jim said, "Suits me."

"Fine," Haynes said. "You haven't had your vacation yet this year, have you? Suppose then we give you a check for what you've worked this month up to now, plus pay instead of the vacation. So it won't hit so hard in the pocketbook."

He nodded.

"Shall we say starting tomorrow?" Haynes said. "Your shift begins at two, doesn't it? I'll have Flannery come in and take it. I suppose either Flannery or Hubble."

"It doesn't matter," he said. "Either of them can handle it."

"How do you feel about this?" Haynes said. "Does it meet with your approval?"

He shrugged. "Why not? Sure it meets with my approval." He went unsteadily into the kitchen and began fixing himself a drink. "Anything for you?"

"Too late at night," Haynes said. He brought out his watch. "You know what I think that mobile is made out of?" he was saying to Posin, as Jim got ice cubes from the refrigerator.

He stood alone in the kitchen, drinking. In the living room Haynes was talking.

"There's only one thing you can be sure of. What sells soap today, stinks tomorrow. There's no charity in the industry. You take somebody like Sherwood; they're reeling him out on a string. A fair question would be, does he know it? Or does he think he's getting away with something? Nobody's going to pay his bills when he stops selling; he's just a new way to sell."

"A new way," Posin said.

"With the illusion of independence."

"A trend," Posin said.

"If you wish, a trend. But suppose he really knocked the sponsors; suppose he stopped smiling as he spills the—what is it?—Falstaff beer. Then they yank him. Of course the problem is that nobody really knows what they want. They're all confused; the whole industry is confused."

"You can say that again," Posin's voice sounded.

"Sherwood is riding on a crest. They're trying him out. If Sherwood went up to the wheels at ABC and said, what is it you really want me to do, they wouldn't be able to tell him."

"They'd be able to tell him, you sell soap," Posin said.

"Yes, they could tell him that. But they wouldn't."

"Pragmatic," Posin was saying, as Jim finished his drink and poured himself a second.

"What happened to Briskin?"

Posin's voice said, "He went into the kitchen."

"Well, go see if he's all right."

Appearing, Posin said, "Are you okay?"

"Sure," Jim said. Leaning against the moist tile of the sink, he drank down his drink.

"I think the thirty-day business is a good all-around solution," Posin said.

"You do?" Jim said.

Haynes, in the living room, said, "I'm going to have to run along. Briskin, you have anything you want to say before we go? Any comments or suggestions?"

Jim walked into the living room. "Mr. Haynes," he said, "what do you listen to when you turn on the radio?"

Gravely Haynes said, "I never listen to the radio if I can help it. I stopped listening years ago."

Both Bob Posin and Haynes shook hands with him, told him when he could expect his check, and then went out of the apartment into the hall.

"Want a ride home?" Posin said to him.

"No," he said.

"You look ready to give out."

37

He began to close the hall door between himself and them.

"Now wait a minute," Posin said. A slow, uneasy flush crept up in his face as he realized that Jim was going to remain behind in the apartment with Patricia.

"Good night," Jim said. He shut the door and locked it. The bell rang instantly, and he opened the door. "What?"

"I think you better come along," Posin said. He was out in the hall alone; Haynes was already on his way to the stairs.

"I'm too sick to come along," Jim said.

"You're not sick; there's nothing wrong with you. You're just too big a slacker to do your job. You got the whole station into trouble and you're just going to stand around slobbering in your drink—"

"Go to hell," Jim said, closing the door. Posin's foot came out, wedging itself in the way.

"Now look here," Posin said shakily. "We're grown men. You were married to Pat, but that's over and done with; you have no claim on her."

"What's your name on the phone book for?"

Ted Haynes, from the end of the hall, said, "Are you coming or aren't you?"

After a brief conflict, Posin withdrew his foot, and Jim closed the door. He locked it and then walked back into the kitchen. Somewhere he had set down his drink; the glass was lost. In the cupboard he found another to take its place.

Good lord in heaven, he thought. The things that could happen to a rational man.

While he was fixing himself another drink, Pat came out of the bedroom in a long, pale blue robe. "Oh," she said, startled to see him.

"I'm still here," he said. "They left."

"I thought you all were gone," she said.

"I'm suspended for a month. Without pay." An ice cube skidded from his hands and onto the floor; he bent to pick it up.

"Starting when?"

"Now. Today."

"That's not so bad. That's not bad at all. He must want to keep you. That'll give you time to think it over." She was watching him warily. The towel was gone; in the bedroom she had combed her hair out, dried it, and fluffed it. Her hair spread out against the collar of her robe, long and soft and dark.

"Nice," he said. Then suddenly he said, "I give up."

She went and got a cigarette. "Go home and go to bed." Clouds of cigarette smoke billowed toward the light mounted over the sink, the plastic-hooded kitchen light. She tossed the match into the sink and folded her arms. "Or do you want to stay here?"

"No," he said. "I'll leave."

Taking his glass from him, she poured the rest of the drink away. "In a month you'll know what it is you want to do."

"I don't want to do anything," he said.

"You will." Again she was watching him, calmly, in her confident manner. "You're lucky, Jim."

"Because he didn't fire me?"

Sighing, she left the kitchen. "I'm too tired to talk about it." She went into the bedroom, put her cigarette in the ashtray on the end table by the clock, and then stretched out on the bed, in her robe, her head on the pillow, her knees drawn up. "What a day," she said.

He came in and sat down by her. "How about getting remarried?"

"What do you mean? You mean you and me again? Are you saying that seriously, or do you just want to see what sort of reaction you'll get?"

He said, "Maybe I'll go up to the cabin."

"What cabin?"

"Yours. On the Russian River."

"I sold it. Last year or the year before. I had to get rid of it . . . I wasn't using it."

"But wasn't that a present from your father?"

"In his will." Her eyes had closed.

"That's too bad," he said, thinking about the cabin, the white boards of the porch, the tank of gas for the stove, half-buried in leaves and dirt, the host of long-legged spiders that had rushed from the water closet the first time he had gone with her to open the cabin up.

"Did you want to go away? Up in the country or something?"

"Maybe," he said.

"I'm sorry about the cabin."

He had met her through the cabin. In the summer of 1951, five years ago, he had wanted to rent a cabin for his two-week vacation; going through the newspaper he had come across the ad for Patricia's cabin and had gone to see her to find out how much she wanted.

"What do you rent it for?" he said.

"Sixty dollars a month. During the summer."

Her family had lived in Bolinas, a fishing town set off by itself on the coast side of Marin County. Her father, before his death, was a rural real estate man, selling lots, farms, summer cabins in the resort areas. In 1951 she was working as a bookkeeper, twenty-three years old, isolated from her family. She had never respected her father; she described him as a windy, beer-drinking old man with varicose veins. Her mother, still living, was a mystic with a tea-reading shop near Stinson Beach. From that had come Patricia's contempt for phony idealism. She lived a brisk, efficient life, rooming with another girl in the Marina, cooking her own meals, washing her own clothes; her only concession to luxury was the buying of an opera ticket or a trip on the Greyhound bus. She loved to travel. And when he had met her, she had owned a set of oil paints and did an occasional still life or portrait.

"Sixty bucks," he said.

It seemed like too much for a cabin. She showed him a photograph of it tacked up beside the mirror of her dressing table. The cabin was on the river. The water was slow, and it spread out into the bushes and grass. In the photograph, Patricia rested with her hand against the railing of the cabin's porch; she wore a wool bathing suit, and she was smiling into the sun.

"That's you," he said.

"Yes. I used to go up there with my brother." Her brother, she told him, was killed during the Second World War.

He asked about seeing the cabin.

"Do you have a car?" She had been hanging clothes on the line in the backyard of the rooming house; it was Sunday, and she was home. "I don't have a car. I haven't been up there since the forties. Somebody up there, a real estate man, a friend of my father's, was keeping it fixed up for us."

He drove her up the coast highway in his car. They left San Francisco at eleven in the morning. At twelve-thirty they pulled off the road to have lunch. They were near Bodega Bay, in Sonoma County, and they ate a meal of prawns dipped in batter, beer, and tossed green salad.

"I like seafood," she said. "We always had fish of some kind. Bolinas is a dairy town, and before my father was a real estate man he was in the dairy business. We used to drive at night in the fog, over Panoramic Highway to San Francisco . . . the fog was so thick he had to open the car door and look down at the white line. Or we would have gone off the road."

She seemed a happy and bright girl. He thought she was exceptionally pretty. She wore a sleeveless blouse and a long skirt almost to her ankles. Her black hair was tied in two braids, and in each braid was a ribbon.

At two o'clock they reached the Russian River. By that time they had stopped for gas and had gone into a roadside tavern, a redwood and neon place where the jukebox was playing "Frenesi." Kids, high school kids in white cotton shorts and shirts, filled up the booths, eating hamburgers and drinking Cokes. The racket was terrific. Both he and Pat had a couple of drinks. They felt good. When they reached Guerneville, on the Russian River, they stopped again at another tavern, also redwood and neon, and had a couple more drinks. By the time they reached the cabin, the time was three-thirty in the afternoon, and they were both pretty well looped.

The cabin was overgrown with weeds and brambles. One of the back windows was broken. The river had, at some recent time, risen and filled the front room with mud. The porch was broken and sagging; the railing, against which she had leaned in the photograph, was gone completely. When they pried the door open—the hinges and lock were rusted—they found that mice and ground squirrels had destroyed the sofa and mattresses and chairs. Somebody had broken in and stolen the pipes from the stove. The electricity was off, and the supply of gas was almost gone.

"Jesus," Patricia said, walking back outside to gaze across the river. "I'm sorry."

He said, "In two or three days it can be fixed up."

"Can it? It looks dreadful." She tossed a stone into the water. On the far side tiny children were paddling. People, on the beach, were sunning themselves. The afternoon air was hot, dry. Around them the bushes rustled with the wind.

"It's nice up here," he said.

He found a shovel and cleaned out the debris, the silt, and rubbish. With the windows and doors open, the cabin aired out rapidly. Pat, using a heavy needle and thread, managed to repair the mattresses to some degree.

"But you can't cook," she said. "How can you fix meals? The stove won't work without pipes."

He had lost interest in that part; he had become interested in her. "They probably have pipes around here," he said. "And glass for the window."

"If you say so," she said.

When the sun began to set, they walked into Guerneville and had dinner at one of the restaurants. After dinner, they sat at the table drinking beer. By nine o'clock neither of them was in any condition to drive back to San Francisco.

"This is a hell of a thing," he said when they left the restaurant. Kids roamed the streets; kids in hot rods screeched by. The night air was pleasant. Off to their left was the river. He could see it glinting. The river did not seem to move at all. Somewhere the Sonoma County people had dammed it up.

Beside him Pat strolled contentedly. "I like it up here." She had changed into jeans and gone wading, her jeans rolled up to her knees. Her legs were smooth, light. She walked barefoot.

"Don't the stones hurt your feet?" he asked.

"Everybody up here walks barefoot," she said. She stumbled a little, and he caught her. "Be careful," she said to him.

"Why?" He held onto her arm.

"I think I'm drunk."

"I think you are too," he said. "I think we both are."

On the bed, her eyes shut, Pat said, "We stayed there that night, didn't we? Was the electricity on?"

"No," he said. "It was still shorted." He had got the lights working the next day.

"Did you make love to me that night?"

"You're darn right I did," he said.

She reached out for her cigarette, stirring on the bed. "Why isn't it like that anymore?"

"Your fault. My fault."

"Nobody's fault," she murmured. He took the cigarette from her fingers; she was dropping it to the covers. "Thanks."

He said, "Remember that beanery down in the Tenderloin?"

"Where we stood," she said. "Where they didn't have chairs or stools. Just the counter. That was where all the longshoremen ate . . . down by the produce area and the docks." Her voice trailed off.

All the various places, he thought. The secondhand record shop on Eddy Street where the old man fussed with the albums, not knowing what he had in stock but knowing everything there was to know about the records themselves. And the nights they had rushed upstairs floor by floor at the War Memorial Opera House, battling to get to the rail first, clutching their standing-room tickets.

And, he thought, the day they had bought the firecrackers and given them to the kids. The illegal firecrackers. They had driven down to San Jose to buy them. Early morning in the San Francisco streets, driving with the car full of fireworks, cones and pinwheels and cherry bombs, giving them away to the kids. And, he thought, then the police.

"They sure got us," he said.

"They?"

"The police. For the firecrackers."

"Yes," she said.

He leaned down and kissed her. She did not protest; she turned a little toward him, drawing her knees up and burying her head down between her arms. Her hair spilled over her shoulders, and he smoothed it away from her face, out of her eyes. "Maybe I will stay," he said. "Can I?"

Presently she said, "Okay."

"I love you," he said. He put his arm under her and lifted her up against him; she was a dead weight, sound asleep, without resistance. "You know that?" he said.

"Yes," she murmured.

"But I'm not good enough for you."

"No."

"Who is?" he said. She did not answer. Her hair brushed against his wrist, and he kissed her again, on the mouth. Her lips gave, and he was conscious of her teeth, her hard teeth, relaxed, apart, and the motion of her breath in her throat.

"No," she said, "we better not." She struggled up. "I'm sorry. I wish we could. We better just go to sleep . . . I think you should sleep above the sheet. So we can't without going to a lot of trouble. Don't you agree?"

"If that's what you want."

She opened her eyes. "It's not what I want. I wish we could . . . maybe we could. No, it wouldn't be right. Come on, get into bed and let's go to sleep. You don't have to get up early tomorrow, but I do; I have to get up at six-thirty."

Going here and there in her apartment, he shut off the heater and the lights and made certain that the door was locked. When he re-entered the bedroom, he found her standing sleepily by the bed, her robe in her arms; he took it from her and hung it in the closet.

"How serious is this business with Posin?" he said.

She shook her head without answering. Already she was in bed, tugging the covers over her; she wore some kind of single-piece material, but he did not see what it was. He did not recognize it. Something new. Something she had bought after she had left him.

As he got into bed, above the sheet, separated from her by the surface of material, she put her arms against him, her fingers pressing against his head. "This is nice," she said, but she was falling asleep; she was drifting away. The outline of her body was vague under the sheet, and he could not reach it. He could not grasp her. When he tried to take hold of her, he found himself holding nothing but material, the uniform cotton material, bleached and absolutely clean and absolutely impersonal. She turned away from him, and that was that.

5

No joy in Fogville.

The other night long- and short-hair disc jock Jim Briskin on radio (recall, you TV addicts?) station KOIF got off a doozy of a reading of a Looney Luke (three ughs and a blah!) commercial right twixt Beethoven and Brahms.

Said Briskin: "Looney Luke sells clean cars." Which Looney Luke thought was fine. And then he said: "That's enough of *that* commercial." Which durn near everyone else in town thought was fine. So now no more Looney Luke commercials on KOIF, because even if you weren't listening the sponsor was.

But now poor Jim's on suspension. Lost a month's pay.

Alas, no justice in this-here world.

From within his concealed and reinforced loft, Ludwig Grimmelman watched the three of them approach. It was late in the afternoon, and the day was hot and fair. The sidewalk sparkled, outlining the figures.

First walked Ferde Heinke in his fairy suit, in his baggy pants and sweater; he wore his glasses and carried a binder full of school and library books and, of course, a number of recent copies of his science fiction magazine, *Phantasmagoria*. After Ferde came Joe Mantila, and then came Art Emmanual.

Grimmelman's loft had once been a union meeting hall. It was a single large barren room with a stove at one end; a small bathroom led to the rear, where the stairs arose. This was in the Hayes Hole section of San Francisco, the slum district of liquor stores and old unpainted rooming houses. Beneath Grimmelman's loft was a series of crib rooms, now used as storerooms for Rodriguez's Mexican and American Foods, the grocery store on the ground level. Across the street was a tiny Catholic church.

As the three of them trudged along, Joe Mantila said, "Let's go get a Coke."

"No," Ferde said, "this is important."

Art Emmanual agreed, "We have to tell him."

They trailed single file along the path of lettuce leaves and torn orange crates by the side of the grocery store. Here and there a chicken stalked, pecking among the weeds. In a rear house an elderly Mexican woman sat on a porch rocking. A gang of Negro and Mexican children scampered after a beer can, kicking it and shouting shrilly as it bounced into the street.

As the three of them reached the stairs, Ferde Heinke stopped. "Of course," he said, "he's probably already heard about it."

"Get going," Art Emmanual said. But he too felt tense. Above them in the loft, Grimmelman was certainly peering; Art could feel the pressure of Grimmelman's eyes, bright little eyes . . . Grimmelman, the hairy owl, in his black wool overcoat, wearing paratrooper's boots, his cheap cotton undershirt showing.

"Okay," Ferde said, starting up the stairs.

At the top was the metal door which Grimmelman had prepared against invaders; it began to open, and by the time they had reached it there was Grimmelman gazing down, grinning and dancing, rubbing his hands together, retreating to admit the callers.

In the light of day he had a ruffled look, a disorder, about him. Expecting no one, he had removed his boots; he waited in his stocking feet. He, in his mid-twenties, born in Poland across the border from Germany, had a round Slavic face; his face was marred with a beard that covered his jowls and neck, a smear like singed pinfeathers. His hair was thinning, and in a few years he would be bald. Art, following Ferde, caught the old-cloth smell of Grimmelman, the familiar staleness of the man's seclusion. Grimmelman dwelt here, laboring on his maps, his revolutionary schemes, the phrasing of his vast theories; in summer, his money gone, he emerged to work day and night in the canneries, a marathon ordeal that brought in enough for the balance of the year.

The long room was littered with books and papers. At the side was a sagging sofa on which at night Grimmelman, in his overcoat, slept. Weapons were mounted on the walls, army pistols and grenades, a pair of swords, and, held by Scotch tape, prints of World War I battleships. Grimmelman's worktables sagged with material. Nobody really knew what he was preparing; its scope shaded into infinity.

"Something's happened," Joe said, settling down on the sofa.

Grimmelman glanced at him, grinned, turned inquiringly to Art.

Art said, "It was in the *Chronicle*. You know Jim Briskin, this disc jock that runs 'Club 17' in the afternoons? He got fired."

"He got suspended," Ferde said. "For a month."

Grimmelman's eyes sparkled. "Oh?" He strode to the metal door and bolted it. "Tell me why."

"He read this commercial wrong," Art said. "This used car commercial, you know?"

Excitedly Grimmelman strode to the giant wall map of San Francisco. On the map, in his cramped hand, he had noted all the significant elements that made up the town. For an interval he studied the map, inspecting the notations at Van Ness Avenue and the used car lots. "Exactly which used car lot was it?"

"Looney Luke's," Art said. "Where Nat used to work."

Grimmelman stuck a pin into the map. "When did this happen?"

"Night before last," Ferde said.

Grimmelman's agitation increased. "Did any of you hear it?"

"No," Art said. "It was later on during the classic music. Not on 'Club 17.'"

At the map Grimmelman said, "This is an important event." He took his fountain pen and jotted a further entry in the notebook open beside the map. From a card file he selected several references, and then he opened a heavy case. "A number of possibilities may now occur."

"Like what?" Art said, experiencing, as always, the radiant energy of Grimmelman's intrigue. What a drab world it was without Grimmelman; his sensitivity to covert forces of mystical power and tenacity colored to a fever glow the most ordinary happenings. And this event, the vanishing of the familiar voice of Jim Briskin, already interesting, became in Grimmelman's hands a prize of much promise. Facing his map, Grimmelman was discovering overtones invisible to the unpracticed eye.

"First," Grimmelman declared, "it may be that he was instructed to read it wrong. We must not dismiss that."

"That's dumb," Joe Mantila said.

Grimmelman favored him with a glance. "It's not probable. But it is possible. In what way did he read the commercial wrong?"

"He said he was sick and tired of it," Art said. "He said the hell with it. And he didn't finish; he broke off in the middle."

"I see," Grimmelman said.

"And," Ferde Heinke said, "that's the last he was on. He wasn't on yesterday or today, and then there was this mention in the *Chronicle*." Unzipping his binder, he showed Grimmelman the item.

"May I keep this?" Grimmelman said. He added the item to a scrapbook, gluing it in and rubbing it flat with his fist.

"It's sure too bad," Art said. "Now there's some joker running 'Club 17,' and he's no good at all. He only plays the records; he don't say nothing at all."

"You think this is the time?" Joe Mantila said abruptly.

Grimmelman said, "It could be."

"The time," Art repeated.

In the environment built up around Grimmelman nothing superseded the idea of *the time*. Art felt the wave of anticipation; a host of emotions swam up inside him. The others, too, were affected; the Organization, as a group, lived for *the time*. Their sorties were arranged in an almost occult pattern of correct moments, conjunctions of astrological bodies. A peasant cunning mixed with peasant superstition welded Grimmelman to the stars. His plans were cosmic and cosmically determined. Always, in everything, Grimmelman consulted for signs to demonstrate that at long last the moment had arrived, the instant in which successful action was finally and absolutely possible.

"Time for the Organization to act," Ferde said, hypnotized by the idea. All of them envisioned at once the ritual of action: the bringing-out of the massive car from its hiding place, the thorough working-over of the engine and electronic controls so that no hitch could occur. And the checking of the weapons.

But Grimmelman was hesitating. "The Horch hasn't been out in months." He studied his charts. "Three months."

"Sure," Joe said, "it's time! Three months, that's a long time."

"Let's get going," Art said, sharing his restlessness.

Grimmelman said, "Hasty action is wasted."

"You and your charts," Joe Mantila said disgustedly.

"Saturday night," Art said, "The Bactrians are having a dance at Bratton's place." The Bactrians were a club of well-to-do youths from Nob Hill. Bill Bratton was their president; his father was a wealthy Montgomery Street attorney. "Afterward some of them'll probably stop at Dodo's."

"There's forty of them," Ferde said. "And only eleven of us. If very many of them show up, we're cooked."

"We'll do like we did last time," Joe said. "Park on the edge, get one of their cars going out. Same deal."

"In any case," Grimmelman said, deep in thought, "we could go ahead and activate the Horch."

In Art's ears the words fell beautifully. Activation of the Organization's remote-controlled car, with its speakers and antennae and fantastic straight-eight engine. The Horch, its lights off, speeding down Highway 99, escaping silently from encounter with the enemy as they drove behind, directing it . . . and, in a ditch, the flipped-over carcass of a '56 Ford.

On the wall of the loft were trophies, remnants taken from the vanquished. The Horch had gotten away each time. Grimmelman was cautious; each incident was scrupulously planned out.

At his worktables Grimmelman pointed to a relay board with its wiring and tubes and booster circuits. A soldering iron was beside it; he was in the process of working on this part of the Horch's system. "I have to get it finished. Or the Horch'll be silent."

The Horch could not be silent. The taunting voices, magnified and distorted, were vital. Otherwise the Horch, as it sped off, could not announce itself. It could not boom out who and what it was.

Ferde Heinke said suddenly, "Hey, you know? Rachael's going to have a baby." He glanced apologetically at Art. "His wife Rachael."

At his worktable, Grimmelman shivered. He did not look at them; he concentrated on his notebooks. The oily girl, he thought. The outsider. He felt fear.

As she walked, the slow, heavy walk of a woman, she gave forth a spearmint smell, spearmint and soap. And the eyes fixed on him, the judgment; she had seen him, judged him, dismissed him. Dismissed all of them and their various plans.

The room had become silent. They all felt subdued. The woman walked among them, taking away their excitement.

On the sofa Ferde Heinke fussed with his school books and magazines. Joe Mantila stared at the floor. Art Emmanual wandered to the door of the loft, his hands in his pockets. The air was oppressive. Beyond the locked metal door the sounds of the Negro and Mexican children filtered to him faintly, a tinny sound, like the rustling of weeds.

At five o'clock in the afternoon Van Ness Avenue lay under blown bits of paper. Wind had left the scatter in each shop's doorway. The waning sunlight made the scatter seem white.

The cars in Nat's Auto Sales were older, pre-war. On the side of the bakery by the lot, a sign was painted:

CARS THAT WORK FOR PEOPLE THAT WORK

At the fourth car, a 1939 Dodge, Nat Emmanual was opening the hood and connecting the battery charger. Here was his lot. Here was he, in cloth jacket and tan slacks, discovering that the battery cable of this car was eroded and would have to be replaced; at the end of the day he inspected his cars and learned the worst about each of them, the tires that had sagged, the batteries with dead cells, the rear main bearings that leaked oil.

He walked across Van Ness Avenue, stopping for the cars and then running, until he was on the far side and entering Hermann's Garage, "Specialists in Carburetors Rebuilt." The entrance was blocked by cars waiting to be fixed. In the back, by the workbench, Hermann had crawled within a Packard to adjust the brake. Nat reached into the litter of parts on the bench, pushing and rooting among the valves, gaskets, discarded fan belts.

"You got such a thing as a battery cable for a pre-war Dodge?" he said.

"Let me tell you a story," Hermann said. He emerged, wiping grease from his face and hands. "You believe in God?"

"No," Nat said, examining a clutch plate, wondering if he could make use of it in one of his cars.

"You believe it's wrong to spray over rust?"

"Naturally."

"So the paint falls off next week. That's the used car business." Hermann nodded his head toward the Packard. "You know whose that is?"

"Luke's."

"Luke sprays over rust. Luke fills up the dents with putty."

"I used to work for him," Nat said. "How about the cable?"

"You like him?"

"I don't care," he said. He had been in the used car business too long to care about paint over rust; he had done a little of that himself. Bending, he picked up a set of discarded plugs. "Can I have these?"

"For nothing? Or what do I get back? How about fifty cents? Something like that, whatever you want—it's up to you."

While Nat was regapping the plugs, Luke Sharpstein walked into the garage to see about the Packard. He wore his usual straw hat, maroon shirt, and flannel slacks. "Fella," he said genially to Nat. "How's it go?"

"Fine," Nat said noncommittally.

Picking at his pale teeth with his toothpick, Luke said, "Moving anything?"

"Not a drop."

Luke said, "Can you use a couple of Lincolns, '49's, good and clean? Give them to you cheap. Too old for me. Maybe swap a couple of Chevies even."

"All I have is junk," Nat said. "You know that. I'm in the yo-yo business." And it was Luke with his powerful sales techniques that had put him there, had put all the small dealers there.

Luke smiled his false-teeth smile. "I can use a few '41 Chevies for my jalopy lot."

"If you have any Willis Overlands, I might take them," Nat said with heavy irony.

Without a trace of humor, Luke said, "Well, I have a Willis station wagon. A '51. Dark green."

"No good."

Hermann, at the valve-grinding machine, said to Luke, "I got your Packard. The brakes are up."

Taking his regapped plugs, Nat Emmanual left the garage and recrossed Van Ness Avenue to his lot. A colored man was kicking the tires of a '40 Ford coupé, and Nat nodded to him. In the office, the cramped basalt-block structure which he had built himself, his kid-brother Art was peering at the naked-girl calendar on the wall.

"Hi," Art said, as Nat carried in the box of plugs. "When did you get this?"

"Month or so ago."

Art said, "How about lending me a car for a couple of days? We sorta wanted to take a drive, maybe down to Santa Cruz."

"You shouldn't be looking at that calendar." He put his hand over it, half seriously. "You're a married man."

"Yeah," Art said. "Hey, how about that Dodge?"

"The battery cable has to be replaced."

Art followed him out of the office, onto the lot, his hands in the back pockets of his jeans. "Just for a couple of days—a weekend, maybe. So she can sit around on the beach."

"How's Rachael?"

"Okay."

"Why's she need to sit around on the beach?"

Art said, "She's going to have a baby." He did not look directly at his brother; he fooled with the antenna on one of the cars.

"What?" Nat said loudly. "When?"

"January, I guess."

"How the hell can you pay for a baby?"

"We'll be okay." He scuffed at the ground.

"You're eighteen years old," Nat said, his voice rising. When he was angry, he had a mean, loud voice; Art knew it from childhood. "You don't know your ass from a hole in the ground. You think you're going to manage on fifty bucks a month? Or—for Christ's sake, do you think she can keep on working?"

The two of them were mute, and both breathed with difficulty. Gloom hung over them; defeat was in the air, a cloud of it from all directions. Nat thought about his used car lot, his row of old wrecks. He was making no money; he was on the verge of going out of business. How could he support a kidbrother with a wife and baby?

Resentment drained his strength. He had never approved of Rachael or the marriage; she had maneuvered the kid into it. This proved it.

"That's what you deserve," he said.

Art said, "Jesus, we're *glad.*"

"Glad!" He was incredulous. "Toss it in the Bay."

Art repeated, "We're glad." He could not understand his brother's attitude; the viciousness, the cruelty repelled him. "You're nuts," he said. "What kind of guy talks like that? You been selling used cars too long."

"You have a strange idea what being a nut is," Nat said savagely. "How about your pal Grimmelman and his bombs and maps? I'd call a guy nuts who's going to blow up the city hall and the police department."

Art said, "They're not going to blow up anything. Natural conditions will take care of it."

"Grow up," Nat said, irritated and discouraged. He washed his hands of them, his younger brother and Rachael. The hell with them, he thought; he had his own problems. "You can't expect the world to look after you," he said. "It's sink or swim. If you want to keep your head above water, you got to keep fighting." His outrage swelled. "How do you think this country was founded? By guys sitting around all day, doing nothing?"

"You talk like I committed some crime," Art muttered.

"Listen here," Nat said, "a couple years ago I was working for that snow-artist Luke. Now I got a lot of my own. That's what you can do in a country like this, you can be your own boss and not take nothing from nobody. If you work hard, you can get your own business; you understand?"

Art said, "I don't want a business."

"Then what do you want?"

After a long time, Art said, "I just want to stay out of the Army."

Nat stared at him, dumb with rage. "You slacker, you know if it wasn't for guys like me going overseas and taking care of the Japs you'd be working for Tojo right now and learning Japanese in school instead of sitting in the can smoking cigarettes."

"Okay," Art said. He felt ashamed and apologetic. "Take it easy, I'm sorry."

"A stretch in the Army'd be the best thing in the world for you,"

Nat said. "That's what you should have done as soon as you got out of school; they ought to make them all go in as soon as they finish school." Instead, he thought to himself, of letting them get married.

Turning to the Dodge, he began removing the defective battery cable.

In the kitchen of the basement apartment in the wooden house on Fillmore, Rachael peeled potatoes at the sink and listened to the radio. She was tired. During the morning, from eight until noon, she had worked at the airline office. The company was a nonentity, four planes in all, but the ex-GI's who ran it were nice; they kidded her, and they bought her coffee, and now that she was pregnant they had stopped making passes at her.

Reaching, she took her cigarette from the ashtray on the table. The radio was playing a Stan Getz record. This was the program she listened to each afternoon; this was "Club 17." But Jim Briskin was not on it. Somebody else was on, and she did not like him; he was not what she wanted to hear.

Outside, on Fillmore Street, a group of men walked by, noisy and abusive. A car honked. Traffic signals clanged. She felt a hollowness inside her. Where was the easy voice, the presence that had comforted because it had not asked for anything? She had grown up in a hostile, quarreling family. Everybody had demanded something; everybody had slashed at her. Jim Briskin had wanted nothing from her. What now? she wondered. What was there to take his place?

When the front door opened, she said, "Dinner's ready."

Art closed the door after himself and Ferde Heinke. "Hi," he said, sniffing the warm smell of food.

Putting the silverware on the table, Rachael said, "Did you tell him?"

"Yeah," he said.

She went over to him and kissed him. Her arms, around his neck, were thin and cold and slightly moist from the dishes. Then she returned to the table. She moved slowly, setting out the plates and cups with care. The set of dishes was a present from Art's great-aunt, one of the few wedding presents they had received.

Ferde, embarrassed, said to her, "Hey, congratulations about the baby."

"Thank you," she said.

Noticing that she was subdued, Art said, "Anything wrong?"

"I turned on 'Club 17,' " she said. "Jim Briskin isn't on it; somebody else is taking his place."

"It was in the paper," Art said. "He's off for a month because he wouldn't read a commercial. They suspended him."

She turned her swift, hard gaze on him. "Can I see it?"

"Grimmelman has it," Art said.

After a pause Rachael said to Ferde Heinke, "Did you want to stay for dinner?"

"I have to get home." He edged toward the door. "My mother's expecting me to get home by six-thirty."

At the icebox, Art poured himself a glass of beer from the quart bottle. "Stick around," he said. "We can go over the dummies for the magazine."

"Why don't you?" Rachael said. During their four months of marriage, they had not had much company.

6

In the early afternoon the telephone rang. Jim Briskin answered it, and a soft little feminine voice said, "Mr. Briskin?"

"Yes," he said, not recognizing the voice. He seated himself on the arm of the couch, avoiding the records; they were a stack belonging to KOIF which he planned eventually to return. "Who is this?"

"Don't you know?"

"No," he said.

"Maybe you don't remember me. I met you down at the station the other day. I'm Art Emmanual's wife."

"Sure I remember you," he said, glad to hear from her. "I just didn't recognize you over the phone."

"Do you have a second?"

He said, "That's one thing I have plenty of. How've you been, Rachael?"

"Pretty good," she said. "It sure is awful your not being on 'Club 17.' Art got the newspaper where it told about you. He didn't bring it home, but he told me what it said. Are you ever coming back?"

"Maybe," he said. "I haven't decided. We'll see at the end of the month."

"That guy, whatever his name is, he's no good."

"What have you been doing?" he asked.

"Nothing much." She paused. "I wondered, we both wondered, if you would like to come over for dinner."

"I'd like to," he said, pleased.

"Would you like to come tonight?" On the phone she had a correct, painstaking manner; her invitation was presented with formality.

THE BROKEN BUBBLE

"Fine," he said. "About what time?"

"Say seven o'clock. You won't be disappointed if it isn't much."

"I'm positive it'll be excellent."

"But if it isn't," she said, still serious.

"Then it'll be nice seeing both of you again."

She gave him the address, and he repeated it back. Then she said goodbye, and he hung up the phone.

Cheered, he shaved and took a shower and put on a clean pair of slacks. The time was two o'clock. He had five hours to fill until dinner with the Emmanuals, the balance of the afternoon and the beginning of evening. Gradually his good spirits left. Time, he thought. It was going to destroy him.

Getting into his car, he drove out toward the Presidio. But his depression remained. He had got to thinking about Pat. That was fatal. That was the one thing he could not let himself do.

For half an hour he drove at random, and then he turned in the direction of Fillmore Street.

The bars and shops were busy and the sight of them restored some sense of optimism in him. He parked his car, locked the doors, and walked along the sidewalk, looking at the numbers.

The house itself, huge and in disrepair, was set back on its lot between a billboard and a hardware shop. A wire fence ran along the edge of the sidewalk, and in the center was a rusty, ponderous gate. He managed to force the gate open. It groaned as he shut it after him.

The cement walk led him to the side of the house. Steps descended to a wooden door, a separate basement apartment. He rapped on the door and waited. There was no response. For an interval he rapped, waited, rapped again. They were not at home. His own fault, of course. This was a wild idea, a long shot.

He started back up the steps, keenly disappointed. What now? he wondered.

On the broad main steps of the building, the steps leading to the front porch, three teenage boys sprawled. They had watched him without comment as he rapped on the Emmanuals' basement door. Now he noticed them for the first time. All three wore jeans and heavy boots and black leather jackets. Their faces were expressionless.

"Are they out?" he asked.

Finally one of the boys inclined his head.

"You know where they went?"

No response. The faces remained blank.

"You know when they'll be back?"

Still no response. He started down the cement path to the sidewalk. As he was closing the gate after him, one of the boys said, "Try Dodo's."

"What's that?" he said.

After a pause, another of the boys said, "Dodo's Drive-In."

"Down Fillmore," the first boy said. The third said nothing; he had a beaked, hostile face, and on his right cheek, by his mouth, was a crescent-shaped scar. "Couple blocks," the first boy said.

"Thanks," he said. They continued to gaze after him as he walked off.

Parked in the lot at the drive-in, its front facing the glass doors of the building, was a pre-war Plymouth. Inside were four or five kids, and one of them was a girl. He walked cautiously up beside the car. They were eating hamburgers and drinking malts from white cartons. The girl was Rachael.

At first neither she nor Art recognized him.

"Hi," he said.

"Oh," she said, "hello." That was all she said. All five kids seemed subdued. They concentrated on their food.

"Is this where you hang out?" he said clumsily.

They nodded, dividing the nod among them. There was just the one nod for all five of them.

Art said, "She's not f-f-feeling too good."

"Anything serious?" he said.

"N-n-no."

Another boy said, "She's feeling blue."

"Yeah," Art said. "She's been feeling blue all d-d-day. She didn't go to w-w-work."

"That's too bad," he said, concerned and knowing no way to show it. All five of them seemed blue; they munched and passed the malts back and forth. Once Art bent to brush bits of fried potato from his pants. Another car, similar to theirs, drove up on the far side of the drive-in building. Kids stepped from it and walked indoors to order food.

"Would anything cheer her up?" Jim asked.

They held a conference. One of the boys said, "Maybe you could drive her to this lady's."

"Her teacher," Art said, "she had in h-h-high school."

"Sure," he said, wanting to help.

The door of the Plymouth presently opened. Rachael stepped out, walked to the trash dispenser with an empty carton, and then returned. Her cheeks were hollow and darkened, and she moved slowly. "Come on," she said to her husband.

"Okay," Art said. "But I'm not going in. I don't w-w-want to see her."

To Jim, Rachael said, "Where's your car?"

"Down the street," he said. "I can go get it."

"No." She shook her head. "I'd like to walk. I feel like walking."

"What teacher is this?" he asked, as the three of them trudged along Fillmore, past the shops and bars.

"My home economics teacher," Rachael said. "Sometimes I talk to her about different things." She kicked a bottle cap along the pavement until it rolled into the gutter. "I'm sorry I'm like this," she said, her head down.

Art patted her. "It's not your f-f-fault." To Jim he explained, "It's my fault; she's afraid because I'm m-m-mixed up with these guys and she don't like them. But I'm through with them; I r-r-really am."

"I don't mind your being with them," Rachael said. "I'm just worried that—" She broke off.

"She thinks they're going to d-d-do something," Art said. "Hey," he said to his wife, tugging her until she bumped against him. "No more for me, you hear? Last time was the last."

Ahead of them was Jim's car. He unlocked the door and held it open for them.

Wonderingly, Rachael said, "It must cost a lot to have a car like this."

"Not worth it," he said. They were starting into the back and he said, "We can all fit in front."

When they were in, he closed the doors and backed out into traffic. As he drove, Rachael and Art put their heads together in an almost wordless discussion.

Art said, "Hey, now she don't want to go there." To his wife he said, "Then where do you w-w-want to go?"

Rachael said, "Remember when we used to go swimming all the time?"

"Y-y-you can't go swimming."

"I know," she said, "but remember we used to go out to the pool at Fleishhacker Zoo? Maybe we could go out there and just sit. It ought to be nice out there."

Making a left turn, he drove in the direction of Fleishhacker Zoo.

"This is sure n-n-nice of you," Art said.

"I'm glad to," he said, and he meant it.

"Did you ever go out there?" Rachael asked.

"Whenever I could. I used to walk around the Park."

"That's over farther," Rachael said. "It's nice there too." Now she seemed less despondent. She sat up straighter and began to look through the window at the cars and houses. The bright July sunlight shone from the pavement.

"Everything okay with the baby?" Jim said.

"Yes," Rachael said.

He said, "I guess you don't have to worry about the Army."

"Oh, they could take him," Rachael said. "Art, I mean. In fact they sent him a notice and he went down. And they classified him 1-A. But he has a kidney condition . . . he can't eat a lot of foods, a lot of sweet stuff. And he didn't tell them; he forgot. So they were going to draft him, and he even had the notice that tells when to report. So I called them up. And I had to go down and talk to them. And then they didn't want him. So I mean they could take him . . . but I don't think they will."

"You don't want to go," Jim said. It was obvious enough.

Art said, "If they want me, sure I'll g-g-go. But I mean, there's no war or nothing."

Rachael said, "They get everybody sooner or later. I think they want to have something so they can get you when they want you. Like in an emergency or something. They have everybody in a classification."

"Not women," Art said.

The sun was warm on the trees and gravel paths and on the water of the pool. On the rim of the pool teenagers sunned themselves in trunks and bathing suits. One or two beach umbrellas had been erected.

Rachael seated herself on the low steps overlooking the pool. In the company of the two kids, Jim began to feel old and overly tall. And yet, he thought, their situation was not so different from his. They were not so far apart in their problems.

"Let's walk," Rachael said. "It's so dull here."

The three of them walked from the pool, in the direction of the Zoo itself. At a wire cage Rachael halted, and when he and Art looked back they saw her in contemplation.

"What is it?" Jim asked, returning.

She said, "I made the puma growl."

The puma rested on an artificial tree branch in his cage. His muzzle was massive, more like a dog's than a cat's. His whiskers were short, stiff bristles. He did not deign to notice anyone.

"He needs a shave," Jim said.

Rachael said, "Growl at him and he growls back."

They went on, plodding listlessly.

Suddenly Rachael said, "What's there to *do?*"

He was at a loss to answer. "Lots of things."

"No." She shook her head. "There isn't anything to do. I don't mean just now, either."

"Pretty soon you'll have plenty to do. When the baby comes."

But even to him that did not seem enough. He wanted to give a better answer than that.

"For a man," he said, "a job is the most important thing. And I don't see anything wrong with that. It's something to focus yourself on. You get better at it, whatever it is. You learn more. You become more skilled. And you can expand that . . . it can be more than just a job."

Rachael said, "I thought that was important, what you did. Not reading that commercial."

"It wasn't," he said. "I was just tired. Fed up. Troubles with Pat."

"That was the day we saw you," Rachael said. "Did it have anything to do with us?"

"Yes," he said.

"Did we upset you?"

"Yes," he said, "you made me feel strange."

"Then your job wasn't the most important thing to you . . . you were willing to give it up for something else."

He said, "Why did you give me that roll?"

"Because I liked you. I wanted to give you something so you'd know. You did a lot for us, with the program. We always listened. You were somebody we could trust. When you said something, it was true. Was that why you wouldn't read the commercial? Was there something in it that wasn't true? Sometimes they're so one-sided: they just say what's good about the product. Did you feel if you read it people would think you believed it, and you knew you didn't believe it, you knew it wasn't true? When I heard what you had done, I thought that was probably the reason. Because if you didn't believe it, I knew you wouldn't read it. You never told us anything that wasn't true. If you had, if you lied to us, we wouldn't have listened."

"You shouldn't expect that much from some guy sitting at a microphone," Jim said. "Some disc jock with a bunch of pop tunes to play and three hours to kill."

"All right," she said, "who should we listen to, then? They used to tell us stuff in assembly . . . we read the same stuff in magazines and they say it in churches. There's always a bunch of old ladies, like the PTA; they're always telling us what to do. But I figured that out a long time ago. It's what they want; it's what would be nicest for them. Wouldn't it be nice if we just curled up and died? If we never asked for anything, wanted anything—never bothered them. They have all this stuff that explains why they're right. But you know, they're always talking about dropping hydrogen bombs on the enemy. I hope when the war comes the bombs get dropped on them, too."

"You mean us," he said.

"No," she said. "Them. What do you mean, us? What do we have for them to bomb?"

"Your lives," he said.

"I don't care. What difference does it make? What do we have to look forward to?" She plodded along, past the animals in their cages. "I read in a book about frontier women. They churned butter and they made their own clothes."

"Would you like that?"

Ponderously, she said, "Who does that anymore?"

She had a point.

"You know," she said, "I know a girl, a Jewish girl. And she went to Israel. And she worked on a farm. And she was out there in the desert . . . she carried a gun while she worked. And they all ate together, and everything they owned belonged to all of them, and they didn't get any money, they were part of this—" She hesitated. "I don't know the name. It's a Jewish word. Sort of a community settlement. And before that, she used to live like us, sitting around doing nothing, wasting her time with nothing to do. Like we all used to walk down to the show together on Saturday night, me and her and a bunch of girlfriends, and just sit there in the show, and usually it was a love picture—you know?—where they finally get together in the end, the good guy and the good girl, and you see him kissing her and everything's wonderful. And they have this place up sort of in the country, with a lot of furniture and one of those big windows."

"Picture window," he said.

"And two new cars. And the furniture is sort of blond and modern."

"Well," he said, "there are houses like that."

Art, ahead of them, pointed and said, "H-h-hey, look over that way."

Speeding along the street beyond the Zoo was a red-and-white convertible; in it were four boys, well dressed. The car was new and shiny, and the boys wore sweaters and their hair was neatly combed. With a scream of tires, the convertible turned a corner and disappeared.

"Bactrians," Art said.

"Never mind," Rachael said.

"They were, though."

She said to Jim, "Did you know, I was engaged to Bill Bratton. When I was in high school. We went steady for a couple of months."

"He's president of the Bactrians," Art explained. "Their families have a lot of d-d-dough; his father's an attorney. A-a-and they have real new cars and they have these d-d-dances."

Rachael said, "Bill used to take me dancing up to these expensive supper clubs. Sometimes we'd drive over into Marin County and up along the highway. We'd have dinner and then we'd dance. I even wore his club pin."

"How'd you meet him?" Jim asked.

"At a school dance. They all used to come into the gym in a group, with their shoes shined and their hair combed; they looked pretty good."

"They danced good," Art said. "They took instructions."

"Bill liked to rumba," Rachael said, "and mambo, and I guess now they're real good at the cha-cha-cha. And I liked to dance, so I used to go around with him. Art never could dance very good. I even had dinner one time up at the Brattons' home, up on Nob Hill. They have a sort of mansion, with a gardener to take care of the lawns, and a library and a lot of rooms, and this huge table; there must have been twenty people sitting at it. And then later on, Bill got into a lot of trouble up in San Rafael."

"Yeah," Art said, "they made a mistake because the police up there d-d-don't know who Bratton is, and they put a whole lot of B-b-bactrians in jail one night."

"They were driving through San Rafael," Rachael said. "They cut up the tires of cars and pushed some cars down a hill, and they beat up some people going home—it was real late—and the car they were in was stolen. But the police caught them on Highway 1 near Olema. And they had beer in the car. And usually their families could get them off, but not this time. And some of them paid a lot of fines and one kid, I guess he was over twenty-one, went to jail for a year. Bill got a suspended sentence. I wasn't going around with him then. I stopped going around with him because of this initiation thing. They were down at Carmel, and I went along with Bill. I stayed at night with these girls, but during the day we went around and had a lot of fun. And then they wanted to make these guys they were initiating do these things . . . it was disgusting and I left, and that was the last time I went out with him. It was really awful. I mean, it wasn't like people; I can't say what some of the things were. But finally one kid was killed and then there wasn't so much of that."

"Boy," Art said, "their families sure p-p-pulled a lot of strings to get them off."

"Are there many clubs like that?" Jim said. "Among the upper-class kids?"

Rachael said, "Most of the kids from good homes belong to one club or another. They have pins and dances and initiations. And the trouble is, the reason the clubs are so strong, is that their fathers used to belong to them. And the dances are held in those big houses up on

Nob Hill. The parents sort of sponsor them. They have a lot of money. Like the Bactrian pin costs around fifty dollars."

Ahead of them were the bear cages. They found a place to buy hot coffee and a place to sit. Rachael seemed tired from the walking; her shoulders drooped. Across from their bench, children gathered to view the bears. One bear lay back on its rump, clutching its hind feet with its forepaws and rocking grotesquely from side to side. The sight seemed to make Rachael uncomfortable.

"What's the m-m-matter?" Art asked, bending over her.

"Nothing. It just bothers me."

Art said, "M-m-maybe we ought to get back. So she can start fixing d-d-dinner."

As they drove back toward the apartment on Fillmore, Rachael said, "Who is Pat?"

"My ex-wife," he said. "She works down at KOIF."

"Is that that woman with the b-b-black hair?" Art said. "I think I saw her; she's real cute. Real cool-looking."

"It must be funny," Rachael said, "not being married to somebody and still seeing them."

"It can be tough," he said.

"Does she like to work?"

"She likes her job."

Rachael said, "I think if a man loves a woman he should never leave her or go around with anybody else."

"Sometimes," Jim said, "the woman doesn't want to have any more to do with him."

Rachael nodded.

"Had you thought of that?" he asked her.

"No," she said.

"I was very much in love with Pat," he said. "In some respects I still am. But she wanted something that I couldn't give her."

"How do you feel when you see her?" Rachael asked. "Do you still want to help her and do things for her and take care of her?"

"Yes," he said. "But I'm realistic enough to accept the fact that I can't. One of these days she's going to get married to the station business manager, a fellow named Bob Posin."

He made a left turn onto Fillmore. Presently they were parked down the block from the house, and he was opening the car door for Rachael and Art.

"Don't be too disappointed," Rachael said, "if I don't cook as well as Pat."

He was amused. "Okay, little Mrs. Wife."

The apartment was below street level, and the living room was cool and damp. Pipes ran along the walls. How few pieces of furniture, he thought. A heavy round oak table was the largest piece, and then two chairs, and the couch, and a dresser on which was a television set, an obsolete twelve-inch Emerson with a rabbit-ears antenna. Standing up in the corner were printer's dummies, titled *Phantasmagoria* in huge Gothic type. Rachael went at once to the kitchen and began preparing the meal. Throwing himself down on the couch, Art lit a cigarette and began to smoke nervously. The man of the house, Jim thought, was feeling the gravity of his position.

"Not bad," Jim said, meaning the apartment.

"We been living h-h-here since we got married." Art puffed more and more rapidly; clouds of cigarette smoke obscured him. With a sigh, he drew in his feet and shifted about on the sofa.

Rachael appeared at the kitchen doorway, looking for dishes. She, too, was anxious, and he thought to himself that this was an occasion for both of them. Probably she had little opportunity to cook for company, to play out her role as hostess.

"Would you like some coffee?" she asked.

"Don't make any," he said.

"It's made; I just have to heat it up."

"Okay," he said, "thanks." When she had returned to the kitchen, he said to Art, "How much do you pay for this?"

"Fifty-five dollars a month," Art said.

He asked how much the two of them earned.

"Counting what I g-g-get," Art said, "we make around a hundred and fifty a month."

Jim thought: And over a third of it goes for rent.

"They really have you," he said, "on rent."

"Yeah," Art said fatalistically. "But this isn't bad for these days. Some places we saw, they w-w-wanted sixty and seventy. And they weren't as good as this."

66

"How are you going to get along when the baby comes? Have you made any plans?"

Art shuffled his feet. "We'll be okay."

"What're you going to buy food with? She can't keep on working."

In the kitchen, Rachael shut off the water and came to the doorway. Her eyes, dilated and dark, fixed on him. "That's what his brother says."

He was cowed. "But what's the answer? You earn two-thirds of your combined income; that'll cease when you quit your job."

"Do you have any money?" Rachael said.

"Some."

"Well," she said, "why don't you give it to us?" Then she smiled. "You're all white. I scared you."

"Yes," he said. "But not the money."

"I know. You'd give it to us, wouldn't you?"

"I would," he said. "But you wouldn't take it."

She returned to the kitchen. "We hardly even know you."

"You do," he said.

"Not real well. Not that well."

Art said, "We got l-l-lots of money. We got over a h-h-hundred bucks saved up."

"Let me match it," he said suddenly.

"Aw, ha, no. Hell." Art laughed anxiously.

"Come on," he said, wanting to.

"Hell, no," Art said.

But he needed to. "What can I do?" he said.

"For what?" Rachael said, appearing with the pot of coffee.

"I'd like to do something to help."

Neither of them answered. They were both a little surly. Like cats, he thought. Like the puma at the zoo. He had pestered them too much.

"You haven't got the slightest ability to deal with your problems," he said. "You're living here in this slum without money—you're not living like adults. You're living like God knows what."

"Because we don't have any money?" Rachael said.

He said, "I'm afraid something'll happen to you. And there's nothing I can do; I can't help you." Powerless, he thought. He was powerless to affect their lives, to alter things in any manner. His program was gone, his contact with them; he did nothing, no work, no act that had any meaning. How futile it made him feel. How superfluous.

"Can't I buy you something?" he said.

"Just drink your coffee," she said, placing the cup before him.

"Do you understand how I feel?" he demanded, ignoring the coffee.

Standing before him with the coffeepot, she said, "You can buy something for the baby. Some clothes. When the time comes, I'll write out what size and color."

Returning to the kitchen, she seated herself at the table; with her recipe books open, she prepared dinner.

7

On Saturday night a visitor rapped at Ludwig Grimmelman's locked metal door.

"Who is it?" Grimmelman said, not recognizing the knock. From a wall rack, he took down an Army M-1 rifle; sweeping up the secret documents and reports he had been preparing, he stuffed them into a briefcase, closed the snap, and pushed them into a hiding place. He turned off the light and stood in darkness, hearing his own breathing. "What do you want?"

"Mr. Grimmelman?" the voice said, a man's voice.

Grimmelman went to a side window, unfastened the catch, raised it, and peered out. A man was standing in the outside stairwell, a heavy-set man in a topcoat, wearing a hat and a pressed suit. He was middle-aged; he seemed to be a salesman, probably an insurance salesman.

Putting his light back on, Grimmelman unlocked and opened the door. "I'm busy. I refuse to buy anything."

The man said, "I'm Ralf Brown. From the FBI." He flapped open a black leather identification folder. "I'd like to step in a moment and discuss a matter with you. If I may."

"What's this about?" He backed away as Mr. Brown entered.

"About a fellow you might know." Brown glanced about the room. "Quite a place you've got here." He strolled leisurely.

"What fellow?"

"Ever heard of an individual by the name of Kendelman? Leon Kendelman? We thought you might know him. Here's his picture." Mr. Brown, from the deep pocket of his topcoat, brought forth a

69

packet; he opened the packet and handed Grimmelman a snapshot, blurred, indistinct.

But nonetheless the snapshot was familiar.

"Why?" Grimmelman demanded.

"Draft evasion."

Grimmelman returned the snapshot. "No, I never saw him. And anyhow your organization is infiltrated by Communists; it's no use talking to you, it goes straight to MVD hatchet men in the Labor School and around the PW."

"You never saw this individual?"

"No."

"Positive?"

"No, I never saw him." He was terrified, because the snapshot, taken from a distance with a telescopic lens, was of him.

Mr. Brown said, "May I see your draft card?"

The card was in a locked box under the table, along with other papers. Larsen, the printer whom Art worked for, had done it; at one time Larsen had been an organizer for a splinter Trotskyist organization of which Grimmelman had been a member.

Studying the card, Mr. Brown said, "You're twenty-six?"

"Yes," he said, "born in Warsaw, naturalized in 1932."

"You're 4-F," Mr. Brown said, returning the card. "How'd you work that? You look all right to me."

"Hernia," Grimmelman said.

"And you're positive you don't know this Kendelman?"

Actually there was no Kendelman. He had registered under that name, and he used it now and then in covert political work, undercover work such as spying on Fascist student groups, Stalinist fronts, and for taking out library books he did not mean to return. "Positive," he said.

He wished Mr. Brown the FBI man would leave. He wished it more than anything else on earth; the wish became a passion. In fact, if Mr. Brown did not leave, he would fall dead in his tracks; the sense of danger was too much. He could not bear it.

"Quite a place you got here," Mr. Brown said, picking up some photostats of *Pravda.* "You're interested in politics, Mr. Grimmelman?"

Mr. Brown showed no sign of leaving. On the contrary, the more he saw, the more interested he seemed to become.

Joe Mantila said, "He says it's time to get out the Horch. He says we're supposed to go start it up and make sure the engine's tuned." He leaned from the window of his '39 Plymouth toward Art Emmanual, who stood at the curb. Behind the Plymouth other cars, the traffic along Fillmore, honked and flashed their headlights, and swung around. "I'll go get Heinke; you can come now or we'll pick you up on the way back."

"Pick me up on the way back," Art said.

"Okay, that'll be in around fifteen minutes." Mantila held his watch up to the light from the cars behind. "Ten-five."

Art walked back up the path and down the steps to the apartment. Behind him the Plymouth, popping and sputtering, gunned off and was gone. The nighttime traffic resumed its regular flow.

Closing the front door, he said to Rachael, "We can't go out tonight. I have to do something."

She said, "Was that about Grimmelman?" She had put on a coat, and now, in the bathroom, she was combing her hair. They had been about to leave for the bowling alley; she liked to watch the players and be where there was noise and activity and kids her own age. Especially on Saturday night.

"It looks like we might be doing something," Art said. He was uneasy; he knew how she felt about Grimmelman and the Organization.

"It's up to you," she said. "But he's so—peculiar. I mean, he sits up there all day; he never goes out. Is that really what you want?"

"I got a lot invested in the Horch," he said. It had been his job to supply parts for engine repair.

"There's something wrong with him," she said, taking off her coat.

"That's what Nat says."

"I think you go over there," she said, "because you can't find anything else to do. If you had something else, you'd do it instead."

"Maybe you're right," he mumbled, standing first on one foot and then the other.

"When will you be back tonight?"

71

"Probably late." He did not really want to go. But he had to. "Will you be okay?" he asked hesitantly.

"I might go to a show."

"I'd kind of feel better if you stayed home."

"Okay," she said, "I will. Could we sometime play poker again?" That was an eternal love of hers; she played a tight game, without talk or motion, straight or draw poker with no variations and no cards wild. Usually she won a dollar or two. She had frightened off most of Art's high school friends, who liked to play goofy, extravagant games with a great deal of horseplay. Once she had slapped Ferde Heinke and knocked off his glasses because, in dealing, he had kiddingly turned over a card.

"They're all scared to play cards with you," he said. "You take it too seriously."

"There's no such thing," she said.

"It isn't a game when you play."

"Poker isn't a game," she said. "What do you think it is? Do you think it's like hearts or something? That's the trouble with you, you can't tell what's important and what isn't. You're going out to fool around, and you don't know if you're playing a game—it would be playing revolutionary, I guess, Nazi or something, with that car. But you also think you really are a revolutionary and it isn't a game. So which are you? You're sort of between. Do you know what this is here, me and this apartment and you? This isn't a game either. And if you go out there and horse around with them and I don't think you're coming back here, not as soon as you should anyhow, then I'm going to bust you one." She looked at him with that sharp, intent look that was so frightening; nobody stood up against that. She would demolish the apartment and everything in it. She would lay it waste. And she would not say a word; she would just go about it. And for weeks she would say nothing to him; she would go to work, fix the meals, shop, clean and sweep the apartment, and never speak to him.

The thing about her that was so awe-inspiring was that she never kidded. She never joked; she meant everything she said. It was not boast. It was prophecy.

Taking her in his arms, he kissed her. Her face was cold; her lips, always thin, were dry. He kissed her on the cheek, and he felt the bone close to the surface; he felt the hardness. "You're pretty tough," he said.

"I just want you to know." She smiled up at him then.

He said, "What else can I do? I have to go."

"You don't have to go."

"I'm supposed to." He was helpless.

"You don't have to do anything. Nobody can make you do anything. All these things they say, it's just a lot of words. Grimmelman is as bad as the rest of them. Grimmelman is like a sign. Do you do what signs say? How about when you read something, do you do that? Do you believe it because it's up there on the wall or somebody mails it to you in an envelope? You know it's just words. Just talk."

He said, "I do some things they tell me."

"Don't do anything they tell you."

"All of them?" Her hardness troubled him.

"Remember all that stuff they taught us in school, all that junk. There never was anything in all of it." With her long, accurate fingers she looped a thread that dangled from his shirt: she broke the thread and put it into an ashtray on the mantel.

He placed his hands on her shoulders. Through the material of her blouse, his hands rested on her, and he felt that she was close to him, close to the surface.

"I wish we could go somewhere," she said. "Not just around here. I want to see different places. Maybe someday we could see the Rockies. We could drive up high; we could even live up there. They have towns up there right in the mountains."

"It's hard to get a job there," he said.

"We could open a store," Rachael said. "There's always things people want. We could open a bakery."

"I'm not a baker," he said.

"Then we could put out a newspaper."

He kissed her again, and then he lifted her up, off the floor and against him. Then he set her down on the arm of the couch.

"Tell your brother Nat," she said, "to give us one of his cars so we can drive. Tell him we need a new one we can sell when we get there."

"You mean it?" he said.

Of course she did. "But not yet," she said. "We better wait until after I have the baby. Then we can go. In a couple of years, when we have some money. When you're finished being an apprentice."

"You really want to get out of here?" After all, he thought, she had been born here; she had grown up here.

She said, "Maybe we could even go up into Canada. I was thinking about that. To one of those towns where they trap animals and there's a lot of snow."

"You wouldn't like that," he said. But, he thought, maybe she would.

The Horch was parked in a sheet-metal garage down in the flat industrial section of the city. Grimmelman, in his black wool great-coat, paratrooper's boots, and army shirt, unlocked the padlock and shoved aside the doors.

The garage was clammy. The cement floor was wet with oil. To one side was a workbench. Joe Mantila put on the overhead light as Art Emmanual closed the doors behind them.

"Nobody's been here," Ferde said. "Nobody's got to it."

The Horch was dented from its encounters, but it was still impressive. It weighed almost six thousand pounds. This car had come up from Latin America; it had been built in 1937 by the Auto-Union, and this model, a five-passenger sport convertible, had been the staff car of the Wehrmacht and S.S. Grimmelman had never told anyone how and where he had gotten hold of it or how much he had paid. The Horch was painted jet black, and with its remote-control system it was unique.

Art got in behind the wheel and started up the engine. In the closed garage, the noise deafened them; exhaust fumes billowed up in clouds, and the smell of gasoline was sickening.

"It's missing a little," Ferde Heinke said.

Lifting the hood, Art began tinkering with the fuel mixture. "How come you decided to roll out tonight?" he said to Grimmelman. He had never seen Grimmelman so agitated, in such a state of anxiety.

"The time has arrived," Grimmelman said, pacing in a circle, his hands behind his back.

"Is that why you're jumping around?"

Ferde Heinke said, "If we're really going to do something tonight, we better get more to go; four isn't enough. We ought to get the rest of the Organization." The Organization faded off indistinctly, without particular edges; beyond the hard core were a number of members who came and went.

"This is more in the nature of a warm-up," Grimmelman said, attaching the relay board of the remote control unit. With a screwdriver, he cinched up the lugs to the terminals. Perspiration streaked his cheeks; his face shone under the light. "A dry run so we'll know we're ready to roll at an instant's notice."

"Roll where?" Joe said.

"The situation is at a critical stage," Grimmelman said. "I want the Horch filled with gas, ready for a long trip. If necessary we may have to move operations to a new area." As he completed the wiring of the vital control unit, he added, "From now on I want the weapons kept here in the Horch."

"Where are we going tonight?" Ferde Heinke asked.

"We'll conduct practice maneuvers in the vicinity of Dodo's. If possible we'll engage a Bactrian vehicle."

"Fine," Joe Mantila said, hating the Bactrians with their cashmere sweaters and slacks and argyle socks, their country club dances, and especially their late-model Detroit stock cars.

"See if the coast is clear," Grimmelman said, panting with eagerness.

Ferde stepped outside and surveyed the street.

"I'll take the Plymouth," Joe Mantila said, passing through the doorway and outside after Ferde. He carried with him the controls and a microphone and a roll of cable with a jack on the end. "Let's see if I can back it out."

Seated in the Plymouth, he punched buttons, controlling the Horch. The power-assisted wheel of the Horch revolved as the car shifted gear and began to back. The original eight-speed manual transmission had been removed and an automatic Borg-Warner transmission installed. The overhead cam engine, with its immense crankshaft supported by ten bearings, was original equipment; nothing else was its match. The engine thundered, and the Horch backed from the garage into the street. Its headlights flashed on; it shifted into a forward gear, and the foot throttle eased. From the grill beneath the

Auto-Union insignia, Joe Mantila's voice boomed, "Okay? Let's go."

"Great," Grimmelman said, hurrying outside. Art closed the garage doors; the three of them hurried to the Plymouth to join Joe Mantila.

Joe drove the Plymouth, while Grimmelman worked the controls for the Horch. The ponderous Horch started out ahead of them, and they followed closely; it was necessary for them to be near enough to see what lay ahead. In the beginning their control car had lagged, and the Horch had been permitted to crash against parked cars and curbs; now they had learned to keep it always in sight. Its headlights swept the pavement, and, over its open top, they studied the street.

"Turn it right," Ferde said.

The Horch turned cautiously, as Grimmelman slowed it almost to a halt. "More traffic," Grimmelman murmured; his face was tense with the strain of operating the controls.

"That's no lie," Ferde Heinke said. "Hey, you want me to go take it manually until we're at Dodo's?"

"No," Grimmelman said. "It's okay."

The open Horch, with no one inside, sailed down Fillmore Street among the buses and taxis and stock cars. As usual, its empty driver's seat was unnoticed.

"Art," Grimmelman said, "you operate the assault weapon."

Reaching around on the floor of the Plymouth—he was crowded in the back seat with Ferde Heinke and piles of equipment—he located the assault weapon: a spray gun filled with white enamel paint. But he did not feel in the mood. The spray gun was a dead weight, and he handed it to Ferde.

"You get them," he said.

"What's the matter?" Grimmelman demanded. "I told you to do it."

He shook his head. "I don't know. I don't feel like it."

Ahead of them was Dodo's. At the curb, a sparkling new Detroit bomb was parked; its occupants were inside the drive-in, at the counter. "Bactrians," Grimmelman said.

The car was a '56 Buick, dark green and white.

"Park the Horch," Joe said excitedly.

Grimmelman caused the Horch to glide to the curb at the end of the block. There, with its motor idling, it parked and waited.

"Now," Grimmelman said.

Ferde Heinke, leaning from the window of the Plymouth, sprayed paint on the green fender of the Buick, spelling out:

FUCK YOU

"Okay," he said, finishing. "Let's go."

Art lay back against the seat as the Plymouth shot forward. His heart was not in it, and he began to think about Rachael. Behind them, the Bactrians were rushing out of Dodo's and into their Buick. But he did not care.

"Stop," Grimmelman ordered Joe. "Around the corner, like before."

The Plymouth screeched around the corner, passed the parked Horch, and came to a stop. At the drive-in, the Bactrians were starting up their Buick. As the Buick left the curb, Grimmelman propelled the Horch from its parking place out into traffic, into the path of the Buick.

"Lily-whiters!" the Horch's speaker boomed at the Buick as the Buick swerved past it, trying to get around it. Now the Horch blocked the side street and prevented the Buick from turning; the Buick went on past with the Horch following.

Joe Mantila backed the Plymouth onto Fillmore and followed after the Horch; ahead of the Horch the Buick snaked from side to side as the Bactrians stuck their heads out and peered back, bewildered.

"Lily-whiters!" the Horch's speaker thundered, a gross and magnified voice directly behind them. They could easily see that nobody was at the wheel; the Horch was frighteningly empty.

"Speed it up," Ferde said to Grimmelman.

The Horch gained on the Buick and slammed against its rear bumper. The Bactrians, in panic, spun around a corner and vanished; they had given up. The encounter was over.

"Okay," Grimmelman said, "That's enough."

Joe Mantila halted the Plymouth in a driveway as Grimmelman turned the Horch in a ponderous U-turn. Presently they were following it back in the direction they had come.

"What's the matter?" Ferde Heinke said to Art, digging him in the ribs.

"Nothing." He felt glum. For the first time he had failed to enjoy an encounter.

Grimmelman said, "He wants to go home."

"That's right," he said.

An uncomfortable silence fell over them.

"Maybe next time," Art said. "I got a lot of worries this week." Both Joe Mantila and Ferde Heinke were glancing at him apprehensively. But Grimmelman ignored him; he concentrated on the task of directing the Horch.

"Christ," Art said, "it's not my fault; I got a lot of responsibilities." His apology went unanswered.

8

That Saturday night Jim Briskin was across the Bay in Berkeley, at his mother's home on Spruce Street. With his key—he still kept a key to the white concrete house in which he had been born—he unlocked the basement door and began sorting among the stacks of boxes piled by the pipes of the furnace. The cement floor under his feet was cold. Spiderwebs had spread over the jars and bottles along the window sills. At the far end of the basement was a combination washer-drier, and that was new; he did not remember that.

Among the clothes and magazines and furniture, he found the camping equipment. First he carried the Coleman stove and lamp to his car, parked in the driveway, and then he gathered up the tent and took that, too. While he was inspecting the air mattresses, the door at the top of the stairs opened, and the stairs lights came on.

"It's me," he said, as his mother appeared.

"I saw your car," Mrs. Briskin said. "What a surprise. Weren't you going to say hello? Were you just going to come and pick up what you wanted and then leave?" With her hand on the stair railing, she descended, a short gray-haired woman, wearing a housecoat and slippers. He had not seen his mother in two or three years, and as far as he could tell she looked exactly the same; she was no more infirm or stooped or halting. She was as vigilant as always.

He said, "I thought I'd take a camping trip."

"Come upstairs and say hello while you're here. There's some rolled roast left over from dinner. I read in the newspaper about your quitting your job at the station. Does that mean you'll be moving back here again to this side of the Bay?"

79

"I didn't quit my job," he said. He loaded the tent and the air mattresses and sleeping bags into the back of his car.

"Is she still working there?" his mother asked. "If you want my opinion, you're a whole lot better off away from there, if for no other reason than because of her. As long as you're both working around each other, you're not really free of her."

After he had closed up the car, he went upstairs with his mother and had a cup of coffee in the long living room with its carpeted floors and picture window overlooking the Bay, its lamps and piano and prints on the walls. The living room was the same, except that the fir trees by the window had grown taller. In the evening darkness the trees blew and rustled.

Seeing the living room again reminded him of his first year of marriage, the year in which he had tried to get Patricia and his mother to come to some kind of terms. Pat, with her preoccupations, had been unaware of Mrs. Briskin, and his mother had responded with hostility. His mother could never accept a daughter-in-law who was not "respectful." As far as he could tell, Patricia had no opinions about his mother; she enjoyed the house, its size and sturdiness, the large rooms and the view of the Bay, and especially the garden. Patricia entered the house as if she were alone in it. The house was "where he had grown up," and during the summer she liked to spend time out in the backyard, in one of the canvas lawn chairs, sunbathing and listening to the radio and reading and drinking beer.

Patricia had one day come indoors in her bathing suit and thrown herself down to have a long talk with his mother. The marriage was already coming apart, and Pat had a lot to talk about. With her was a bottle of Riesling. Lying on the floor, on the rug, in her bathing suit, she drank and talked, while his mother—as the old woman related it—sat stiffly in a chair in the corner, disapproving and unsympathetic. Pat's erratic sorrow had gone on and on until finally the afternoon was over, and still she lay on the floor; the Riesling was gone, and she was either sound asleep or had completely passed out. His mother had telephoned him, and he had come and gotten her; he found her still in her bathing suit, at seven o'clock in the evening, still on the living room floor. On the trip back across the Bay to their apartment in San Francisco, she had mumbled, and it had seemed funny to him; he could not work up the indignation his mother felt. The scene was the last between Patricia and his mother. As far as he could tell, Patricia remembered almost nothing of it. She thought that she had gone to sleep in the garden, by herself.

"What about this camping trip?" his mother asked, seated across from him. "How long do you expect to be gone?"

"I just want to get away," he said.

"You're going by yourself? I noticed you took both the sleeping bags." His mother went on to recall the camping trips he had made with his father, the excursions up to the Sierras. She did not mention the trips which he and Pat had made together.

"I have to go somewhere," he said, interrupting. "I have to do something."

His mother said, "I wish you could meet some nice girl."

He thanked his mother for the coffee and drove back across the Bay to San Francisco. Parked before his apartment house, he opened the glove compartment and brought out all the road maps. But he was not going on a camping trip; he had already given up the idea.

Putting the maps away, he drove in the direction of the station.

An hour later, in a back room at station KOIF, Jim Briskin sat sorting through the station's record library. On the floor was a carton half filled with albums he was taking; beside it was the carton he had brought back. On the table were his personal items, his bottle of Anacin, nosedrops, a hat he wore on rainy days, pencils and pens, letters he had saved that had arrived over the years, and odds and ends that he had stuck away in the desk at which he worked. Nothing, in all, of particular value.

Frank Hubble kicked open the door from the broadcast studio. An LP of Gershwin tunes was on the turntable, twenty minutes of music. Hubble, lighting his pipe, said, "What are you doing?"

"Taking home my stuff. Bringing station stuff back."

"Why don't you leave it all here? You'll be back in August."

"Maybe not," he said.

Tossing a dead match across the room to the wastebasket, Hubble said, "Patricia was in earlier."

"That's why I'm in late," he said. It was after ten o'clock.

"I don't mean during the day. I mean around fifteen minutes ago. She was supposed to meet Bob, but he's out closing some deal. You know how he operates."

"More used car lots?" Jim said. He could imagine Bob Posin still out, still chasing down contacts.

"No, this is for a food account. She was all dressed up. I guess they were going out for a good time."

Jim continued sorting the records from the cabinet. A Fats Waller disc slipped from his fingers, and he seized it and stuffed it into the carton. It was not his, but the hell with it, he wanted to finish and get out of the station.

"Take it easy," Frank said. Puffing on his pipe, he strolled back into the studio and closed the door.

While he was returning the station's records to the cabinet, a woman's voice said from behind him, "Hello, Jim."

"Hi," he said, continuing to work.

Pat entered the office. Her clothes, as always, were the best, he thought, noticing her shoes, her high heels, the straps at her ankles. She wore a rust-colored suit; a coat was over her arm, and on her hair was a small, simple hat. How red her lips are, he thought. Her figure was remarkable, but he was wise enough to recognize it from the bra ads; it was a professional figure, done with wire hoops and cones and straps. Too much pointing. Too much of an upward angle.

"What time did you get up?" she said. "The next morning."

"Around ten," he said.

"I thought you should sleep. So I didn't wake you up. Did you see my note?"

"No, I cleared out as soon as I could."

Pat said, "I said in the note that you should go ahead and have breakfast. There was bacon and eggs in the refrigerator. And if you wanted lunch there was a frozen chopped steak in the freezer."

"To tell you the truth," he said, "I saw the note. But I wanted to get out."

"Why?" She walked over beside him and the hem of her coat dangled by his shoulder. Close beside him her legs were smooth in that fine, regular manner that was so gratifying to the touch.

"Because," he said, "I was miserable enough as it was."

"You saw the write-up in the *Chronicle*?"

82

Pouring the odds and ends into the carton, he prepared to carry his possessions downstairs. "I'm parked in the taxi zone," he said. "I don't know how long I can get away with it."

"Are you moving out your things?"

"Pretty much."

She followed as he lugged the carton along the hall to the stairs. "Can I carry anything?"

"I can manage," he said.

"Use the elevator."

"Habit." He returned to the hall and, with the corner of the carton, punched the button for the elevator. "You're going out tonight?"

"Yes," she said.

"You look good," he said. "When did you get that suit?"

"I've had it."

The elevator arrived, and Pat held the door aside for him.

"Don't come down with me," he said.

"Why not?" She was already in the elevator; she touched the button, and the elevator descended. "I can help you with the car door."

When they reached the ground floor, she went ahead of him. He carried his load outside onto the sidewalk and to his parked car. Sure enough, a San Francisco cop was prowling at the license plate, considering it for a ticket. His motorcycle leaned by the curb, and he was already reaching his gloved hands toward his pad and pencil.

"Station business," Jim said, balancing his load to get out his keys. "Records and scripts."

The cop eyed him.

"We always use this loading zone." As Pat opened the car door, he shoved the carton inside onto the back seat and went quickly around to the wheel.

"This is a taxi zone," the cop informed him.

"I'll be right out of here," he said, starting the motor.

The cop shook his head and returned to his motorcycle. Jumping bodily on the accelerator, he roared off into the nighttime traffic and was gone.

"I have to go back up," Jim said. He had forgotten his hat and Anacin bottle.

"Will he be back?" Pat said.

"No," he said, shutting off the motor. "Not for a while."

They went back up, this time walking up the flight of stairs. The building was cold and deserted, and the stairs were gloomy. Beside him, Pat put on her coat; he helped her with it.

"It's scary," she said, "this late at night." She held onto the bannister.

He said, "I appreciated that, your letting me stay."

"I wish—" she said. "I wish we could have gone ahead." She stared down at the steps.

Upstairs on the station floor, she caught Frank Hubble's attention through the glass window of the broadcasting booth. When he stepped out, she said, "Has Bob been in?"

"No," Hubble said, "not since you were in last."

While Jim got his hat and Anacin bottle, she telephoned Bob Posin's apartment. Hanging up, she said, "No answer."

"He's out making money," Jim said.

They went back down the flight of stairs. There, under the windshield wiper of his car, was a ticket.

"He came back," Pat said.

"He or one of his kind." Furiously, Jim tossed the hat and Anacin bottle in with the other things.

"You should have moved it," she said, "when he told you to."

"How do you like that," he said, trying to control himself. "You can't believe in anything anymore."

"You always hated to get a ticket."

He stuffed the ticket into his pocket. "Don't you? That's ten bucks shot. For nothing."

"Calm down," Pat said.

"Good night." He started into the car.

"Wait," she said hesitantly. "I don't want you to go off like this. Why don't you take me across the street? That wouldn't do any harm."

He looked to see what was across the street. Most of the shops were closed and dark, and he dismissed them, but the Roundhouse cocktail lounge was open, and he realized that she meant it.

"The bar?" he said.

"No," she said, changing her mind, "let it go."

"Why not?" he said, taking hold of her arm. Why not indeed, he thought to himself, not letting her go.

"I better not," she said.

"If it was all right for me to stay with you the other night—" He led her across the street—the traffic was held up at a light—and onto the far curb. "This certainly ought to be okay."

She was nervous. "It's so much like a date. As if you were taking me out again."

"I am," he said, keeping tight hold of her.

Pulling away, she walked a few rapid steps; her heels clacked on the pavement. "I was just afraid if you drove you might be under too much strain; you are, aren't you? You might hit something. And I'd blame myself."

"Suit yourself," he said, pushing open the doors of the bar. With all his willpower, he kept himself from looking back; the doors swung shut, and he was inside, alone. The Roundhouse was a small high-class bar where the drinks were mostly water and cost more than he could afford; he traditionally avoided the place. The booth seats were red leather with brass studs. Quite a number of women were at the bar, and they were all well dressed. At the rear, a jukebox played dance music, strings and winds. The air was close. Everyone seemed to be smoking as well as talking.

He stood for a moment, and while he was standing the doors opened behind him, and Pat entered. Her face was pale.

"Come sit down," he said, leading her to a booth and feeling, inside him, a terrible sweep of hope; he was in a state of tension, and as he helped her take off her coat his hands shook.

"You're worked up, aren't you?" she said, touching his wrist.

"No," he said, seating himself across from her. "Just about to go out of my mind."

"Do you expect much out of this? Don't expect much; for my sake, please don't make something out of this. I just want to sit here and have something to drink."

The waitress appeared.

"What do you want?" Jim asked the woman across from him.

"Just order me something I can finish." She placed her hands together before her, touching her purse. What she wanted was Scotch or bourbon and not a mixed drink, a sweet drink. Too many sweet drinks made her sick, and he remembered mornings when he had fed her tomato juice and soft-boiled eggs and dry toast until she was able to get out of bed and onto her feet.

After he had ordered, he said to her, "Remember that New Year's Day we drove over to Sausalito to that joint out over the water . . . you lost your shoe; you sat down on the curb and wouldn't get into the car."

She said, "I think I should call Hubble and tell him if Bob shows up to come over here."

"Don't play coy," he said.

"I'm not." The drinks arrived, and she picked up hers. "Do you think I am? Do—you think I'm a tease?"

"No," he said.

"I am."

"Because of the other night?" He drank his own drink.

"It only made things worse. But it's as bad for me as it is for you . . . I feel terrible, I really wish I could die." Already most of her drink was gone: when she was in a crisis, she drank, and this was a crisis for both of them.

At each booth was a ceramic ashtray, as large as a pipe tray, and gray. He inspected the one by his elbow. While he was holding it, he realized that Pat was on her feet.

"I'm going to go phone. Order me another." She walked off, gliding forward without individual steps. Her coat was over her arm; the fall of it blended with her carriage, her upright posture. She lifted her chin and straightened the lines of her neck. At the same time, she seemed to know exactly where her feet were; he could not imagine her stumbling.

"Get him?" he asked, when she returned.

"Still no answer." She picked up her fresh drink.

"He's probably reading Looney Luke plugs."

After she had gone deep into her second drink, she said, "I want to show you something. It's a present." Opening her purse, she lifted forth a small tissue-paper package. "For Bob. I got it in Chinatown." She unwrapped a deity figure which he had seen many, many times. "It's a god. It brings luck . . ." She ran a nail across the stomach of the deity. "What do you think of it?"

He had to tell her it was trash.

"Oh," she said. "Well, what do you think of this? Or maybe I shouldn't show it to you." Another package was visible, but she put her hand over it, concealing it.

"I'd like to see it," he said.

With great deliberation, she unwrapped the package.

"A bracelet," he said, taking it.

"Silver. Handmade." She reached for it, and he wound it around her wrist: the bracelet slipped to the table. It was massive. He helped fasten it for her.

"Thanks," she said. "See the jade?" Dull stones were set in the silver fret- and scrollwork.

"It's Indian," he said.

"India?" she said doubtfully.

"American Indian. Probably Navajo."

"What do you think of it?"

"You know I'm not much on that sort of stuff. Too heavy, too much bulk. I like those thin hoops you used to wear." Reaching up, he touched her ear. "Those earrings."

"They should have told me it wasn't Chinese," she said. "It was a Chinese store; the man was a Chinese." She finished her drink, and he thought that she was beginning to get that fixed look; her features were becoming rigid. She had worked hard all day, and she was too tired to cope with the situation between them. Too much, he thought. For both of them. His old tenderness sprang to life inside him, his feeling for her; he knew how unhappy she was, sitting here, across from him. She could not leave and, for her, remaining was unbearable. So she was drinking.

"Let's go," he said, rising. He put her coat around her, handed her her purse, and with his hands on her shoulders persuaded her to get to her feet.

"Where?" she said. In her fatigue and confusion, she was malleable; she wanted him to take charge. "I should be over at the station. Suppose he comes and I'm not there?"

"All right," he said, "we'll go back there."

They left the Roundhouse and recrossed Geary Street. As they passed his parked car, he saw that a second ticket was stuck under the windshield wiper. The hell with it.

Upstairs in the station, he switched on the Best amplifier and turntable. From the studio, Hubble watched, smoking his pipe, as he fiddled with wires. Pat had withdrawn into a corner, taking no part in what he was doing. He plugged in a jack, closed a toggle switch, and as the tubes of the Bogen amplifier reddened, he rasped his finger against the diamond needle of the transcription arm.

From the speaker, a gross *fwwfh-fwwfh* sounded, an enormous tumult. This was quality equipment; over the years he had helped assemble it.

When he looked for Pat, she was gone.

The door of the broadcast studio opened, and Frank Hubble said, "What's going on, pal?"

"Nothing."

"You going to hold forth here?"

"No," he said. Over the years, he had come here and used the station's playback equipment; in a sense it was his.

Hubble said, "Of course it's fine by me. Like old times. But I'll be locking up at twelve. And you don't have a key anymore."

He started to go through his pockets, and then he remembered that of course he didn't have a key; he had given it to Haynes. Without answering, he went searching for Pat.

The door to the roof was open, and he stepped outside, onto the rickety wooden catwalk. Pat stood leaning with her elbows on the railing, smoking a cigarette and gazing across the roof at the lights and traffic of the street below.

"I wanted to clear my head," she said.

"Did you have that much to drink?"

"Yes." She lifted her face. "Before I came up here, before I ran into you . . . I was already over at the Roundhouse."

"How many?"

"I don't know."

"You look all right," he said, his fingers on her neck, at the line of her chin.

She said, "I feel as if I'm walking along a long drainpipe. One of those pipes we used to crawl through when we were kids. Bent over . . ." She drew away from him. "You were going to play records for me, weren't you? Like we used to before we were married."

"May I?" he said.

"Do you have to? I just want to stand out here. I don't think Bob's coming. Please—you go ahead on in. I'll stay out here. Please?"

Going back in, he took an album from the record cabinet, an old

Victor 78 r.p.m. set of the Sibelius Symphony No. 7. Hubble had returned to the broadcast studio; he was reading a commercial into the boom mike. His voice was audible from the wall monitor, and Jim shut it off.

The discs were in manual sequence. He put side one on the turntable and lowered the arm. Now Frank Hubble was watching through the window of the studio; he scowled with disapproval. How wicked, Jim thought, to be playing records. A man trying to draw out and hold his own wife.

The music, with its progression upward, its heavy quality of darkness and isolation, helped clear his mind. The weight seemed to pass from him into the music. The great structure of the music absorbed it and accepted it from him.

So, he thought, he discovered at this late date that the stuff had a use.

He got the music up loud enough to reach across the station, from one room to the next, out onto the roof where Pat stood in the darkness. At such volume, the music could not be evaded. Listening, he paced back and forth; he became restless, and suddenly he was afraid that no time was passing. The music had put an end to everything.

As he was putting on the second record, Bob Posin appeared. "What a racket," he said. "I could hear it all the way downstairs. Isn't it getting over the air?"

"No," Jim said, demoralized. In his mind he had written Bob Posin out of existence.

"Is Patricia here?"

Entering the room, Pat said, "Where have you been?"

"I was tied up. Straightening out the Granny Goose potato chip material." He said it with anger.

Pat said, "I can't go out. It's too late. Take my word for it; you wouldn't want to be with me tonight. I've had too much to drink, and all I want to do is go home. We can go out some other time; she'll be there for a week at least, and if she's gone we can see her when she's back this way." She seated herself with her coat and purse on her lap. The drinks had begun to affect her outwardly; her face was waxen. "Just go off and leave me. Will you do that?"

Standing his ground, Bob said, "At least let me drive you home."

"Have you ever seen a woman throw up nine drinks?"

Bob Posin left. "I'll see you tomorrow. Good night."

"Don't come near me," Pat said, as Jim approached her.

"I know you," he said. He led her from the station and downstairs to his car; she walked slowly, step by step, her eyes on the ground. In the lobby she halted, and try as he might he could not budge her.

"I'm scared," she said. "I'm too drunk to go with you. I know how you feel about me. Honest to God, Jim, I can't go with you. There's no point in talking about it; I mean it, and you know me well enough to know I mean it. And if I passed out, would you want me like that? That isn't what you want. I'm going to sit down here." With care she went to the lobby couch, the old ratty, bedraggled couch, and stood beside it. "Go away," she said. "In the name of Jesus Christ, leave me alone!"

He walked out onto the sidewalk and then around the block, past bars and closed-up shops, until he reached the side entrance to the station's parking lot. By the long route, he came back to the McLaughlen Building. In the lot was Pat's car, and she was trying to start it. The headlights were on, and with each turn of the starter motor the lights dimmed to a feeble yellow.

In the darkness he watched her, feeling compassion for her; the car door was open, and she was crouched over the wheel, her arm resting on it, her coat spilled onto the floor by her feet. She was crying; he could hear her where he stood. At last the engine caught, and the headlights flared up. Pat slammed the car door, threw the gear into drive, and drove directly into a car parked across from hers. The bumpers tangled with a grating metallic shriek. The engine died, and Pat sat without moving, her hand over her face.

Walking over, he saw that no harm had been done; both bumpers were scratched, but that was all. Nobody would care. He opened the car door and said, "Sweetheart."

"I won't let you," she said. She was clutching the wheel, and on her face was the set, fanatic look that she got once in a long while; she was terrified of him and of what she had done. Probably she thought she had demolished the other car.

"Look," he said. "I don't want anything to happen to you. You can't drive. You'll kill yourself."

She nodded.

"Let me drive you to your place. I won't go in; I'll park you in front of the building and I'll leave you."

"How'll you get back here? You have to come back for your car."

"I'll walk. Or take a cab."

"That isn't right."

He said, "Then I'll send you home in a cab."

"Don't." She caught hold of him; her fingernails dug into him. "It's dark there. I want to be out somewhere." Tears shone on her cheeks. "It's awful living alone; I have to marry Bob Posin—don't you see? I can't stand living alone. I can't stand waking up in the morning alone and going to bed alone at night and eating alone."

Kneeling against the seat, he put his arms around her and pulled her to him. Kissing her, he said, "Then let's go to my place."

For a moment, for the passing of one breath, she seemed to give in. Then, without pulling away from him, she said, "I can't."

"What then?"

"I—don't know." Her voice was bleak. Tears fell onto his face; tears rolled onto his nose, tickling him. "I wish I hadn't let you stay with me the other night. I just can't stand it without somebody any longer."

"Somebody!" he said, enraged.

"You, then. Oh god. All right, take me to your place, and let's go to bed and get it over with. Hurry." Jerking away from him, she scrambled over to make room for him. "Let's go. Drive me there. I'm tired and I give up."

He sighed. "I tell you what," he said. "I have a couple of friends. Two kids."

Her head turned, and she was looking at him. In the darkness, her gaze was fixed on him; he was aware of it, the intensity.

"They invited me for dinner last night," he said. "Suppose we go over there and stay awhile. Until you're sobered up. Okay? They're nice kids; they've been in the station. You've probably seen them."

Pat said nothing. But the struggle reached him, the sense of torment.

"The girl's pregnant," he said. "She's seventeen; the boy's eighteen. They live in a broken-down flat on Fillmore. They don't have any friends and their families aren't speaking to them. They don't have any money, and they'd like to see somebody once in a while."

After a long time, Pat said, "What—are they like?" Rallying, she said, "Is she pretty?"

"Very pretty," he said. He was still kneeling against the seat, and now he stood up. He was stiff, cramped. "Very sweet, very bright."

"She doesn't sound very bright. She could have taken precautions." For a time she was silent. "How did you meet them?"

"They came into the station. I took them with me when I went to dinner."

"What's . . . their names?"

"Rachael. Art."

Pat slid away until she rested against the far door. He gathered up her coat and purse and put them into her lap. "Just until I feel better," she said.

"Okay." Relieved, he got in behind the wheel and started up the engine.

"Did I damage that car? I never hit anybody's car before."

"It'll live," he said. He backed her Dodge away and then drove from the parking lot.

9

On Fillmore Street the neon signs of bars and shops put on color haphazardly for Saturday night; their arrangement had been built up over the years by businessmen. Spots of gum on the pavement formed dark circles near the entrance of a movie theater, a bowling alley, the illuminated door of a coffee shop.

As late as this a flow of persons, white and Negro and Mexican, passed the shops. In doorways, figures had left the flow and were by themselves. They were mostly boys. They wore black-leather jackets and jeans, and for the most part they were surprisingly lean. They stood with their thumbs hooked in their back pockets; they twisted to follow elements within the flow, as if they had some special interest. At the popping of an exhaust, they raised their heads. They listened; their mouths opened. They caught signals. Then they looked back at the individuals and made judgments about them. Spectators, they saw everyone and had an opinion.

In the middle of the block Jim located the house set back from the pavement, the fence and iron gate. "That's it," he said.

"Maybe they're not up," Pat said.

He was able to park near the house. Together he and Pat walked up the sidewalk; he opened the gate, and they passed on in, to darkness and the sudden loss of street sounds. The cement path was ahead, but neither of them could see it. Reaching, he took Pat's hands. Her fingers were cold, and he enclosed them.

To the right of the porch, the basement window showed a rim of light. "They're awake," he said.

"It's so late," Pat said. She stumbled, and a metal object rolled away, a tin can that glinted and then vanished into weeds.

He went down the steps, leaving her behind him. Against the streetlights she was slim and small, buried within her coat; her head was up, and she walked in a circle, her heels making sharp, staccato clicks on the cement. He knocked on the door.

The door opened and light flooded out. Rachael recognized him and said, "Oh. Hello." Backing away from him and holding the door open, she said, "We were playing cards."

He said to her, "This is in the nature of a favor. I have somebody with me and she isn't feeling well. We thought maybe we could drop by for a while. Were you just about to go to bed?"

"No," she said. She seemed to accept the situation. "Come on in."

Going back for Pat, he led her down the steps and into the apartment. "This was a sort of inspiration. You can throw us out any time."

Cards and poker chips were scattered across the top of the massive oak table. Something about the room had struck him as odd, and now he knew what it was; the walls were bare of pictures.

"This is Patricia Gray," he said. He did not try to describe their relationship. He was not certain what he had said to them.

"I think I've seen you a-a-at the station," Art said. He started to put out his hand and then hid it in his pocket.

Rachael said, "Can I fix you some coffee or something to eat?" She was standing close to Pat, and she had ducked in what seemed a survival of a curtsey. She wore a print dress, a bright summery frock, strapless; her shoulders were bare. Her skin was fairer than Pat's. Her hair was much lighter and cut much shorter. Possibly she was smaller, but her expanded middle made it hard for him to tell.

As he helped Pat off with her coat, she said, "It's warm in here. It's nice."

"You bet," he said.

"What huge lovely eyes she has." Turning to Rachael, she said, "You make me want to take up painting again." During the first year of their marriage she had cleaned a few brushes and made a few sketches, but nothing had been completed. The set of paints, as far as he knew, was now stored or thrown away. Certainly she had given up all pretensions along that line.

Art hugged Rachael close to him. "She's going to have a baby."

"Why, you're just a little doll," Pat said. "I can't get over her," she said to Jim.

"You're not only drunk," he said, "you're also queer."

"I mean it. I'd like to paint her sometime. Those eyes . . ." And then she moved off.

Following her, he said, "What would help? Coffee?"

"Yes," she said.

He went with Rachael into the kitchen. "She's under a lot of strain," he said, as Rachael put the coffee pot on the burner and got down cups and saucers.

"She's high-strung, isn't she?" Rachael said. "I kind of like her."

"You're sweet to let us in," he said. "I'm grateful. We were out roaming around . . . it was no good."

"How long were you married?"

"Three years," he said.

"I wanted to meet her; I'm glad you came. I know she means a great deal to you."

"That's true," he said.

"I can see why," Rachael said. She seemed shy and conscientious, concerned with doing what was right. She carried the coffee cups into the living room and began clearing the table.

"What were you playing?" he asked.

"Blackjack." She swept the deck of cards together and put it in its box. "One time we drove to Reno . . . we stayed there overnight. We played at the different tables."

Art said, "She's a real cool poker player. She takes it real seriously; one time she knocked off F-f-ferde Heinke's glasses because he was fooling around." In his nervousness he avoided looking at Jim and Pat; he grabbed up the poker chips and concentrated on them. He pretended that he was talking to no one in particular.

Several times in his visits to station KOIF, he had noticed Pat. He considered her beautiful; she reminded him of the women in fashion ads. The idea that such a woman would visit his house filled him with excitement. Only once had Rachael worn heels, and that was on the day they had gotten married. Glancing at Pat, he was aware of her dark hair and the intense color of her mouth. Makeup, he thought. He wondered how old she was. She was sitting by the table and he was attracted to her legs; they seemed to him long and curved, and he wondered if she was a model. She was so well dressed and beautiful that he went off into the other room and tried to think how he might improve himself. He examined one of his sport coats and a pair of slacks.

When he re-entered the living room, Rachael offered him a cup of coffee. Jim Briskin was standing by the table, holding a cup and saucer; his head brushed close to the ceiling of the room, and in such small quarters he seemed especially tall. He wore a loose coat, his regular coat, and no tie. Art wondered how he could go around with Pat and not dress up; his own mind was filled with notions and schemes about clothes.

Taking the coffee cup, he paced about with it. He was this close to such a woman, and at the same time he was farther away than ever. He had no idea what he might say to her. He was afraid to open his mouth. His own muteness offended him; probably she would never come back and he would never have this chance again. In agitation he said to her.

"H-h-hey, how long've you worked at the station?"

Pat said, "I don't know." To Jim Briskin she said, "When did I start?" Bending, she unfastened her high-heeled shoes and slid them off. She saw him looking at her and she smiled.

"How is it, working at a station?" Art said, as calmly as he could.

Pat said, "It's noisy."

"You want a month off?" Jim Briskin said.

"Sure," she said. In her stocking feet she went across the room to the radio. "Can I turn it up?" Dance music was playing; she made it louder.

"Not too loud," Jim Briskin said.

"Is this too loud?" Remaining by the radio, she closed her eyes. Art thought she looked tired. But he did not know what he could do for her; he walked in her direction without any plan.

Jim Briskin said, "You better come sit down and drink your coffee."

"It's excellent coffee," she said. "Is there anything to drink? I don't feel like coffee."

"You don't feel like drinking," Jim Briskin said.

"I do." She opened her eyes. "Not very much, just something."

Art said, "There's some beer in the icebox." She paid no attention to him and he went toward the kitchen. "I'll get you some."

Still looking at Jim Briskin, Pat said, "You want to dance with me?"

"You're in no state to dance."

"Then you don't want to dance with me."

"Come sit down." Jim Briskin reached out his hand toward her. "What do you want to do, sit in my lap?"

"No." As Art went into the kitchen, she was beginning to idle back and forth, a restless motion; her hands were up and she had shut her eyes again. His heart ached at the sight of such a pretty and tired woman, in her stocking feet, swaying beside the radio, her hands empty. The feeling was familiar to him, the yearning without an object. She did not really want to dance; she wanted to not be still, to be in motion. She could not bring herself to sit down.

Taking out the quart of beer, he poured a glassful and carried it into the living room. "Here," he said.

Pat shrank away. "What?" she said. "Oh. Thanks. No, I don't want beer." And his contact with her was broken; she no longer was aware of him. Gliding away, she hummed to herself, the tuneless, jangling release of pain.

"That's all we have around," Art said.

Now she returned; her motion carried her back toward him. Her eyes opened, and she focused on him as if she were awakening. "Will you dance with me?" she said. "Art? Is that your name?" Her hand came to rest on his shoulder, and her other hand was up, waiting to be grasped. Before he had time to make a decision, he had let her slip within his arm and he had set down the glass of beer and was dancing with her; her body was warm, and he could feel her backbone beneath his fingers. Her face, close to his, shone damply. Above her lips tiny drops of perspiration glinted from the line of fuzz. It was a lovely foxlike face, new to him, and yet it was almost touching his. Now she turned her head, sighing, and then looked down. Her black hair tumbled forward, and strands of it swept along his cheek. On his shoulder her hand rested heavily.

"Y-y-you dance good," he said.

Suddenly she broke away. "Don't you really have anything but beer? Did he tell you to say that?"

97

"You're turning paranoid," Jim Briskin said. "And sit down before you fall over."

She directed a hard, calculated glance at him, and then she walked to the kitchen. Art followed her.

In the kitchen she had the icebox door open and was kneeling down, reaching in among the milk bottles. "It's true," he said. "We don't usually—"

"I believe you," she said, straightening up beside him. "Do you know I'm drunk? I feel so—" She shook her head. "Not in a drainpipe anymore. That's something, at least. Maybe I feel romantic. Do I look okay?" Lifting her hands, she smoothed her hair.

"You look f-f-fine," he said.

"Did she get pregnant on purpose? You're very lucky, you know . . . to have a little doll of a wife like that. Did you go around together in school?"

"Yes," he said. "We had c-c-classes together."

"God," Pat said, "you're only eighteen. And what's she, sixteen? When I was sixteen, I still thought babies were supplied by the hospital doctors . . . the woman just got large to make a place for it. Like kangaroos. Kids get older faster, now. Why don't you go somewhere and get us a bottle?" From the pocket of her skirt, she took out folded bills and handed them to him; she stuck them between his fingers. "I saw a liquor store up the street. Get a fifth of rye or bourbon. No Scotch; I've had enough Scotch."

Humiliated, he said, "I c-c-can't buy liquor. This beer, some guys picked it up, you know? I mean I can go into a grocery store, I know some of these g-g-grocers around here. In a bar usually they'll serve me. But at the liquor stores they're real tough; they w-w-won't sell liquor to you if you're under twenty-one." It was living death. He slunk in shame; he cringed.

But she thought it was funny. "You poor damn kid." She reached up and her arms folded about his neck. The pressure of her mouth slid in a trail across his face; he felt the moist, clinging smear as she kissed him. Unbelievable. She had kissed him. Breathing into his eyes and nose, she said, "I'll walk you down. Okay?"

Coming out of the kitchen with her, he said to Rachael and Jim Briskin, "We're going down to the corner. W-w-we'll be right back."

"What for?" Jim Briskin said, not to him but to Pat.

"None of your business," Pat said. Stopping by him, she kissed him, too; she seemed gay now.

"Put on your shoes," Jim Briskin said.

Supporting herself with her hand pressed to the wall, she bent her leg, lifting her foot behind her, and slipped on her high-heeled shoe. As she did the same with the other, she said, "I want you to realize I'm paying for this."

"I hope so," Jim Briskin said. "And you'll pay for it a couple times again tomorrow morning. Who's going to feed you tomato juice?"

"Come on," Pat said to Art. "Where's my coat?"

Finding it for her, he started to hand it to her. Both Rachael and Jim Briskin were watching. Should he hold it up and help her into it? While he was floundering, she took the coat from him and opened the door that led out.

"Goodbye," she said. "We'll be right back."

To his wife, Art said, "See you in a minute."

Rachael said, "You might get some potato chips and maybe some of those cheese things."

"I will," he said, and he closed the door after himself and Pat. "Be careful," he said to her. All at once they were in complete darkness. He wanted to take her arm, but he was afraid; he did not understand what was happening—he could not believe it—and so he merely walked beside her up the steps to the cement path. "It's sure d-d-dark," he said. "It's funny, I saw you at the station, but I never said nothing to you. A lot of times we used to come in a group. Around four in the afternoon. We always listened to 'Club 17.' We came to talk to Jim Briskin. I guess he isn't on it now. What is he, off for a while?"

The woman beside him was silent. At the gate she stopped to let him push it aside for her. The gate groaned. She went on ahead of him. In the night wind her hair blew, long and untied; such hair, he thought, as he had never touched. She walked much more slowly than Rachael, but he thought, as she had said, that she had had a lot to drink. Now, on the sidewalk, she wrapped herself in her coat and seemed unaware of him; she gazed at the signs of stores, at the bars, into doorways.

"It's cold," he said, "for July. It's the f-f-fog." The air was heavy with fog; around each streetlight was a ring of misty yellow. Traffic sounds had receded and the footsteps of other persons were muffled, remote. The shapes that passed by were indistinct.

"Do you want the baby?" Pat said.

"Yes. Sure."

"A baby will hold you and her together. You're not a family without children; you're just a couple. Do they all tell you not to have a baby? I wish we could have had children. Maybe we'd still be married."

"Were you married?"

"Jim and I," she said.

"Oh," he said, taken by surprise.

"How long did you know her before you got married? If I told you how I met Jim, you wouldn't believe it. We went up the coast and we got crocked, and we went to bed together and that was it. We were up there on the Russian River for a week . . . six days, drinking and going to bed . . . walking around Guerneville barefoot. Going swimming. Have you ever been up there?"

He was able to say, "Sure, a couple of times. We used to drive up Friday night, a bunch of us. And st-st-stay for the weekend."

"Did you go up there with Rachael?"

"No," he said, "but we went to Reno once."

"Do you like to go out?"

"Sure," he said. "We used to go bowling a lot. And over to Dodo's. A-a-and she likes to play poker. And dancing; she's a cool dancer. And a lot of times we used to go to record shops. And stock car races . . . we drove down to Pebble Beach one time, for the races. When we had a car, we drove around. It broke down and we sold it."

"So you don't have a car?"

"No. I tried to get my brother Nat, who runs this used car lot on Van Ness, to lend me one, but he won't."

Pat said, "Did you go around with other girls before you met her?"

"No," he said.

"Then she's really your girl. Like in the movies. The girl you grew up with. The one woman for you." Her hands in the pockets of her coat, she said, "You think there's one girl for every boy? You believe that?"

"I don't know," he said.

"That's what they say."

"Maybe so," he said uncertainly.

Reaching out, she ruffled his hair. "Do you know you're cute? You're so young . . . and you have your one girl. I'll bet you still know kids you hang around with."

"I guess so," he said.

The liquor store was to their right, and Pat entered it. "Give me back my money," she said to him as they stopped at the front counter.

"What'll it be?" the clerk, a middle-aged bald man, said. He smiled a pale, false-teeth smile.

"A fifth of Hiram Walker's," Pat said. She took the dollar bills from Art and paid for the liquor.

"Good night, folks," the clerk said as they left the store. The cash register jangled.

"What are you going to be," Pat said as they walked back, "when you're old and broken down, like Jim and me?"

"A p-p-printer," he said. "Hey, when we get back you want to see the dummies for our science fiction mag? It's called *Phantasmagoria*. Ferde Heinke's president of the fan club. It's called the Beings from Earth."

She laughed. "My lord."

"It's multilithed . . . we've got pictures of fans and some drawings. If you can draw, m-m-maybe you could draw for the mag. You know?" It seemed a luminous hope; he exploited it for all it was worth. "What do you say?"

Pat said, "I'm no good. I can't really draw. I took a couple of art courses in college." Her voice was empty. "Don't look to me for anything, Art. Look what I did to Jim. I can't give. All I wanted to do was take. It was my fault. I know it, but I still can't give him anything. Even when I try, I can't. The other night I wanted to . . ." She broke off. "Have you ever had a woman hold out on you, Art? They're supposed to do that. One kind, anyhow. I never thought of myself as that kind. I just couldn't do it. Maybe I was still resentful. I was punishing him. Or maybe I've lost the capacity to give anything to anyone. I never gave anything to Bob Posin . . . I told Jim I did, but it was just to hurt him."

She stopped walking.

"That's my car," she said. "What do you think of it?"

Going to the curb, he identified it as a new Dodge. "Not bad," he said. "Too much chrome, but not a bad p-p-p-power plant."

"Can you drive?"

"Yeah," he said.

Reaching into her coat, she brought out car keys. "Here. Open the door."

Dumbfounded, he opened the car door. Pat motioned him in, and he crept in behind the wheel.

"Where do you go," she said, "when you take a girl for a drive?"

"Twin Peaks," he said. "I guess." He was beginning to tremble.

She slammed the door on her side. "Take me up there. Do you mind? I can't go back; he's waiting for me and I can't; honest to God, I want to, but I can't."

On the descending mountainside, cars were parked, most of them off the road or against the railing. In the cars shapes stirred slowly, in cumbersome positions. Below the road the pattern of lights flickered on the streets and houses of San Francisco. A field of lights as far as the eye could see. Fog drifted between the lights, and here and there the lights faded out. There was no sound except from the distant motors of cars.

"Here?" Art said. "Okay?" He took the car off the road, onto a dirt shoulder. Tree branches scraped the hood. He shut off the headlights.

"Turn the motor off," Pat said.

He did so.

Beside him she opened her purse and brought out a pack of cigarettes. He found matches and lit one for her; the match shook and she steadied his hand.

"What's the matter?" she said.

"N-n-nothing."

Blowing smoke from her nostrils, she said, "It's peaceful up here. I haven't been up here in ten years. Not since I was your age. You know where I grew up? Near Stinson Beach."

"That's cool up there," he said.

"We used to go swimming. Every few days. Do you like to swim?"

"Sure," he said.

"Are you good?" She handed him the package containing the bottle. "Maybe you can open it. There's a corkscrew in the dashboard."

He managed to get the bottle open.

"I shouldn't do this," Pat said, taking the bottle. "I know I shouldn't, but I have to do something; I can't go on this way. You think he'll forgive me?" Rummaging in the glove compartment, she came up with a plastic handleless cup. "God," she said, "it's still got Band-Aids in it." She tossed the cup back in the glove compartment. "I don't want to drink. Here." She handed the bottle back to him. "Put it away or drink it or something. You know what I came up here for?"

"What?" he muttered.

"I'm looking for something. I'm twenty-seven, Art. I'm ten years older than you. Do you realize that? When I was your age—you were seven. You were in the first grade." She sat smoking, her legs crossed. In the dull light entering the car her legs sparkled; he made out the line of her ankle, her heel.

"You're sure nice-looking," he heard his voice say.

"Thank you, Art."

"I mean it," he said.

"Let's go," she said. "Let's get out of here; I don't want to stay here."

Obedient, crushed with disappointment, he started up the engine. As he shifted into reverse, Pat reached out her hand and turned the ignition key; the engine died.

"You actually would," she said. "You're so—what is it? Let it go." She put out her cigarette and lit another with a shiny metal lighter. "You'd drive me back if I asked you to . . . you wouldn't put up a fight, you wouldn't argue with me. Do you really like me, Art?"

"Yeah," he said fervently.

"What about your wife?"

For that he had no answer.

"You're going to be a father. Do you realize that, Art? You're going to have a little boy. Have you thought what name you want to call him?"

"No," he said, "not yet."

"How will you feel?" She was staring out at the lights below them. "You're a seventeen-year-old boy and you're going to be a father."

"Right . . . ," he said.

"Eighteen," he said.

"The world's so goddamn peculiar . . ." She turned on the car seat, facing him; she had drawn up her legs and tucked them under her. In the light her cheekbones were radiant, and he traced, in his mind, the line of her forehead, the ridge of her eyebrow, and then her nose. She had thin lips. In the half-light her lips were black. Her chin and neck were in shadow.

"Come on, Art," she said.

"Come on what?" he said, afraid of her.

"Before I change my mind." Rolling down the window, she tossed her cigarette out; it fell into darkness. "I feel so awful. This is a terrible thing to do . . . it isn't fair to you or your wife or Jim or any of us. It's so mixed up. But what else is there, Art? I've been going around and around. I don't know, I really don't know."

Her fingers reached up and touched his face. Moving toward him, she brought her lips close to him; he felt the pressure of her mouth, the hard, sharp pressure of her teeth as she kissed him. Her breath smelled of flowers and cinnamon. As he put his arms around her, he heard the rustle of her clothes and the faint giving of muscles and ligaments and joints, the stirrings of her body. Her sleeve brushed his eyes; she was clinging to him, resting her head against his neck. How heavy her head was. She lay on him, breathing shallowly. Panting, he thought . . . not moving but content to lie against him with her eyes shut, her arm up so that her fingers curled into his hair. She was discouraged and lonely, and he knew what she wanted: she wanted to lie close to him, turning her face up to be kissed. He held her face between his hands and lifted her; at once she let her lips slacken so that he could find her mouth. She was back into the past, living out her own young days. She was with him, in the romance and excitement of a first date, wrapped up in his arms on the front seat of a car, parked at the side of the road above the lights of the city, overlooking the darkness, the night and fog. In other cars other boys held their girls and petted them and kissed them; he ran his hands along the fabric of her blouse, along her shoulders and arms. He avoided her breasts because that was not what she wanted. Holding his mouth against hers, he poured out of him and into her the love she wanted; he lost nothing and yet he felt her fill out and become powerful with it. She had to take it from him. But he had it to give her.

"I love you," he said.

She sighed. She said nothing. Her face lay pressed to his shoulder; time passed and she did not stir, and at last he realized that she had fallen asleep.

Gently, he lifted her back until she rested against the door. Then he covered her with her coat. Starting up the engine, he drove down the hill, back into town.

As they drove among the lights of Van Ness Avenue, she stirred a little, sat up, and then said, "Do you know where I live?"

"No," he said, "but we're not going there; we're going back to Fillmore."

"Take me home," she said. "You can call your wife from my place. Please."

He had been wrong. "Tell me where," he said. He felt leaden, but he did as she said; he could not back out. Beside him she was opening her purse to get out her cigarettes. Neither of them spoke, and then she said, "Turn right here."

He turned the car.

"What are you going to tell her?" she said.

"I don't know. I'll tell her something. I ran into these guys. Grimmelman, maybe."

"You've never done anything like this before, have you?"

"No," he said.

"Do you want to? You don't have to. I won't make you do it."

"I want to," he said. And he did want to. "You're really cute," he said. "You're really pretty."

"Thank you, Art." she said. "I know you mean it. You wouldn't say so if you didn't." She seemed calm, at this point.

10

After her husband and Pat had left the apartment to go to the liquor store, Rachael went into the kitchen and washed dishes. Ten or fifteen minutes passed, and then she dried her hands and walked to the front door.

"They're not coming back," she said, standing at the door.

Jim Briskin was slow to agree. "Sure they are," he said.

"No." She shook her head. "I knew this was going to happen sooner or later. But I thought it would be with the different guys . . . Grimmelman and those people."

Jim opened the door and started up the steps. "They must have gone off in her car."

"Where are you going?"

"Hell," he said, "I'll try her apartment."

"Let him go ahead," Rachael said. Her eyes were dry; he was amazed at her self-control. "She's very lovely and look how grown-up she is. If he wants to, then he should. What difference does it make if they go ahead or not? I couldn't keep him here . . . could you have kept her here?"

"No," he said. But he did not come back inside. He remained on the steps, the door open behind him.

"You can't control other humans," Rachael said. "You can talk to them, but it doesn't make any difference. Maybe in little things, or if they believe it already. Anyhow, I'm glad she's so nice."

He said, "I'll kill her." He meant it; he could feel her neck between his hands.

"Why? You know she's had a lot to drink. You know Art and I have had trouble . . . he wanted to go out. There's so many things he hasn't done and he wants to do them. He's too young. I was the only girl he dated. I guess I'm the only girl he ever—however you say it. People say it different ways. I don't know any good way."

"There isn't," he said, "not in a situation like this." He blamed himself. It was his fault. "Rachael," he said, coming back into the apartment, "I did it. I brought her here. And I knew she was in a state; I knew she was ready to try anything. We both were."

"It's a bad thing for you," Rachael said, "since you're in love with her."

"Look." He picked up his coat from the chair. "You stick around here. I'll go over to her place and try to round them up. I'll see you later." Without waiting, he left the apartment and went along the path to the sidewalk. Pat's car was gone, all right. He hailed a taxi and gave the driver the address of her apartment.

The lights in her windows were off, and nobody answered his rings. Another tenant entered the building using his key for the main door, and Jim went into the lobby behind him. Upstairs, at Pat's door, he knocked and then tried the knob. Still there was no answer. He listened, but he heard nothing.

Going back downstairs to the street, he searched in vain for a sign of the Dodge.

They were not here at her apartment. Where else, then? The only remaining place was the radio station. The time was twelve-thirty, and Hubble would have locked up; Pat had a key, and she and Art would have the station to themselves.

Again he flagged a cab. As it took him toward Geary Street, he thought to himself that at least he could pick up his car; it was still parked in the cab stand in front of the station.

When he had paid the driver, he saw that his car was gone. The cab stand was empty. And, peering up, he saw no lights in the top-floor windows of the McLaughlen Building. He walked around to the parking lot and still there was no sign of his car and no sign of Pat's Dodge.

107

A drugstore down the street was open. He entered it and, in a phone booth, called the station's number. The phone rang on and on; at last he gave up. They were not there either.

He located the number of the Kearny Street police station and called. "My car's been stolen," he said. "I left it parked in front of where I am and now it's gone."

"Just a moment," the police voice said. Clicks deafened him and then, after an endless pause, the voice returned. "What is your name?"

He gave them his name. "It must have happened within the hour," he said. He felt absolutely futile.

"The make and license number?"

He gave that, too.

"Just a moment, sir." Again there was a wait. "Your car was towed off," the police voice said. "It was parked in a hack stand, and the cab company phoned in a complaint."

"Oh," he said, "then where is it?"

"I don't know; you'll have to enquire about it tomorrow morning. Be here at Kearney Street at ten-thirty and arrangements will be made to return it to you."

"Thanks," he said, hanging up.

Without a car he was more helpless than ever. He walked out onto the sidewalk, and when a cab passed he waved to it. Again he was riding in a cab, and again he had given Pat's address. In his mind he was positive that they would show up there. Maybe, he thought, they had gone for a ride.

When the cab let him off before the apartment building, he saw the Dodge, moist and gleaming, parked by itself in a slot near the entrance.

He rang the bell by her name, but there was no response. Again he waited. Presently a figure appeared on the other side of the door. A heavy-set man stepped out of the building, glanced at Jim, and went on. He caught the door before it shut. Somebody was always going in or out. He climbed the stairs to her floor.

The door to her apartment was closed, and no light showed. He knocked. She did not answer, but he knew that this time they were here. Finally he tried the knob; the door was unlocked.

"Pat," he said, opening the door. The room was dark.

"I'm in here," she said.

He went into the bedroom. "Just you?" he demanded, fumbling to find the lamp.

"Don't turn the light on." She was lying on the bed. "Wait a second." In the darkness she rose up and moved; he was aware of her motions. "Okay," she said, "I wanted to put something on." Her voice was relaxed, and she sounded drowsy. "When did you get here? I was asleep."

"Where's Art?" he said, snapping the light on.

She lay stretched out in the bed, wearing a slip. Her feet were bare. Beside the bed, on the chair, was a neat pile of her clothing; under the slip she had on nothing at all. Her hair, dark and heavy, lay spread out on the pillow. He had never seen her so lacking in turmoil, so content. Smiling, she said, "I sent him home. I gave him money for a cab."

"Well," he said, "you've destroyed their marriage."

"No," she said. "I've been thinking about it. I'm a girl he went with before his marriage. Do you see? This is what he missed . . . do you know that Rachael is the first girl he ever took out?"

"I took you over there," he said, "and you wrecked those kids—you went right to work."

Sitting up, she said, "No, you're wrong."

"You wanted to go to bed with somebody, and you couldn't go to bed with me. So you went to bed with him."

Pat said, "It isn't just him. When I saw Rachael, I wanted to have her. Try to understand. I'm in love with both of them, and so are you. When I saw her, I wanted to make love to her; I wanted to kiss her and pet her . . . I wanted to take her to bed and fondle her. But of course I couldn't. But it doesn't matter which one of them. I'm glad you took me over there because now I've finally come back to life . . . it's the same with you, too. Isn't that so?"

"Christ," he said, "don't include me in this."

"They're our children," she said.

He sat down on the bed beside her. In a sense she was right. He could not deny what she had said.

"They hold us together," she said, gazing up at him, her arms loose at her sides. Under her slip, her small unsupported breasts hung forward. At each, pressing against the slip, a dab of shadow rose and fell. Her face had a scrubbed look, and her makeup was gone. "I can't bring myself to trust you, and I can't come to you because of that. And you haven't been able to trust me, have you? Neither of us has any trust in the other . . . but we trust them. You knew this was my fault, didn't you?"

"Yes," he said.

"That's what I mean. For years we've had no confidence in each other. But we love them, and we believe in everything about them. So we can go to them. They're the only persons in the world we can really go to. I think we get to each other through them. We can let go with them . . . we can get the peacefulness we need."

"What a miserable rationalization," he said. "You ought to be weeping in agony instead of lying there."

"I'm very happy," she said. "I feel close to you. Don't you feel you've been with me? It was you I was with, here, not somebody else. Don't you remember how we used to lie together afterward . . . remember when we were up in the cabin, how we used to just lie around—I guess we were exhausted. But there were no tensions, we were just limp and fagged out. I always felt closer to you afterward, even more than when we were actually doing it. To me, doing it is—" She was silent a moment. "Just a means. Isn't that so? God, and at first, before I got my diaphragm. When you used those awful things . . . we were so far apart. It wasn't until afterward that we could come together, that we could lie around."

"I remember what you said," he said.

"About what? Oh, yes. Those things you used."

"Before we found out we didn't have to use anything."

She said, "It was like having a length of green plastic garden hose inside me. I never got anything from that . . . did you?"

"No," he said, "not completely."

"What about now? Have I cheated you again? Do you feel that way?" She caught hold of his arm. "We're going to have to go on reaching each other through them . . . you know that, don't you? We're too involved now. We can't break away."

"Where were you?" he said. "Earlier. I came by."

"We drove up to Twin Peaks and parked."

"Why didn't you do it there?"

"If the police caught us, they'd send me to prison or something.

110

And anyhow it's ugly in a car. I wanted to do it here, where you were, the other night."

"You're really heartless," he said.

"No," she said, "I'm not. You'll see. You'll get to me through the girl . . . we'll live through them."

"What about them?"

Her eyes rose to focus on him. "This will be a great and tremendous thing for them. It already is."

"How do you figure that out?"

"Because," she said, "they love us; they admire us. We're what they want to be. We'll all merge together . . . the four of us, we'll be complete. We'll be able to walk around on the face of the earth again. And we can throw out the trivial people, Bob Posin and all of them. I mean it. I feel so much love for you; it's inside me, and I feel you got to it tonight."

"If I did," he said, "I don't know it. I was somewhere else at the time."

"Hand me my clothes," she said. "Would you?"

He gave her the pile of clothes. Still lying propped up on the pillow, she sorted through them; she untangled her underclothes and stockings.

"I'm going on with this," she said. She hugged the clothes to her breast. "It's going to save both of us, and I'm not going to give it up. Tonight I found what we needed. You knew that, or you wouldn't have brought me there."

"That was such a mistake," he said, "such a terrible goddamn mistake."

"You know I'm right."

He said, "This is just a lot of hot air to justify taking that kid and seducing him."

"Yes," she said, "I guess that's what I did." Now sitting up, she bent forward and tugged her slip off over her head. She stood up, naked. Her body, smooth and pale, disappeared into her underclothes, and then she was buttoning her dress. "If it was wrong," she said, shaking her hair back from her eyes, "I wouldn't feel like this. I wouldn't feel so completely good."

"A length of green garden hose," he said.

111

"What's that? You?" Standing up on tiptoe, she kissed him on the mouth. "No, you were perfect. Everything I could want, everything I ever hoped for."

"That kid," he said.

"That kid," she said, "was you. Still is you."

"Is the girl safe?" he said.

At the dresser she brushed her hair with a hairbrush, her head down, her arms raised. "They're both safe. So are we. We're in together; we can't menace them . . . can we? How is this a menace? Have I taken anything away from him? Have you taken anything from her?"

"No," he said, "and I'm not going to."

She had stopped brushing her hair. "Jim," she said, "if this doesn't heal you and me, then nothing ever will. Do you understand? Do you see that?"

"I see," he said, "that after you finish messing around here and wrecking these kids' marriage and lives, you're going to say that's it and you're going back and marry Bob Posin."

"I won't marry him," she said, "under any circumstances. Whatever happens."

"Thank god for that," he said.

"If this doesn't work out—I don't know what I'll do. Anyhow—" She tossed down her hairbrush and ran over to him; her eyes were bright with joy. "I'm so happy. It was like nothing on earth; he just never got tired or wore out, the way we used to. We could have gone on forever, all night and all day tomorrow and on and on, not even eating or sleeping, just going on forever."

"How about your job?"

His tone made the color and glow vanish from her. She finished dressing, and then she said, "How's Rachael?"

"Okay."

"Did she say anything?"

"Not much."

Pat said, "I'm—a little scared of her."

"I don't blame you."

"Would she—do anything?"

"I haven't any idea. But," he said, "I'm glad I'm not in your shoes."
He patted her on the back. "Think about that for a while."

"She's just a kid," Pat said. "She's only sixteen." But in her voice
was a thread of concern. "That's silly. She'll mope for a while, like
you. But my god, he's going back to her; does she think this is going
to last forever? It's not—"

He said, "We'll see."

Leaving her apartment, he walked downstairs.

When he got home to his own apartment, the phone was ringing.
Leaving the hall door open, with his key in the lock, he crossed the
dark cold living room and groped on the table at the end of the couch.

"Hello?" he said, finding the receiver. An ashtray tumbled to the
floor, disappearing from sight.

"This is Pat." She was crying, and he could barely understand her.
"I'm sorry, Jim. I don't know what to do. I'm so unhappy."

Softening, he said, "Don't feel bad. It can probably be patched up."

"I—wish we hadn't gone over there. I didn't mean to get involved
with him."

"It wasn't your fault," he said. It was his fault, not hers.

"They're both so sweet," Pat said. She was blowing her nose and
undoubtedly wiping her eyes.

"Better go to bed," he said. "Get some sleep. You have to go to
work tomorrow."

"Do you forgive me?"

"Don't be silly," he said.

"Do you?"

"Of course."

She said, "I wish we could get along. It's so miserable. What do you
think will happen? Is Rachael out gunning for me? Do you think she'll
be after me?"

"Go to bed," he repeated.

"I guess you don't want to come back here tonight. Even for a
while."

"I can't," he said. "The cops towed away my car."

"I—could get you in my car."

"Go to bed," he repeated. "I'll see you in a day or so. I'll call you up."

"Is it too late for me to call her tonight?"

"If I were you," he said, "I'd stay away from them."

"All right," Pat said.

He hung up, and then he went stiffly into the bathroom and turned on water for a shower.

11

In the course of keeping strong ties with his various clients, Bob Posin met Hugh Collins, the wealthy San Francisco credit optometrist, for lunch.

"Hugh, old man," he said.

Across the table they shook hands. Collins was a balding middle-aged person with the grimacing smile of the successful businessman. Station KOIF had carried his ads for three years: hourly spots before and after the summary of the news. Dr. H. L. Collins's offices were located on Market Street and in Oakland and down the coast in San Jose. He was a major account.

"You're looking well," Posin said.

"Same can be said for you, Bob," Collins said.

"How's the eye business?"

"Can't complain."

"Still selling glasses?"

"Plenty of them."

The baked salmon steaks arrived; both men began to eat. Toward the conclusion of the meal, Hugh Collins mentioned why he had got hold of Posin.

"Guess you know about our convention."

"Say," Posin said, "that's right. What is it, all the optometrists in North America?"

"Just in the West," Collins said.

"Big doings," Posin said.

"Plenty big. We're holding it at the St. Francis Hotel."

"Starts this week, doesn't it?" Posin said; he had only a hazy idea of such convention activity.

"Next week," Collins said. "And I'm heading the entertainment committee."

"Yeah," Posin said.

"Look here," Collins said, leaning toward him, "I want to show you something I picked up for the boys. Not all of them; just the fellows, if you get me. Personal pals." From under the table he slipped Posin a flat, disclike container.

"What's this?" Posin said, holding it cautiously, suspecting a trick.

"Go ahead, open it."

"What'll it do, give me a shock?" He was familiar with convention gimmicks.

"No, just open it."

Posin opened it. Inside the container was a pornographic gewgaw, brightly colored, made of durable plastic. The kind that in the old days had been made from ordinary red-phosphorus kitchen matches and was imported from Mexico. During World War II, he had been stationed at El Paso and had gone down to Juárez and brought such items back; he had made a steady profit on them. It was a shock to see such a thing again after so many years.

This one was better made. He put it through its limited paces; it had only two postures. Going to and doing.

"What do you think?" Collins said.

"Great," he said, closing the gewgaw up in its box.

"That ought to go over."

"Absolutely," Posin said.

Folding and unfolding his napkin, Hugh Collins said, "Of course that won't hold them for long."

"It'll give them something to fiddle with," Posin said. "So they won't stick their hands up girls' dresses along Market Street."

At that, a queer, strained look appeared on the optometrist's face. "Look here," he said hoarsely.

"Sure, Hugh."

"You run a radio station . . . you must see a lot of folks in the entertainment field. Singers, dancers."

"Sure," he said.

"You got any ideas? You know, for our entertainment program."

Posin, out of spite, said, "Like a young fellow to sing pop ballads?"

"No," Collins said, perspiring. "I mean—well, some gal who can really entertain."

"Afraid it's out of my line," Posin said.

Disappointed, Collins said, "I see."

"But maybe I know a guy who can help you. An agent. He handles a bunch of singers and similar stuff in San Francisco . . . for different supper clubs and night spots and the Pacific Avenue places."

"What's his name?"

"Tony Vacuhhi. I'll have him give you a call."

"I'd really appreciate it," Hugh Collins said. Behind his glasses his eyes sparkled moistly. "I really would, Bob."

That evening Tony Vacuhhi, seated at the desk in the front room of his flat, dialed the official phone number of the optometrists' convention.

"Let me talk to Hugh Collins," he said.

"Dr. Collins isn't here," the voice, a functionary's voice, answered.

"Well, I gotta get hold of him," Vacuhhi said. "He wanted some information, and now that I got it for him I can't get hold of him."

"I can give you his private number," the functionary said. "Just a moment." And right then and there Tony Vacuhhi got the number he wanted.

"Thanks for your help," he said and hung up.

Leaning back in his chair, he dialed the number.

"Hello?" a man's voice answered.

"Dr. Collins? I understand you're in charge of the entertainment for the convention. My name is Vacuhhi, and I'm a representative here in San Francisco. I represent various top-line entertainers and artists in this area. As a matter of fact, we specialize in the type of entertainment appreciated by the various conventions, and we make it a sort of special effort on our part to satisfy the convention people when they get here in town, and save them a lot of effort and embarrassment in procuring this kind of entertainment on their own. Especially where they might not know exactly how to go about it, if you understand what I mean."

"Yes," Collins said, "I see."

Swiveling in his chair, his feet upon the window sill, Tony Vacuhhi

continued, "As you're probably aware, this variety of enterprise re-
quires tact, and we have to be delicate and we need to be certain we're
dealing with the proper persons. So is there any way I can come down
and talk this over with you face-to-face? I assure you I won't be
wasting your time; you can depend on that."

"You can come over here," Collins said, "or I can meet you someplace."

"I'll come over," Vacuhhi said, flipping a pencil eraser up into the
air and catching it in his coat pocket. "Now it might even be possible
for me to arrange to bring along one of these particular entertainers,
who has special experience along the lines we're discussing. She's a
young lady quite popular in this area. Her name is Thisbe Holt; you
may have heard of her. What would you say if I brought her along
and then we could settle the deal right there on the spot and you could
get it off your mind once and for all and turn your attention to the
other various items you have to work on?"

"Suit yourself," Collins said. "She's—the right kind for this?"

"Absolutely," Vacuhhi said. "She has a great deal of visual appeal,
and that's generally appreciated at conventions."

Collins gave him the address and said, "I'll expect you then."

A yellow-and-black Mercury convertible crunched up into the driveway before Hugh Collins's home. The top was down, and in the
convertible were a man and a woman; the man was lean-faced and the
woman was young and pretty, with reddish hair and a full, unlined
face.

Hugh Collins thought how lucky it was that he knew a guy like
Posin, who could put him in touch this way. Opening the front door
of the house, he stepped out to greet Tony Vacuhhi and Thisbe Holt.

"Keep your coat around you," Vacuhhi was saying to the girl. She
seemed quite young, not more than twenty. In the evening wind her
hair fluttered and sparkled. "What do you mean this is costing you
money? Where would you be earning money this time of day?"

"I could be at the Peachbowl," she said.

"Yeah, except the Peachbowl doesn't open until nine o'clock. If you
have any sense and—" He noticed Collins. "Are you Mr. Collins?"

"That's right," he said. They shook hands. "Come on in and I'll fix you a drink." He could tell little about Thisbe because she kept her coat tight around her.

"Nothing for us," Vacuhhi said, "but thanks anyhow." As they passed into the house, he nodded to Thisbe. She slid her coat off and laid it over her arm, seeming to rise up at the same time, as if she were stepping out of warm, undulating water.

"Hello," she said to Hugh Collins.

She was a tidy enough girl, with rather stocky legs. Her breasts were the largest he had seen in years, and they were placed very high; they wagged from side to side as she pushed her coat out of the way.

"Is that really her?" he asked Vacuhhi. "That's not something she's got stuffed in there?"

Thisbe wore a tight silk dress, already stretched and wrinkled. The dress could not survive such pressure; it was beginning to give at the seams.

"That's a size forty-two chest," Vacuhhi said.

"Cut the kidding." But Collins was impressed. The girl, Thisbe, walked stagily about the room, her shoulders back and her buttocks tightened, so that both breasts lifted, wobbling a trifle, an engaging and outlandish sight showing that they were really part of her, not just stuck on afterward.

"Imagine growing up with those," Vacuhhi said excitedly. "All the way through grammar and junior high school."

"Does she know?" Collins said.

"Sure she knows. But she thinks they're just flesh; she don't think anything particularly about them. Like they were hands or something."

Thisbe had come close now. "I'm very glad to meet you, Mr. Collins."

"Same here," he said. "But if you're going to talk to me, put your coat back on."

She did so, struggling with the sleeves. Neither man moved to help her; the two of them stood together, looking on.

"What do you do?" Collins asked.

"I'm a song stylist," she said. "You know, like Lena Horne." With her coat on and buttoned, she seemed quite ordinary. Her face was actually plain, plump enough to sag at the jowls; her skin was clean but not a good color. Much too pale. Her chin lines were indistinct. Despite her mascara, her eyes seemed small, almost malformed—bad eyes, he decided, and damn near crossed. Her hair was really her strongest point—not considering her mammoth breasts. But at least she was young. He could not help contrasting her with his wife, Louise, who was currently visiting her family in Los Angeles. This girl was fifteen years younger. Her red hair looked quite soft. He wondered how it felt to the touch.

"You could certainly do with another name," he said.

She leered at him, a frightful smile made up of jagged teeth and white, expanded gums. Never, he decided, would she get anywhere. Chest or no chest. She had a gross, aggressive quality—or lack of quality—as if she were physically shoving herself forward. Wiggling, pushing, trying to get just one more step up. He felt oppressed by her.

Still, she did have an overabundant "visual appeal," and in a hotel room, among ten or eleven men, she would be a sensation. Just exactly what he needed for the show after and above the public entertainment. Guffy had already made his room available for this, and they had all chipped in money.

"I made up the name," Vacuhhi said. "Don't blame her."

"Don't you know who Thisbe was?" the girl demanded. Evidently she had read up on it. "She was in Shakespeare's *A Midsummer Night's Dream.*"

"She was a wall," he said.

"No, she wasn't a wall. She was the girl in the play they did; she was separated from her lover by a wall."

"Well," he said, "what do you do? Get up and read?"

"I told you very clearly, I'm a song stylist in the manner of Lena Horne. You surely have heard of Lena Horne."

"Get off it, Thisbe," Vacuhhi said. To Collins he explained, "She does a bubble act, but it's not like anything you ever saw in your life. Wait a minute and I'll go get the bubble."

He went out to the car and returned carrying a gigantic plastic bubble.

"Developed by the United States Navy," he said, tossing the bubble down; it struck the living room floor and rolled without breaking. "A float, a marker float." The bubble was transparent, but its texture was uneven; the rug and floor beyond it were magnified, distorted.

Thisbe said matter-of-factly, "I get inside the bubble."

"You do?" Collins said, enthralled.

"Yes, I get in it. Of course, I can't do it now. I can't do it without removing my garments."

"Jesus Christ," he said.

"Yeah," Vacuhhi said, "she really gets into it. It's a tight fit, but she manages. There's this aperture." He showed Collins how a section of the bubble could be twisted loose. "It didn't come that way originally; we altered it for her. She crawls into the bubble with nothing on—" He led Collins off where Thisbe could not hear. "And then they sort of boot her around, you get me?" He gave the empty bubble a shove with his foot and the bubble rolled across the living room, striking the far wall. "Like that. Only she's in it. She turns with it on account of it's so tight in there."

"How does she breathe?" he asked.

"Oh, there's a bunch of tiny holes. You think you could use this for your entertainment program?"

"Yes," he said, "I certainly can."

Thisbe said, "But you guys have to be careful and not kick the bubble too hard. Sometimes I'm black and blue for weeks afterward, after a lot of you convention guys have kicked me around."

After Thisbe and Tony Vacuhhi had departed, Hugh Collins began to dwell on the arrangement he had made, the acquisition of Thisbe for the entertainment of himself and his fellow optometrists.

Good lord, he thought, feeling weak. A girl who would get into a plastic float and allow herself to be rolled around on the floor would be willing to do anything.

This was going to be the best doggone convention yet.

12

Jim Briskin spent most of the next day getting his car back from the San Francisco police. They neither recognized him nor knew where his car was; according to a well-padded cop in a blue shirt, his car could be at one of several tow-away depots. Along with a group of others in the same fix, he trailed off in search of his car. At one-thirty in the afternoon his car was found. He paid his fines and the amount virtually wiped out his cash on hand. He emerged in the midday sunlight blinking, shaken, and scathingly hostile to the San Francisco police department.

A punishment, he thought.

After he had eaten lunch in a downtown café, he got his car from the lot—this time he had taken it off the street—and drove, alone, to Golden Gate Park.

Under his shoes the lawns were wet. He walked with his hands in his pockets, his head down. Ahead of him was Stow Lake. In the center of the lake was an island connected to the shore by a stone bridge. At the peak of the island was a grove of trees, and a Jesus Christ cross, and an artificial fountain, the waters of which were pumped up and released. Ducks paddled in the water of the lake, small brown ducks, not the eating kind. Boats with children were here and there. At the boat house was a candy counter. Old men dozed on benches with their legs stuck out.

As a boy of nineteen, he had come here with a notion which at the time had seemed illicit and lewd, not to say uncommon; he had arrived with a portable radio and a blanket, hoping to meet some pretty girl in a bright, colorful, laundered dress. Now those days, those desires, did not seem lewd; they seemed to him sad.

He thought, I can't blame him. Any boy of seventeen or eighteen or nineteen with a grain of sense in his head would have done the same thing. I would have. How perfect Patricia was. What a wonderful woman for a boy to get hold of. For any man, he thought. But especially for a boy, aching to touch and hold a full-grown woman. A woman who wore a coat and rust-colored suit and whose hair was dark, long, soft to the touch. Once in a lifetime. It would have been lunacy to turn her down.

A dream, he thought. Fulfillment of a dream. A dream of pure life.

Anybody, he thought, who would call such a response a sin was either a hypocrite or a fool.

A fat, dangerous-looking squirrel was preparing to approach him. First the squirrel advanced and then retreated, his brush undulating. What sturdy hams the squirrel had. And the grip of his claws. Revolving, the squirrel again came in his direction, halting to rise up, clasping and unclasping his paws. He had a mean expression; he looked like an older squirrel, a veteran.

Jim stopped at the candy window of the boat house and bought a package of peanuts.

Once, years ago, when he and Pat had walked through the Park, a squirrel had followed them for blocks, hoping for a handout. But that time, alas, neither he nor Pat had had anything to give him. Now, if they were in the Park, they bought peanuts.

"Here," he said, tossing a shelled peanut at the squirrel.

The squirrel scuttled after it.

Off on a slope a gang of kids in jeans and T-shirts were playing softball. Jim seated himself to watch. Eating the peanuts which he had bought for the squirrel, he enjoyed the noisy, disorganized game.

He thought to himself: I'm glad I'm not in her shoes. I'm glad Rachael isn't after me.

A baseball rolled across the grass and stopped at his foot. One of the kids cupped his hands and yelled. Jim picked up the baseball and tossed it. The ball fell short.

Christ, he thought. He could not even do that.

If he were in her shoes, he thought, he would be scared. Because Rachael was a tough little urchin, and she would not listen to the

123

usual hocus-pocus, the verbal clouds thrown up to protect the guilty. She knew Pat was guilty. She knew how her husband's mind worked, how it had to work under the circumstances.

He thought of Jim Briskin, the nineteen-year-old kid, back in the early days, the kid mooning along the path by Stow Lake; his head was too big, too heavy, and his arms flapped foolishly. He was altogether a dopey kid. He was not good in sports, and his complexion was only fair; like Art Emmanual, he had a tendency to stammer, and when it came to girls, well, the truth of the matter was that at nineteen he had never done more than put his arm around a pretty, bouncy-haired high school girl in skirt and blouse. Once, at a dance, a girl had kissed him. Once—and what a once that had been—he had talked a girl (what was her name?) into sliding off her shirt long enough for him to see that it was true, it was all true; what they said was so—the source of immortality on earth, the source of everything warm and good and important in life, was somewhere inside a girl's blouse, if the girl was fresh and pretty and as shy as that girl. But he did not count that; he still thought of himself as not having done more than walk a girl to the show and put his arm around her when the lights were down; the reaching into the girl's blouse did not belong to him because he had gotten nothing, he had gained nothing permanent. For that, he realized, for that kind of moment to mean something, the woman had to be completely taken over. It was nothing to peek, to touch, to be present. That was a mockery. That was pain the like of which he had never again experienced.

At nineteen he had strolled around Stow Lake, hoping plaintively. He had strolled literally for months, in all varieties of weather, and one afternoon on a cloudy day, about four o'clock, he had come upon a girl and a man waxing a diminutive foreign car. The car was parked out of the sunlight—what little there was—and the two of them were working vigorously, both of them perspiring, both in cotton shorts and heavy gray sweaters.

As he passed, the girl had smiled at him and he had said, "A lot of work."

"You want to help?" the man said.

So he took a chamois rag and helped. When the car (a French Renault) was shiny and the rags and wax cans were put away, the two of them invited him to come along with them and have a drink. They were a young married couple with a six-month-old baby; they lived in a housing development, and the man was an engineering student at Cal. They lived in Berkeley—so did he—and he hung around them, off and on, for almost a year. Then the husband, who, it developed, was queer, disappeared with a queer friend, leaving his wife and baby. And with her Jim Briskin had a long, involved, deeply experienced affair, his first affair, until all at once the husband came back, beating his chest with remorse, and the family re-formed.

Now, walking along, he smiled to himself. The illusions of youth. Joanne—her name was Joanne Pike—was about the sweetest, most considerate girl he had run across. She had never understood what ailed her husband, and when he returned, she simply wrote the interval off and made up with him.

And, he thought, Rachael probably would make up with Art. But she would not make up with Pat, and, he thought, perhaps she really would seek her out and do her harm.

At that thought he felt a slow, dreadful coldness grow inside him.

Among all the people in the world, Pat was the most precious to him, and he wondered if he was supposed to protect her from Rachael. He wanted to take care of her, protect her, and be responsible for her. Even last night. Even at the time when he had sat on the edge of the bed listening to her as she lay stretched out in her nylon slip, looking down at her and hearing her account of what she had done and why, hearing how she had gone to bed with somebody else.

What a mess it was. But they were in it now; they were in it to stay.

13

At three-thirty in the afternoon, Art Emmanual, in a sport coat and pastel slacks, his shoes shined, his hair oiled and combed, entered the McLaughlen Building. He pressed the elevator button. With rumblings and clankings the elevator, the iron trap of scrollwork and springs and cables, descended to the lobby. Three men and a woman, in business suits, stepped off and went past him, out of the building. He entered the elevator, started it up, and ascended to the top floor.

Ahead of him was the barren, unpainted hallway. To his left was the high-ceilinged front office of the station, and at her desk Pat sat typing. Her hair was tied back in braids; she wore a jacket and a blouse with buttons running up the middle.

"Hi," he said.

Startled, she stopped typing. "Hello." On her face was an expression of fear.

"I thought I'd drop by," he said. "H-h-how are you?"

"I'm fine," she said. "Did you get home all right?"

"Yeah," he said.

Standing, she came toward him. She wore a long skirt and low-heeled slippers. "What did Rachael say?"

"She was in bed." He shuffled his feet. "She d-d-didn't say much. She knew we went somewhere. I don't think she knows, though. What we did, I mean."

"Really?" Pat said.

He said, "I thought maybe you could get off for coffee."

"No." She shook her head. "I don't think you ought to come here. I might as well break it to you now." Taking him by the elbow, she

126

led him down a hall and into a small back room. "I'm engaged to the station business manager, Bob Posin. He's around somewhere. So you go on home."

Abashed, he said, "Yeah? I didn't know that."

Now she was aware of his sport coat. "That's a good coat for you. I'm not so sure about the slacks."

He said, "You always dress real good."

"Thank you, Art." She was preoccupied. Then she smiled a thin, worried smile and said, "Look, you go on home or wherever you were going. I'll try to call you sometime this evening. Or maybe that wouldn't be so good."

"I can call you," he said, with hope.

"Would you do that? I'm sorry about now, but when you know somebody who works in an office, you want to be pretty careful about dropping in on them. You understand." She passed by him, then, her long skirt swirling. "Goodbye, Art," she said.

As he left the station, she was back at her desk, involved in her typing.

Anguish, he thought to himself.

Going down by the elevator, he experienced all the misery possible; the pain went with him all the way to the ground floor and out onto the sidewalk. He carried the pain block by block as he walked aimlessly. The pain was there as he got into a bus and rode out toward Fillmore Street. At Van Ness he got off the bus, and the pain was right there. He knew it would not leave; it would have to recede gradually, over a period of weeks. It would have to wear out of him; he could not shake it.

Stopping by Nat's Auto Sales, he said, "How about a car?"

"No," his brother said, painting the tires on a Chevrolet. "Ask me tomorrow. I'm getting in a couple of turkeys on trade. Maybe you can have one."

"I want a clean car," he said angrily. "Not some old broken-down turkey."

Nat said, "Go to Luke."

"You son of a bitch," he said, and went on.

At home he threw himself down in the living room to read the paper. Rachael was nowhere around; probably she was shopping. The texture of the paper hurt his hands. Rough texture . . . his flesh crawled. Sensitive, he thought. He could not bear to hold anything. Throwing the paper onto the floor, he went outside onto the front walk; he went past the gate and down the sidewalk. At the corner he stood watching the people and cars.

When he returned to the apartment, he found Rachael in the kitchen. Unloading a brown paper bag—taking out soap and tomatoes and a carton of eggs—she said, "Where were you?"

"Nowhere," he said.

"Did you go see her?"

"N-no," he said. "What do you mean? Pat?"

"She's probably down at the station," Rachael said. "If you want to go see her."

"I know," he said.

"What's she like?" Rachael said. She gave no sign of hostility; her manner was placid but, he thought, unusually deliberate. "I'm kind of curious. She's almost the same size as I am. I think she's a twelve. Did you get a look at her without anything on?"

"I don't know," he said evasively.

"You don't?" She stared at him.

"F-f-forget it," he said. "Sure I got a look at her. And that wasn't all I got."

Rachael went into the other room and put on her coat.

"Where you going?" he said.

"Out. For a walk."

"When'll you be back?"

"We'll see," she said. The door closed and she was gone.

Feeling angry and ridiculous, he began putting away the groceries. For the first time it occurred to him that she might walk out and not come back; she was capable of doing anything she thought was right. He worried about her and about their marriage, and then he worried about dinner. Was she coming back for that?

By five o'clock he was convinced that she was not coming back. She had been gone an hour. Opening a can of soup, he fixed dinner: soup and a sandwich and a cup of coffee. While he sat alone at the kitchen table, he heard steps on the front walk; he put down his spoon and hurried into the living room.

Jim Briskin was coming down the stairs. "Hello," he said, as Art opened the door. "Where's your wife?"

"Out," Art said. "She'll be back."

"I wanted to drop by and see how she was." He looked around the room. "What time did you get in last night?"

"Not too late," he said evasively. And then he thought to himself how he had gone off with Jim Briskin's girl. The emotion he felt was pride. He felt a kind of triumph. "Did she used to be married to you?" he said. "She sure is s-s-something."

"Look, kid," Jim Briskin said, "don't ever talk about a girl like that. It's between you and the girl."

Flushing, he said, "It was her idea; don't start yelling at me. She wanted to go down to the liquor store, and then when we got there, then she w-w-wanted to go for a drive."

"Christ," Jim Briskin said. "Anyhow—" He glanced into the kitchen. "You don't know when Rachael will be back? How did she seem to be? Was she angry? Was she upset?"

"She's okay," he said.

"What are you going to do next?" Jim said. Then he said, "It doesn't matter. When Rachael comes in, tell her I was by. If I don't hear from her, I'll be around again."

"You're pretty sore," Art said. "Aren't you?"

"I'm not sore," he said. "I'm just trying to keep something worse from happening."

Now he felt embarrassed. "She wanted to go there," he said.

"Where? To her place?" Jim nodded. "I know. I saw her afterwards; I got the whole story. She must have had a hell of a hangover this morning."

"I saw her around four," Art said. "She seemed okay then; she acted like she felt okay."

"You went by the station?" Opening the door, Jim started up the stairs.

"She's real cool-looking," Art said.

"Yes." He halted. "She's at least that. What are your plans? You going to give up your wife and baby and start hanging around her?"

"I don't know," Art muttered. "I'm supposed to call her; she said for me to."

"She was pretty damn drunk, last night."

"I know."

Jim said, "Let me tell you something. Not for your own good; for mine. I was married to her three years. I'm still in love with her. All you know is that she's attractive and last night she was available. I doubt if she'll be available again very soon. Either to you or me or anybody else. That was once in a million. You were handy; it's your good fortune."

He saw the torment on the boy's face. Coming back into the room, he closed the door after him. It was Rachael that he wanted to talk to, but now he was here and talking to Art. So he said, "Don't press your luck. Just write it off as a break and be glad. I was walking around the Park today thinking how much I would have given when I was your age for something like that to happen to me. But if you expect it to happen again, you're just tormenting yourself. Believe me; I'm not kidding you. She can cause you a lot of suffering."

"Yeah," Art said, and the expression remained on his face. The acute suffering, more acute than any other kind of pain.

"Be glad," Jim said.

"S-s-sure," Art said violently.

"Wait'll you're in love with her," he said, his own pain rising. "You think you're bad-off now; wait until you've known her and lived with her. What do you know about her? All you know is the way she dresses and how she looks, something you saw when she walked in here."

"I saw her before," the boy said.

Jim said, "I know everything about her. And I'd do anything for her. So for my sake keep your hands off her. The next time she's drunk and wants to go to bed with somebody, you turn around and go back to your wife; let her sober up and she'll forget about it. I'll tell you one more thing. You try and talk her into it again—you'll find out what I mean. Nobody ever talked her into anything, and especially that. You'll wear yourself out, and when you're finished you'll feel like the goddamnedest fool that ever lived. She can make you look sillier than any woman you ever met. Get out of it now while you have something good to think about." Again he opened the door; he had not meant to talk in that direction. "And the next time you think you've accomplished something like this, don't go around with that silly smirk on your face."

Slamming the door, he went up the steps and along the path to the sidewalk. Getting into his car, he backed out onto Fillmore Street and drove off.

Several blocks away from the house, he saw a figure toiling along the sidewalk. She carried a package and she walked slowly; at a discount clothing store she wandered in to study the window displays. How sad she looked, he thought. How woebegone. Signaling that he was stopping, he double-parked and watched her. When she went on to the next store, he drove ahead, keeping up with her.

Compared with Pat, he thought to himself, she did not dress well. Her coat was brown, without particular color; it dragged shapelessly, a cloth coat whose pockets sagged. Her hair was cut in no fashion whatsoever. She wore no makeup; in fact he had never seen her with makeup. Now, as she wandered along, her eyes were dulled. And the bulge of her middle was gradually distorting her figure; the lines were starting to flow and waver. Under certain conditions, he thought, she might be quite plain. But she was not plain. She had a critical, intent expression; even now she was drawn tight by some attitude, some careful holding of herself. The energy was there. The source of strength that he admired so much. Probably as she walked, she was mulling over everything that had happened. She was not going to do anything until she was certain of what was right.

As yet she had not noticed him.

Holding her package in both arms, she walked step by step, making little progress; she was deflected by each store and each passing thing. Her outward attention wavered and fixed itself on first this and that, without order or sequence. If he had not known her, he would have said that at this point she could be led anywhere; she had no direction. But he knew better. She was out by herself, making her decision. She was still very hard and firm, still rigid.

At a grocery store she disappeared from sight. Behind him a car honked and he was forced to pull out into traffic. He made a U-turn at the corner, drove back, came around again searching for her. Now there was no sign of her; he had lost her.

He saw a parking slot and quickly drove into it.

On foot he hurried along the sidewalk to the grocery store. It was a small store, with nothing to offer but vegetables and fruits; he could see at once that she had departed. Two middle-aged women were inspecting potatoes. The proprietor, in the rear, was seated on a stool with his hands folded.

Going on, he peered into a shoe store and then a café, a drugstore, a dry-cleaning shop. She was not in any of them and she was not ahead of him.

"Goddamn," he said.

The late-afternoon sunlight was white and glaring; it made his head hurt. The drugstore had a soda fountain, and he went in and sat down, his head in his hands. When the waitress appeared, he ordered coffee.

Well, he thought, she had certainly gone on home. He could catch her there.

Resting his elbows on the counter, he drank his coffee; it was weak, hot, tasteless. His run-in with Art had left him in no shape to plan, to cope. A downgrade, he thought, the argument with Art. No point to it, no purpose or hope of improvement. What did he expect? What was he after?

Paying for his coffee, he left the drugstore. Now he did not feel able to go back to the house, to the Emmanuals' place. Some other time, he thought.

Across the street Rachael was standing before a magazine rack, reading the covers of the pocket books.

He crossed the street. "Rachael," he said.

Her head turned. "Oh," she said.

Taking her package he said, "Let me carry it."

"Did you find them last night?" She fell in beside him and they walked together. "Art came home. He didn't say anything about seeing you."

"I got there," he said, "but Art had gone."

She nodded.

"Do you care?" he said. "Do you want to hear about it? Or are you tired of hearing about it?"

"I'm tired," she said. "You know, I hate to talk. I hate to listen to talk."

"I do know," he said.

"So let's just walk," she said.

They went on, across another street, onto another block of small shops and stores and bars. Rachael gazed up at a display of television sets; the display seemed to absorb her.

"Did you ever think of going into television?" she said. "Instead of radio?"

"No," he said.

"I was watching Steve Allen the other night. You ought to be good in a program like that . . . where you could say what you wanted."

"He doesn't say what he wants," Jim said.

She dropped the subject.

"Can I say one thing about Pat?" he said.

"Why?" Then she was apologetic. It was impossible for her, evidently, to be mean. She could not act out such a petty role. "If you want to say something, go ahead. But—"

"I just want to say this," he said. "I don't think she'll do it again. She was drunk; she saw Art, and there was this tangle with me—"

Rachael said, "I don't really care. What do I care why she did it or whether she's going to do it again? I've been walking around wondering what I should do. About her, I mean. I don't care about Art."

"Have you decided?" he said. "Because as much as I think of you, I think more of her, and if you have anything planned, I wish you'd drop it and forget about it."

"How far did they go?" Rachael said.

"Don't talk like a child. I'm ashamed of both of you, both you and Art."

"I just wanted to know."

"How the hell far do you think they went?" he said. "If that's the kind of language you have to put it in. How far do you think a very unhappy woman with too much to drink would go with a good-looking eighteen-year-old kid after they had parked up on Twin Peaks at twelve o'clock at night? Can't you tell when your own husband has had intercourse with another woman?"

Curiously, she remained unmoved. "I don't know what to call it.

When we were in school we had a lot of words, but they weren't words you can use. It's hard, not knowing the words."

"Go learn them," he said.

"You're mad at me," she said, "because I can't discuss this with you the way you like to discuss it." Her chin lifted, and all at once her enormous eyes were fixed on him; she brought the full weight of her contempt onto him. "Did you say once you wanted to help us? We don't know anything. Nobody ever taught us anything we can use. I'm not going to go over and—cut her head off or something. I'd just like to know people who don't do things like this to other people."

"She was drunk," he said.

"So what? I'd like to ask her how she feels now. I'd like to go up to her and see if she's sorry or what."

"She's sorry."

"Is she?"

"She called me up last night," he said. "She was wailing and sobbing; she knew she did something wrong."

They had walked almost back to the house. Ahead of them was the fence and gate. Now Rachael stopped.

"What if I didn't go back?" she said.

"That would be a mistake."

"I'm not going back."

"What then?" he said. "Are you going to your family's and stay there awhile? Get a divorce? Never forgive him?"

"I saw that in a movie," Rachael said.

"And you know what you think of movies."

"All right," she said, "I'll go back." She took her package from him. "Would you come inside with me?"

"Sure," he said.

They walked up the path and down the steps to the basement door. The apartment was empty and on the table was a note from Art. Holding her package, Rachael read the note.

"He went out," she said. "He says Grimmelman called and they're over at the loft. I guess you don't know Grimmelman."

"Do you believe him?" he said. "You suppose it's true?"

She tossed her package onto the couch. "No. I'm going to fix dinner. You can stay if you want." She went into the kitchen, and soon he heard the sounds of water running in the sink, the clatter of pans.

"Can I help?" he said.

On her face was a hopeless look. "I didn't get any meat."

"Let me get it." He led her to a chair and sat her down. "I'll be back in a minute."

He left the apartment and went up the street to a meat market. The market was about to close and nobody was waiting at the counter; he bought a New York-cut steak, fidgeted while the butcher wrapped it, and then carried it back to the apartment.

"How's this?" he said, unwrapping the steak before her.

She accepted it gingerly. "I never saw this cut before. It isn't sirloin, is it?"

"No," he said. "I thought it might cheer you up. You ought to eat more."

Going into the kitchen with the steak, she started to take down the frying pan. "Should I fry it?"

"Broil it," he said. "It's too tender to fry."

"Will you stay with me?" she said.

"I'd like to," he said.

"What about afterwards?" she said. "After dinner?"

"He ought to be back."

"Suppose he isn't. Would you stay until he comes back?"

"I don't know," he said. "I don't see how I can."

Rachael said, "I lived with my family until we—Art and I—ran off to Santa Rosa. Last night when you left here, I felt very bad. I'm not used to being alone."

"You always struck me as being independent."

"Maybe we could go to a show."

"No," he said, "I can't take you to a show, Rachael. I'll eat dinner with you and then I have to leave."

"What'll I do?" she said.

He said, "I've been in this spot for years. When Pat and I separated, I thought I'd go crazy. For a couple of weeks I didn't know what I was doing. It's something you have to live through. And you probably won't have to; I think he'll be back. But if he doesn't come back, you'll have to stand it alone. Isn't that right? You're about the only person I'd say this to outright."

"It's the idea of him over there," she said.

"I know it is. But for a year now she's been going around with Bob Posin, and I've gone to bed every night with that on my mind."

"Is this the way it turns out?"

"Not always."

Putting on the burners in the oven, she set the steak under them.

"Rachael," he said, "if he is there, and I went over and got him, that wouldn't solve it. And you were the one last night who saw that. You were the first one to see that."

She said, "I want to go to the show. If you won't take me, I'll go alone. Or I'll go up to Dodo's, and when I see one of the kids or even somebody I don't know I'll get him to take me." With her back to him she said, "So please take me."

"Would you do that?" he said. He knew she would.

"Take me to that movie about the whale. We have a jar full of nickels and dimes; we're saving up. What's it called?"

"*Moby Dick.*"

"It's from some book. I read it in an English class. We read a lot of old books. It's supposed to be a pretty good movie, isn't it?"

"Yes," he said.

"And then maybe we could go somewhere else." She put on water for the vegetables. "I want you to stay with me," she said. "In January I'm going to have my baby, and I have to be able to count on something. You brought her here and you know you're in this. I've been thinking it over and I'm not kidding. If he's gone, you have to take care of me. Have you ever heard of a thing like that? But it doesn't make any difference; you have to. I have a lot of respect for you. I don't even feel bad about this. There isn't anything else I can do. What would you do if you were me?"

"I don't know," he said.

"This will be very practical," she said. "You came here originally and said you wanted to help me."

"I meant both of you," he said.

"All right." Her voice was reasonable, measured. "You helped Art. Now you can help me. You gave him what he wanted; now see to it that I have enough money and a place to live and something to do. Maybe this sounds—wrong."

"No," he said, "just ruthless."

"You got yourself into this," she said.

He could not help admiring her. She was certainly brave; she had worked out the best solution she could think of. She did not give up or break down into self-pity or sentimentality. This was something out of her own mind, from her own system.

"I'll think it over," he said.

She continued fixing dinner.

14

The front door of the apartment building was locked, and he knew that this was the policy of the big apartment houses. He also knew that there was a back entrance by which the women took wash down to the lines. Going around to the rear of the building, he saw the lines, the recessed garages. A flight of spindly wooden stairs led up to a door, and as he had expected the door was not locked; a housewife had blocked it open with a rolled-up copy of *Life* magazine.

He entered the building and went along the carpeted halls until he came to her door. Without hesitation he knocked.

"Who is it?" Patricia said from inside the apartment. "Just a minute."

"It's Art," he said.

The door flew open. "What?" she said. She had on a heavy cord robe; she had been taking a bath. Her hair was tied up in a turban, and her cheeks were dark, glowing. Tightening the sash of her robe, she said, "I didn't expect you; I thought you were going to call." She was indecisive, and while she tried to make up her mind, he entered her apartment.

"I called," he said. "I didn't get any answer."

"What about Rachael?" In consternation she moved away from him.

"She went out," he said.

"I have to finish taking my shower. Excuse me." She hurried into the bathroom.

Listening to the rush of water, he wondered if she had been here

138

when the phone rang. The time was a quarter to six. "How late do you work?" he said.

"Five-thirty."

So, he decided, she probably hadn't been here. "Have you eaten dinner?" he said, standing by the bathroom door.

"No, I'm not hungry. I don't feel well today. I want to go to bed early."

Waiting for her, he roamed all around her apartment. Last night he had seen nothing of it; they had gone directly to bed, and Patricia had not even turned on the living room light. The prints on the walls interested him. And the mobile in the corner. He touched it, examined the materials, the workmanship. Handmade, he realized. From the metal strips of coffee cans, and from eggshells delicately tinted and glazed, undoubtedly by her. The furniture was low, light in color; he liked it. He tried out several chairs. Their lines were simple. He was a little awed, and at the same time he felt a full measure of confidence. This seemed to him a place where he had won out; he had nothing to fear from this room or this woman. He was excited and keyed up, but not apprehensive.

When she came out of the bathroom, he said, "Let's go have dinner in Chinatown." The restaurants there were cheap and the food was good. "You could maybe have some tea." He was positive that she would want to eat.

"My head aches," Patricia said. "Please, Art, not tonight. Okay? I just want to go to bed." Going into the bedroom, she shut the door partly. The rustle of clothing reached his ears. In the darkness of the bedroom—the shades were down—she was dressing.

"I want to take you around," he said.

"No," she said. "Have some consideration. I had to work all day."

"You'll like this," he said. "H-h-hey, I want you to meet some guys." He was thinking of the loft.

Pat emerged, wearing leotards and a sweater. Her hair was still up in the turban. She looked cross and beset; she said, "Leave me alone tonight, Art. Please? As a favor to me?"

He put his arms around her waist. She was so small and light that he had no trouble with her; kissing her tight, inactive mouth, he said, "Come on. Let's go."

139

"I don't want to go out."

"You want to stay here?" he said, not releasing her. In her eyes panic appeared; she darted a glance up at him, her body stiff. If he let go of her now, she would talk and keep away from him, and in the end he would be maneuvered, step by step, out of the apartment. She was on the verge of some quick flight. But as long as he held onto her, she was afraid; she was too close to him to do anything.

"If you expect to take me out," she said between her teeth, "you have to dress better than that."

"I look okay," he said.

"You look like a drugstore delinquent."

"Too bad," he said, enduring.

"I'll go out with you tomorrow night. I promise."

"No," he said. "Maybe I can't get away tomorrow night." His arm around her, he reached to pull down the shades in the living room. "You feel like dancing?" he said. He turned on the console radio and tuned in dance music.

Still resisting, she said, "I'm no good at dancing. I hate dancing. You wouldn't want to dance with me." Suddenly she broke away. Before she had gone a step, he grabbed her; she fought, straining and twisting, and then gave up.

"I—have nobody to blame," she said faintly, "but myself."

He waited by the door to the hall while she got her coat and purse.

After they had eaten dinner, they remained in the curtained booth. The Chinese waiter cleared the dishes away and brought a fresh enamel pot of tea. Beyond the curtains customers and waiters stirred and made sounds; Art listened amiably.

Across from him Patricia seemed less restive. Now, pensive, she lit a cigarette with her lighter and said, "I always like Chinatown. But you shouldn't have brought me here."

"Why?" he said.

"You shouldn't try to take me anywhere, Art." She smiled. "You have a crush on me, don't you? But I'm too old. One of these days Bob and I'll be married."

"I thought you were Jim Briskin's girl," he said, not able to understand.

She said, "I'm his ex-wife!"

"But you were going around with him."

"What a special world you kids live in," Patricia said. "Dates, going steady . . . do you feel you're dating me now, is that it? Taking me out to dinner, holding doors open for me. When you take me home, are you going to kiss me good night? Or have we passed that? It seems a little misplaced . . ."

"I think you're pretty swell," he said, "you know? I mean, the way you dress and look."

"Yes," she said, "I know, Art." After an interval she said, "You kids are almost—what do I want to say? Archaic. So sort of formal and stilted. Old-fashioned. And they say you're wild beasts. It's not true. You're courtly. Do you realize that? I suppose I like that. Last night it was fresh for me because of your preparations. You had to say this and go through that. Each step of the way. It took so long, you almost drove me crazy. But it was worth it, I thought. It made a lot of difference. Starting over again, like that. As if neither of us had ever done such a thing before . . ." She tapped her cigarette on the rim of her empty cup.

"If you were a kid," he said, "in school, you know? You would be the best-looking. Your hair's so nice." He meant, by that, that she was beautifully built; he thought her body was fabulous, but he could not conceive of saying it.

"I think that's what I responded to," she said. "You were conscious of a lot of little things. You seemed to notice not just one thing but all the different things about me. But you have so much to learn. For instance—" She glanced up. "Never tell a woman any part of her is large. Her hands or her legs or her bosom. And for heaven's sake, remember that you can injure a woman if you go too fast. Especially a woman who's"—she raised an eyebrow—"let's say small. What I mean to say is, at that point go slow. Let her decide. Sometimes she can't relax; she stays constricted."

He said, gazing down at his hands, "Rachael was like that to start. It took a week. A lot of times."

"If I were a man," Pat said, "I'd go after her. What do you see in somebody like me? I can't give you anything she can't. Don't you really see her? I just don't understand. Maybe it's because you have her and you know you have her. I'd like to give her some clothes; I think she could wear them. She needs clothes, but you can't buy them now. Not on what you make."

He nodded.

Pat said, "There's nothing for you here. Don't get a crush on me. I'm not worth it. And anyhow we can't do that again."

"That's what Jim Briskin said," he said, opposing the words, the statement of it.

"What did he say?"

"He said it was because you were drunk."

"It's true," she said. "When did you see him?"

"He came over tonight."

"How did he act?"

Art said, "He wanted to talk to Rachael."

"Yes," she said, "I expect so. He's very responsible, Art. He's concerned about you and her and about me."

"He said not to try to take you around. He said you would cause me a lot of suffering."

"He's right, Art, I will."

"He's just jealous."

"No," she said, "he knows what he's saying. He knows me. In some ways he's like a child . . . he has an irrational streak. He gets excited and he acts on impulse; he gets carried away, especially if he thinks it's his duty. But he has perspective. I don't think it's only jealousy . . ." She put out her cigarette.

Getting to his feet, Art said, "Hey, let's go. I want you to meet this guy; he has this place with a bunch of maps and papers. It's our organization. We have a Horch, a Nazi car."

"Do you want to take me there?" she said, seated, gazing up at him.

"S-s-sure," he said.

"All right, Art. If you want to." She arose; he held her chair awkwardly. "What does your organization do?"

"It's sort of revolutionary," he said, finding money to go with the check.

"Really?" Again she was lost in thought. "When I was a kid, I was a socialist. A Shavian socialist. Did you ever read *Man and Superman*? Any of Shaw?"

"No," he said, pushing the curtain back and leaving the booth. She

142

walked slowly, her coat over her shoulders. Three men, seated at a table, studied her, and one of them made a remark and whistled.

In a flurry of clumsiness, he paid the bill at the front cash register and started out onto the street. Pat came after him, expressionless; she did not seem to have noticed the men.

But, he thought, he certainly had.

The path that led to the stairs was littered with debris; he kicked at the bottles and paper rubbish, saying, "This sure is run-down around here. Can you get by?" The sun had set; darkness was appearing.

Since she did not answer, he assumed she could. He started up the stairs to the metal door. Behind him she had halted to reach into her shoe. Then she came on.

"He's up there," Art said.

The metal door opened a crack. "Who's that?" Grimmelman demanded in his shrill voice.

"It's me," he said. "Hey, I got someone with me."

A blinding light shone in his face; Grimmelman had lit his carbide lamp and was swinging it out above the stairwell. "Emmanual? Step up. Identify your companion."

Annoyed, he said, "Open the door."

With reluctance Grimmelman admitted him. "Is that Rachael? What's your motive in bringing her here? You've been informed—"

"No," he said, "it's somebody else."

The door was open, and now Pat entered the loft. Her arms folded, she walked up to Grimmelman and said, "Are you Art's revolutionary friend?"

"This is a classified area," Grimmelman said.

Her lips moved. Without a word she passed Grimmelman to examine the maps mounted on the wall. Making no sound, she traveled the length of the loft, inspecting the papers and books and reports and heaps of information on the tables. Grimmelman, shivering with displeasure, said, "You're not permitted to handle that material." To Art he said, "Who is she? Is this authorized?"

Pat said, "This is an SWP paper, isn't it?" She held up a newspaper with heavy black banners. "During the war I knew a boy in the SWP."

"Are you politically active?" Grimmelman demanded.

Tossing down the paper, she walked toward him. "No. Should I be?" She cleared papers and books from a chair and seated herself. "You know what you remind me of? The French students after the war. Living in Paris on bread and margarine. Kids who were in the Resistance in their teens."

Grimmelman said, "Were you in France?"

"For a few months in 1948. On a scholarship."

"What was it like?"

"They were very poor. What's all this for, up here? Are you part of an organized group?"

Art said, "H-h-he's going to overthrow the existing order."

"I see," Pat said.

"This is not something to be discussed," said Grimmelman. "If you were affiliated with the SWP, you probably have contacts with elements hostile to us." He busied himself with papers; he ignored her. It was clear that he disapproved of her. He was not going to talk to her.

Art said, "Look at this." He showed her the M-1 rifle; as always, it was oiled and shiny.

"I see," she said, without taking it.

"Don't show her those," Grimmelman said.

"Aw, hell," Art said, exasperated. "What do you think she's g-g-going to do? I told you she's okay; I know her." He pushed the M-1 rifle at Pat, wanting her to take it. But she did not. Baffled, he returned it to its wall rack. From one of the work tables, Pat took a book, opened it, and then put it aside.

His back to the two of them, Grimmelman shuffled papers. He carried the papers to a map in the corner and transferred information from the papers to the map. Except for the wheezing and scratching of Grimmelman, the room was quiet.

"Let's go," Art said.

She remained seated, and he thought that she did not intend to leave. But then, almost as an afterthought, she arose and walked toward the door.

"What time is it?" she said to him as she started down the stairs. Neither she nor Grimmelman said goodbye; at the map, Grimmelman devoted himself to his papers, his shoulders hunched, his nose bent and twitching. He snuffled, lifted his head to rub his cheek with the back of his hand. Seeing them leave, he whinnied, a half laugh; as Art closed the door, Grimmelman started over to lock it.

Pat had already reached the path and was starting cautiously in the direction of the street.

Art said, "That's sure strange up there."

"He takes it seriously, doesn't he?" Pat said. "How old is he? He's older than the rest of you."

"I don't know," he said, wishing to forget the whole business.

Pat said, "It smells stale. Like food. Does he eat and sleep up there?"

"Y-y-yeah," Art mumbled.

"What's he do for a living?"

"Works at the cannery, I guess. During the fall."

"How did you run into somebody like that?" She stood at the sidewalk, by the car.

"He used to hang around Dodo's," Art said.

"He's a crank. He must have put a lot of money into those books." Getting into the car, she said, "Do you want to drive? Is there somewhere you want to take me?"

At the wheel he said, "How'd you like to see the H-h-horch?"

"Whatever you want."

"It's real rare," he said. "You never saw one like it." As they drove along the dark street, he said, "Maybe you d-d-don't care."

She repeated, "Whatever you want." She sounded indifferent, as if it was all the same to her. To him she sounded far off.

On both sides of the car, industrial installations and warehouses passed. Streetlights were few and far between. Once he saw a bus parked at an intersection; the driver, alone inside, was reading a magazine.

No good, he decided. He turned right and headed back into town.

When they crossed Columbus, Pat said, "Are we going any place in particular?"

"No," he said.

"Then why don't we stop over there." Ahead of them was a night spot; a green-and-blue neon sign whisked on and off. Cars and taxis were parked close by. An awning stretched from the door of the club to the curb; several men in dinner jackets stood in the entrance. A woman in an evening gown and fur joined them.

"There?" Art said.

"I'd like something to drink."

"I can't go in there."

Pat said, "Then let's stop somewhere else. Over in North Beach somewhere."

"No," he said.

"They don't care how you dress in the North Beach places."

"I can't go in because I'm under age."

"You haven't got anything you can show them?"

He had only one piece of forged identification, a borrowed Air Force pass. It was too risky. If they asked for his driver's license or his social security card, he was sunk.

"Let's just go home," he said. "To your place."

"Then we're through going out?"

He did not look at her, but he knew she was smiling.

"It wasn't much of an evening," she said. Stretching her arms, she said, "I shouldn't go out on workdays anyhow. I have to be up at seven tomorrow."

"You want to just drive?" he said.

"No. I'd just as soon go home."

And still, he thought, she was smiling. She was enjoying this; she was amused.

"What does Rachael think of your revolutionary pal?"

"Not much."

"I don't think—what's his name?—likes girls."

"No," he said.

"Did he ever make any passes at you?"

"No," he said.

"There're a lot of them in San Francisco. Once Jim went around with a girl whose husband was queer. He had an affair with her. That's what he said, anyhow. That was years ago."

He grunted.

"Sex is mysterious," Pat said presently. "Sometimes I think it isn't an instinct . . . it's what you're accustomed to or what you think you should want. Or something you haven't ever had and you wonder how it would be. There's a certain element of illicitness in it. The concealed . . . the denied. Something you're not supposed to have. The ads hint; they never say exactly. They build it up, with mentions and elusive words. Like the lyrics in pop tunes. When I was in my teens, we were still listening to Glenn Miller. I remember during the war . . . we used to get our Benny Goodman and Glenn Miller records together, six or seven of us, and we'd play the records and lie around on the floor. Frank Sinatra." She laughed. "I remember Frankie . . . on the 'Hit Parade.' He and Bea Waine. 'I've Got Spurs That Jingle, Jangle, Jingle.' " She began to hum. "That was—when was that?—1943, I guess."

He said nothing.

"That was when the Russians were our friends," she said. "When they stopped the Germans at Stalingrad." Rolling down the car window, she rested her arm on the sill. Cold evening wind rushed in, mixing with the warm air from the heater. "When I was growing up," she said, "we sang all the different pop tunes. What was the first one? *Bei Mir Bist Du Schön.*' I was in grammar school. And 'The Lambeth Walk.' We actually believed the different lyrics. Do the kids believe them now?"

"No," he said.

"About June and the moon?"

"No."

"I remember one I always thought was beautiful. Do they ever play it anymore? 'I'll Build a Stairway to the Stars.' I liked that about the best. The stuff Jim plays on 'Club 17' . . . I can't get used to Mitch Miller's echo chamber. It's so—bloated. And the styles, you can't tell if it's a woman or a man. Like Johnny Ray. And it's everything mixed together, Western and Negro jump and sweet sentimental . . a mish-mash."

"Some aren't so bad," he said.

"You listen to 'Club 17'? Yes, I think you said so. Until this last week."

"Rachael likes it," he said.

"Don't you think it's about the best kids' disc-jockey program in the afternoon?"

He nodded.

"How about these ballrooms? Do you have to be twenty-one to get into them?"

"No," he said.

"Thinking about the old tunes makes me feel like dancing. But it's

147

too late. Maybe some other time. I never could get Jim to go dancing. He's always so self-conscious. Did you used to have high school dances?"

"Yes," he said.

"Every week?"

"Yes."

"On Fridays?"

"Yes."

"Do the boys all line up on one side?"

Ahead of them was the apartment building. He slowed the car, looking for a parking place.

"Are we there?" Pat said. "Too bad."

"Why?"

She shrugged. "It's still early. I'd like to go somewhere and sit. And maybe listen to a small combo, nothing noisy. Just a rhythm-and-blues group. Or maybe some folksinger. Bob Posin and I were going to hear June Christy . . . she's in town. She used to be with Stan Kenton. Jim and I go to hear Kenton when he's in town." She added, "We used to, anyhow."

He parked and turned off the motor.

"Well," she said archly, "I guess that's that."

"You sure change your mind," he said.

"Do I?" Her nails tapped on the metal side of the car, a rhythmical drumming.

"You know I can't take you to those places."

"I wish you could." Opening the door, she stepped out onto the curb. When he came around he found her strolling toward the door of the apartment house; she seemed animated and he could not understand why.

A passing car honked. She turned.

The car stopped beside the Dodge. The window was rolled down, and a man slid across the seat and stuck his head out. "Where you been?" he called. "I came by a couple of times tonight."

Advancing a step, she said, "Oh, I've been out."

"Who's that with you? Just a second." The man tugged on the parking brake and climbed from the car. "You kinda had me worried; the last time I saw you, you said something about being sick. I thought maybe you'd come down with ptomaine poisoning."

"Bob," she said, "this is Art Emmanual."

The man stuck out his hand. Still addressing Pat, he said, "You know where I was all day? Talking to the Bürgermeister beer people. They may take a full hour every night, the eleven to twelve spot. Wouldn't that be something?"

Pat said, "Would it be pops or classical?"

"Sort of semi. Boston Pops and Morton Gould. Nothing too heavy." He raised an eyebrow. "You all beat out?"

"No, not particularly."

"Want to . . ." He gestured.

She glanced at Art.

Grimacing, Bob said, "How about Scoby's Place? Ralph Sutton's there. We could drop by for an hour or so."

"Good enough," she said.

"Then it's a deal," Bob Posin said.

To Art, Pat said, "You can't come along, can you? They'd want to see your identification."

Scrutinizing Art, Bob Posin said, "Haven't I seen you around the station in the afternoons? Around four?"

"Art listens to 'Club 17,' " Pat said. "Or did. Before the blowup."

"Oh, I see." Bob nodded. "Well, shall we go?" To Art he said, "Can I drop you anywhere?"

From his coat pocket Art lifted out a switchblade knife which he had picked up from among the weapons at the loft. Pat saw the knife, the glow of light from the blade. "Bob . . . " she said in a weak, constricted voice. She put up her arm, a gesture of defense. "You run along. I don't want to go anywhere."

"What?" he said. Bewildered, he opened and shut his mouth in exasperation. "What the hell's happened between us?"

"Just go," she said. "Please." She started away from him toward the entrance of the apartment building.

"I don't get it," he said. Shaking his head, he stepped from the pavement to the side of his car. "You sure you're all right?"

"Yes," she said, "I can handle this. I'll see you tomorrow at the station. Please?"

Still holding the knife, Art stepped after Bob Posin. He had never before carried a knife this big, and in the actions of the Organization a knife had not been a factor. Not knowing how close he had to be—he

149

could not conceive of throwing it—he moved up to Posin and stood by him as the man opened his car door. The knife was hidden by the folds of his sport coat. In the doorway of the apartment building, Pat watched, her hand up to her face, her fingers spread apart.

"Glad to have met you, boy," Bob Posin said sourly. "I'll probably see you again."

Art said nothing; he did not know if he would be able to speak. His throat was choked and he could hardly breathe.

"Well," Posin said, "good night." He slammed the car door, moved over behind the wheel, and waved to Pat.

"Good night," she said.

Bob Posin drove off.

Returning to her, Art said, "What do you want to do?" He closed up the knife and put it away in his pocket. The knife weighed down his coat on one side; the pocket bulged.

"Nothing," Pat said weakly.

"Let's go inside," he said.

They went up the stairs to her apartment. When she had unlocked the door, she said, "What would you have done?"

"I just wanted to get rid of him," he said.

"Would you have done anything?"

He closed the door after them.

"I'm engaged to him," she said. "I'm going to marry him."

"So what?" he said. "What do I care?" He walked away from her, feeling upset and angry.

"What have I got myself into," Pat said. Going into the kitchen, she stood by herself at the sink, her hands pressed together. She was pale, and her voice was thin and unsteady.

"How about letting me stay here tonight?" he said.

"I—don't see how you can."

"Why not?"

She turned. "You're nuts. You're as bad as that queer pal of yours. How did I get mixed up with you? Christ." She put her hands over her face. "You nutty kid. I'd give anything if I hadn't gone there with Jim. But there's no use blaming him."

"I just want to stay," he said. "What's the matter with that? How's that d-d-different from what we did?"

"Look . . ." She walked toward him and then over to a chair. Seating herself, she said, "I'm tired and I don't feel good and I couldn't go through last night again for anything. What is it, you're all ready to start over again?" She took a deep shuddering breath. "And all I did was want to go down and buy a bottle. I didn't even want to go down; I wanted you to go down."

Suddenly she was on her feet.

"Stay here if you want," she said, "I'm going." She walked to the door without looking back.

He went after her, caught her by the shoulder, and socked her in the eye. Not making a sound, she tumbled away with her arms out; she fell against the wall and then to the floor. Her head struck and she lay with her eyes shut, one arm bent under her, both her legs drawn up. Beside her waist her purse had spilled open; lipstick and pencils and a mirror had come out of it onto the rug. He was a little amazed that she had gone down so readily; he picked her up and carried her to the couch.

Her body was limp and she did not stir. She was completely out. When he let go of her, she slumped forward; her chin came to rest against her collarbone. Curls of dark hair fell across her forehead. The flesh near her eye was beginning to swell; she was going to have a shiner. Several times in his childhood, his dad had beaten up his mother; once she had worn a shiner for a week. Once, he remembered as he stood by the couch looking down at Patricia, the police had been called in by neighbors. His parents had scrapped, month in, month out; it had been a part of his life.

Stirring, Patricia moaned. Her hand came up; the fingers groped at her forehead, her eye.

"Don't touch it," he said.

Gradually her eyes opened. They were glazed and empty. For a long time she did not seem to see him.

"What do you want?" he said.

Still her eyes were unfocused. Her nose was beginning to run; he bent down and wiped it with his forefinger. Then he went to the kitchen and fixed a cold pack of ice cubes wrapped in a towel. Returning, he found her conscious. She was propped up, her hands to her face.

"Oh my god," she whispered, a quavery, almost inaudible voice.

He sat down next to her and put the cold pack against her eye. Finally she took hold of it.

"Did you hit me?" she managed.

"Yeah," he said. "You were t-t-taking off."

Leaning back, she rested. Neither of them spoke.

"Art," she said finally.

"What?" he said.

She put the ice pack down on the arm of the couch. "Art, you never should hit a woman."

He said nothing.

"Bring me a mirror," she said, "will you? From the bathroom."

When he had brought the mirror, she examined her face; she touched herself, pressing at her eye.

"It's going to be b-b-black," he said.

She put down the mirror. "How could you hit a woman?"

"You were leaving."

"That's the first time anybody ever hit me," she said. "I can't believe it." She sat up, drawing away from him. "I just can't believe it. My god, Art, you hit me." Now she was staring at him; she continued to stare.

Feeling uncomfortable, he got up and paced around the room.

"I don't see how you could do it," she said. "I've never even seen anybody hit a woman. Can a thing like that happen?"

Again she picked up the ice pack and held it to her eye. The incredulous waver remained in her voice as she said, "Could you really do that? Did you ever—hit your wife? Do you beat her up?"

"No," he said.

"Oh my god," she said. "My good god."

152

15

The alarm clock woke her. The bedroom, with its indistinct shapes, was gray with early-morning light; she struggled up and found the alarm clock and shut it off.

Her body ached, and all her muscles, all her joints were sore. Her ribs—she remained motionless, wincing—felt as if they were cracked and broken. Reaching down, she massaged her waist. Her skin was tender to the touch. The night, the whole night long—they had gone on and on. And then, as she pushed the covers away, she put her hand to her face and felt the hardened, swollen ring around her eye.

Beside her, still asleep, Art Emmanual lay with his head buried in the covers. His blond hair, in the first sunlight, looked clean, bleached white, completely pure.

She did not know how she could get up. For a long time she simply sat; she left her eye alone and tried not to think about it. At eight o'clock she at last slid from the bed, put a robe around her, and went stiffly along the hall to the bathroom. Even the soles of her feet hurt; her flesh was dry, brittle, unyielding. She was, she thought to herself, a kind of dried corn husk.

In the bathroom mirror she inspected her eye. The flesh around it was bluish black, swollen so that the eye was almost shut. When she lifted cold water to it, the eye closed; for a time she could not get it open. The eye burned furiously and she thought: So that's how it feels. That's what it's like.

Going to the station was out of the question. She wondered how long the discoloration and swelling would remain. Two days? Three? And in addition the urgent, ceaseless sex had worn her out. Once, in

153

her high school days, she and two other girls had hiked to the top of Mount Tamalpais. At the end of that hike, she had been tired, but she was more tired now. This was complete; this was absolute exhaustion. She fixed coffee. While the coffee heated, she lit a cigarette. By the time the coffee was ready, she felt better. She ate a little cottage cheese and dry toast, drank the coffee, and then washed the dishes. Her head ached and she swallowed two aspirin tablets, standing at the sink in her robe, her feet bare. After that she walked back into the bedroom.

In the bed Art Emmanual slept on. One arm was thrown out, the hand open, fingers trailing from the bed. His clothes, with her clothes, were piled upon the chair by the bed. He did not look tired at all, and she thought to herself: This was what she had talked about. This vitality.

Now, she thought, she had it. Here, sleeping away in the bed, here it was.

From the chair she took some of her clothes and started to dress. But she did not have the strength. The time was eight-thirty. She went into the living room and telephoned the station.

"Hello?" she said. "This is Patricia."

Ted Haynes said, "What is it, Patricia?"

"I wonder if it would be all right if I didn't come in today?" Her voice was a rasp; she did not have to force it. "I've got the flu or something. What do you think? I haven't missed any time so far this year."

Ted Haynes outlined a long list of medicines to buy, told her to stay in bed until she was well, wished her good luck, and then hung up.

Stay in bed, she thought. It was funny. It was really funny.

Returning to the bedroom, she tossed her robe over the chair with the rest of the clothes and then, lifting the covers back, got into bed beside the sleeping boy.

In the half-light of the bedroom, she leaned above him, her elbows resting on the pillow, her face close to his. Her mouth brushed across him, and she brought her hands to the sides of his face. She lifted his head with her hands, gazing down at him. Presently she pushed aside the covers and lowered herself onto him; she rested her body against his chest, his face, his legs and hips and feet. How warm he was. She felt his heart beating; it moved at her breasts, his heart deep inside him, stirring and awake. She heard him breathing; she put her ear to his chest and crouched there, listening, holding on to him. In that position she dozed.

Some time later, when the room was full of light, she was awakened by the pressure of his arms. His eyes were open and he was grinning up at her; he had taken hold of her and was holding her in his grip, clutching her where she was sore, where she hurt the most.

"Oh no," she said. "we can't . . . we've had enough."

"Sure," he said.

She slid away from him, but he held on to her. "You ought to be exhausted," she said, marveling. "You ought to be dead."

"Did you get up?" he said. "A little w-w-while ago, you were gone."

"I ate breakfast."

"Your eye looks awful."

She said, "I can't go to work. I can't go outside like this." Sitting up, unfastening his fingers from her, she put her hand to her face, exploring the flesh by her nose, by her brow. "Is it going down?"

"Some."

"What can I do?"

"Just wait," he said. "You n-n-never had a black eye?"

"No." She lay back, her knees drawn up to keep him away. "Leave me alone," she said. The covers scratched her cheek; he was lifting them around her, covering her. That made her feel better. "Thanks," she said.

"You still look okay," he said. "Even with it."

She said, "You remember when we were up on Twin Peaks? You said you loved me."

"Yeah," he said.

"Do you?"

"Yeah," he said, "sure I do."

"Then how could you hit me?" She shifted to face him. "How can you do that to somebody you love? Don't ever do it again, Art. Promise me?"

"You were leaving."

"I was going out. I wasn't leaving."

He said, "What was I s-s-supposed to do, just stand there?"

"And that knife—where did you get it? From that creepy pal of yours? You shouldn't be mixed up in things like that, Art. Don't you know that?"

"That was the first time," he murmured.

"Throw the damn thing away somewhere."

"Okay," he said.

"Will you do that? If you're going to go around with me, you can't do things like that. You know that, Art."

He said nothing.

Beside him she waited, she listened. When he did not answer, she reached out her hand and placed it on his body. This was not so bad, surely. This was nothing to complain about. She lay in bed, and time passed; hours went by. The sun climbed in the sky, and the room became warmer, brighter. The air became stuffy.

Art said, "Hey, I'm hungry. How long are we going to stay here? Let's get up."

"You won't always be able to do this, Art," she said.

Restlessly, he shifted about in the bed. "It must be almost noon."

"Yes," she said. "It's eleven-thirty."

She rolled over until she lay against him. She put her arm under him, bearing his weight on her wrist, her elbow. Then she drew herself up onto him, but only her head and shoulders; with her hand she held him away from her.

"No," she said. "I just want to look at you."

That seemed to trouble him; he did not enjoy being looked at. Gradually he became embarrassed.

"What's wrong?" she said.

"I don't know, it's so light in here."

"The light?" She raised herself up. "Oh," she said. "You think it's wrong for me to see you. Is that it?"

"I just don't understand why you like to lie around doing nothing."

But still she sat, resting back on her heels, her bare knees jutting out before her, her palms resting on her thighs. And his dismay increased. "There's nothing wrong with this," she said. "Are you ashamed of me? Are you ashamed of yourself?" She tossed the covers away from him; the covers settled to the floor, leaving both of them uncovered. "You have a nice body . . . you should be proud of it."

He got up, picked up his clothes, and dressed. And she watched that, too.

"Let's eat," he said.

Remaining on the bed, she said, "I just want to lie here."

"Come on!" His face was sullen.

She said, "Lie here with me." Stretched out on the bed, she lifted up her hand, reaching toward him. "I thought you were insatiable." His discomfort struck her as ironic. "Now that I'm rested up, you don't want to. Or do you just want to do it at night?"

"You're only supposed to do it at night," he said.

"Why?"

"Because it's dark," he said.

She laughed. The bizarre modesty . . . the stilted ideas. Old teachings: concealment and—the word that came to her mind was *prudery*. During the night he had battled with her until she was sore and worn out, but now, in the sunlight, he refused even to stay in the room.

"How was it?" she asked.

"Okay," he said angrily.

And, she thought, he could not bring himself to speak of it. Wrong to speak, she thought. And she thought: My god. Wrong to talk about it in front of a woman. He can talk about it with his drugstore pals; they probably talk about it all the time. But I'm like his mother or a teacher, I shouldn't hear about it.

And she thought that in a stupid sense she was in love with him. She had a crush on him, an adolescent crush; the kid in her was aroused.

But she could not help being contemptuous. What did he have to say? He was ignorant, young; he shuffled his feet and stood inert. But he was nice-looking. He was strong and, she thought, he had a natural purity. From his youth. The fact that he was so young. He had done so little; he knew so little.

"How did you imagine it would be," she said, "when you were a child? Is it anything like you expected? Or did you have a lot of idealistic dreams and notions . . ."

He grunted.

"Do you know anything about erogenous zones?" she said.

On his face was an expression of distrust and horror: he did not know what she meant, but he did not like the sound of it.

"I think there're nine of them," she said. "In a woman. Probably it differs between different women."

At the door he lingered; he was unable to leave. But he wanted to leave.

157

She said, "Would you feel better if I put something on?"

"You ought to get up," he said.

"Did you know that some women can come to a climax by fondling their breasts?"

He left the room. In the kitchen he collected eggs and bacon from the refrigerator. For a while she remained on the bed, and then she got up and put on a skirt and blouse. And then she changed her mind. She put on only a half slip, from her waist to her knees. Wearing that, she followed him into the kitchen and sat down at the table.

Smoking a cigarette, she watched him fix himself breakfast.

"What is it?" she said. "Do I bother you?"

"Go put something more on," he said.

"I don't get a chance to do this," she said. "How many times in my life can I loll around like this? I don't have to work today . . . I can't go to work with my eye the way it is."

"Suppose somebody comes."

She shrugged. "Suppose they do. You can answer the door."

"Suppose Jim Briskin shows up."

"Oh," she said, eyeing him, "does that worry you?"

"I d-d-don't like it."

"What do you want me to put on? Do you want me to dress up? Are we going somewhere?"

He seated himself across from her and began to eat. The smell of bacon made her ill, but she remained at the table. Smoke from her cigarette drifted around him; turning his chair, he ate with his plate between his knees.

"That's no way to eat," she said.

"Go to hell," he mumbled, his mouth full, his face flushed.

"Didn't your mother teach you how to act at the table? Does Rachael let you eat that way? There's so many things you're going to have to learn. What about your clothes? You can't wear those again today. Don't you have anything else you can wear?"

"They're home."

"Then buy some more. Or go get them." Lazily she leaned back, her arm over the top of the chair. "Why don't you take the car and go by your place and pick up your clothes? And you need a shave." Reaching, she touched his chin; he ducked away. "It's true. You can't go out like that."

158

Throwing down his fork, he left the table.

She went into the bedroom and finished dressing. When she came out, he was standing at the living room window, his hands in the back pockets of his slacks. The crease was gone from the slacks, and they hung unevenly, bagging at the knees. All night his clothes had been piled up on the chair.

"How do you like this skirt?" she said; she had put on a bright blue skirt and a white frilly blouse.

He said nothing; he did not look.

"I thought I'd go downtown and shop," she said. "If I'm not going to have to go to work, there're some clothes I want to buy. I have a list of errands."

"How about your eye?"

"It's improving." She went to the basin in the bathroom and splashed cold water on it. The skin was discolored, but it was not as hard, not as distended.

"You can't go outside looking like that," he said at the bathroom door. "You look awful."

"Okay," she said. "We'll stay here, then."

"I'm not sticking around here," he said vehemently. "I can't stand just s-s-sitting around. Anyhow, I have to get over to Larsen's. I'm supposed to be there every day."

"All right," she said, "you do that. I'll stay here and catch up on my letter writing." As an afterthought she added, "There's another thing you probably should do."

"What?"

"Shouldn't you call Rachael and tell her you're okay? She's probably worried about you."

Art said, "Let's go away."

"Go away? With you?"

He gave her a deadly, impassioned look.

Sobered, she said, "What do you mean? For how long?"

"Let's just go."

"My job," she said.

"The hell with your job. Pack your stuff up and let's go."

"Do you have any money?"

"No," he said.

"Then," she said, "how can we go away?" Now she felt more

secure. "And I don't have any money. If you want, you can look around; look in my purse if you care to."

"You can sell your car."

"No, I can't." The presumption shocked her, the absolute disregard of her interests. "I don't have the pink slip. I still owe eighteen hundred dollars on it. I won't own it until May 1958."

"You can borrow on it." He seemed to have made up his mind. Dealing her possessions out, she thought.

"Why do you want to go away?" she asked, unable to follow the process involved. Impulsive, she thought; it was a boy's whim. But the coolness was shocking. The assumptions.

Art said, "Somebody might c-c-come here."

"Like who?"

"Jim Briskin."

"Why does Jim Briskin worry you?"

"Because," he said in his brusque, unreasoning voice, "you're his girl."

He made her pack all her things: her clothes from the closet, medicine from the bathroom, the cosmetics from her vanity table in the bedroom, the slips and bras and underpants and stockings and sweaters and blouses from the dresser drawers. As fast as he could, he carried everything to the bed, on which her suitcases rested end to end, one of them already full, the next half full. Whenever she looked up, there he was with more things. No limit, she thought. How systematic he was. And, she thought, in the face of this flow she drifted along; she was captured and held fast.

"What else?" he demanded.

"There's enough here already," she said. "I don't really need all this."

He said, "I don't know what you need. Let's not take it; take what you need."

"If you won't tell me where we're going or how long we'll be gone, I can't tell what I need. Isn't that so?"

But his mind was on the car. "People sell cars they don't own. You can get something out of it." Picking up the telephone, he called a number. As she packed, she listened to him; he was asking questions in monosyllables and grunts.

She thought: If I am not careful and do not keep some control, I will give him the car. I will let him take everything.

"Who was that?" she said when he hung up. "Who did you call?"

"My brother."

"I didn't know you had a brother. Is he older than you?"

"Yes," he said.

The idea was ominous: a bigger, more formidable Art. The same, she thought, the same but larger.

"He says you can sell your equity," Art said.

"How does he know?"

"He has a used car lot."

"It doesn't make any difference," she said. "I'm not going to part with my car."

"How big's your equity?"

She said, "You can forget it, Art. I have to have that car." From the heap which he had assembled on the bed, she separated towels; they would not need towels.

"Once you get on something," she said, "you just go on and on. If you'll shut up about the car—" She pretended not to see him; she carried the towels back to the dresser. "I have some money in a savings account."

"How much?"

"The passbook's in the drawer." She indicated the table. "I forget. Whatever it is, you can have it."

He opened the passbook. "Two hundred dollars," he said, pleased. "That'll do."

"What are you going to do about clothes?" she asked. "Your own clothes."

Reluctantly he said, "What kind of clothes do I need?"

"Don't you know? Good god, don't you buy your own clothes? Does she buy them for you?"

His eyes on the floor, he said, "Socks, I guess."

"Socks and shirts and a suit of some kind and underwear." Her voice was rising, and she remembered the trouble it had caused, the fights with Jim; she heard herself gain the acrimonious tone, the animation. And underneath it was something different, something that she did not recognize. "You're as helpless as a baby. Go out and go to some men's clothing store and tell them your stuff was destroyed

161

or it was all lost. Get a neutral suit, blue or brown or gray, single-breasted. Don't get any sport coats."

"Why not?"

"Because," she said, "sport coats make you look like a kid dressed up for Saturday night."

He was attending, aware of her conviction.

"Get a couple of sport shirts," she said, "and some plain white shirts." And then the yearning beneath the anger came out, and she said, "I'll go with you."

"No," he said.

But she had made up her mind. Going through her purse, she kept alive a running patter of talk; her eagerness was working through her, and she could not shut it off. "Why should I stake you to an outfit? What kind of a thing is this? Am I supposed to buy your clothes and feed you and support you? Am I keeping you, is that it? What am I supposed to be getting out of it?"

He had no answer; he hung his head.

"I'll tell you one thing," she said. "You're supposed to look out for a woman, not live off her. I even have to think for you; I have to tell you how to dress yourself and cross the street. How long do you think I'm going to put up with this? I think I've had just about enough. This really is something. You better take a good look at yourself."

"Calm down," he said.

But she could not calm down. "Do you know what's going to happen?" she said. "I'm the one who's going to have to suffer for all this. I'll lose my lease here. I'll probably lose my job. And Rachael's probably after me, and Jim Briskin too. And I'll wind up borrowing on my car. I can't afford to do that, Art; I just can't. And that's the last of Bob Posin. You don't have to worry. If the police show up, it'll be me they'll arrest. Contributing to the delinquency of a minor. God, you're just a child; you're like a baby, a little boy. My little boy." She swept past him, hurrying away from him so that she was not close enough to touch him; she did not trust herself so close to him.

Going into the bedroom, she closed the door, stood for a moment, and then she thought, what's gone wrong with me? What is it? Taking off her skirt and blouse, she changed to a blue suit. She made herself up with more powder than usual; she obscured the discoloration around her eye. Then she put on stockings and heels and a white hat with a veil. That does it, she thought. Except for the purse and gloves. She put her things into a dark leather purse, tugged on her gloves, and opened the door. Her muscles were so unresponsive that she thought some blight had fallen onto her; she was dominated by invisible fluids. As if the blight had made a passage into her nerve centers and had lodged there.

"I don't think my eye will be too noticeable like this," she said.

Art said, "You look like you're going to a wedding."

"Do I?" Approaching him, she said, "What about my eye? How does it look?"

"Not too bad. You c-c-can still see it."

But she saw his admiration; she knew how good this suit was for her. She saw the response. "Jim likes this suit," she said.

"You look okay," he said, and that was as much as he would say. Disappearing into the bathroom, he spent a long time with his hair. She waited, knowing that he was fixing himself up as best he could.

Her suit made her feel superior. She was raised up, maintained. She went about the apartment, smoking, pausing to watch his progress. In this high state she was lazy and at ease. Art, in the bathroom, labored at the mirror; she walked in to inspect his progress. The mirror gave back their combined reflection. How much larger he was than she. But, she thought, she looked good with him; she looked trim and tidy. This was a deep pleasure for her, and she made the most of it. She felt wealthy, expansive; supervising him, she felt aristocratic.

"You have to shave," she said.

"With what?"

Returning to the bedroom, she rested one of the suitcases on the chair arm; opening it, she took out a plastic-wrapped package from a side pocket. "You can use mine."

He was astonished to see a regular razor and blades. Beside the plastic package was a blue box; on its side were elegantly printed letters, and as he accepted the razor, he read the letters, slowly, unbelievingly. On his face the dismay was so great that she had to cover her mouth to keep from laughing.

"What's wrong?" she said.

No words were audible. He stared at the box.

"Oh," she said innocently, "my diaphragm. I had that out the other night. Didn't you notice?" Still he said nothing. "No," she said, "I

163

guess you didn't. I have to use it." She was curious. "Doesn't Rachael own a diaphragm?"

"No."

"Do you know what a diaphragm is?"

His lips moved. "Sure."

"She can get one now," she said. "Now that she's married. She ought to have one. Tell her. What do you use instead?"

"N-n-nothing."

"She should use something. A diaphragm is the safest. She can go to a gynecologist and get herself fitted. They'll measure her, and then she can get it at any drugstore. This one belongs to me and Jim . . . I got it when we were married. By the California Joint-Property Laws half of it is his." She was enjoying herself, and she pursued him back into the bathroom. His arms and face vanished under the spray of water in the bowl; his back to her, he began industriously to wash and lather himself.

While he shaved—stripped down to his pants—she was leaning against the doorjamb, her arms folded. The bathroom was steamy and warm, and she thought how much it was like some safe cavern; it was womblike, isolated from the world. The noise of the water blanked out other sounds. The smell of lather filled her nose, the sweet, wet smell.

"Jim shaves twice a day," she said. "His beard is heavy; it's like steel wires in the morning. Do many men shave that often? I guess having to shave is really the worse of the two."

"Two what?" Washing his face, he began to dry himself; he buried his face in a towel.

"You wouldn't want to know," she said, teasing him, playing with him. She walked nearer to him, and then all at once her delight vanished. In its place was lust, and she put her arms around his bare waist and clutched him as lightly as she could; she prevented herself from laying hold of him with her real devotion.

"Watch it," he said, a little apprehensively. And then she thought, with clarity, that her ambition had been opened to him at last. At once she released him; flustered and embarrassed, she retreated.

My child, she thought. Now he put his shirt back on and began to button it. A sullen boy, she thought, controlling her hunger, permitting the mere dreams, the desires and hallucinations, to gallop through her mind. The scenes fled past and she reviewed them; she identified them as old fantasies that had always been with her but could never be acted out. She waited and remained placid until they subsided. But they were not gone. They would never be gone.

"Maybe we ought to leave," Art said.

She said, "I want you in the most awful kind of way. So maybe we should. Have you ever seen a woman with a new baby?"

"That's not me," he said.

"I won't hurt you," she said. "I just want to be close to you; I'll be careful. But at least let me buy your clothes for you." She wanted to dress him and comb his hair, but she kept her hands away from him. A great expanding bloom of love and weakness loosed itself inside her; it detached itself from her and rose up. It hovered within her throat, and then it came forth in a muffled shriek; she walked hurriedly away from him, not wanting him to hear. But he was aware, in some dull fashion, so it made no difference. She could not conceal it from him, and anyhow, she thought, he did not care.

"I don't expect you to give me what I want," she said.

"You want a baby," he said knowingly. "That's what it is."

"Don't hate me," she said, trying not to plead. But it did not matter what she did because she was not going to be able to get what she wanted. He did not have it to give her.

The suitcases were packed in the trunk compartment and in the back seat of the car. She shut off the gas in the kitchen of the apartment; she made certain that the faucets and lights were off and that the door was locked.

"That does it," she said. They got into the car and she watched the apartment house disappear behind them. They stopped at the bank and then at a men's clothing store on Market Street. When they left the clothing store, Art drove in the direction of the freeway. He paid no attention to her; he was involved in the driving.

"South?" she asked. "Do you like it better down south?"

Without answering, he made a left turn onto the freeway. Now they were above the houses and streets of the city. Everything was grimy, she thought. Rundown and dismal.

"Art," she said, "I want to ask you something. If you weren't married, if you didn't have a wife and you weren't expecting a baby, and say you were a couple of years older and I was, say, twenty-four instead of twenty-seven—" She turned to face him. But when it came down to it, she was unable to say it.

"What?" he said.

Struggling, she said, "Would you want to marry me?"

"S-s-sure," he said, "I want to marry you now."

"You can't, Art," she said. "Don't even think about it."

"Why not?"

"Art," she said, "you'll just make yourself more miserable." In that instant she felt like crying; with effort she said, "You can't leave Rachael. She's a wonderful person. She's a lot finer person than I am. I know that."

"No," he said.

"It's the truth. If I were anything at all, I wouldn't be here with you. I'd have broken it off after that first night. But I don't have the strength. I'm too weak, Art." And it was true, she thought, it really was true; she could not deny it. "It's just delaying it. Sooner or later we have to break it off. I keep telling myself: we had to now, right now. I'm too old and you're too young. But we keep on going along. Someday we'll have to pay for this."

"No," he said, "why do we have to stop?"

"We'll want to. This isn't healthy or right. There's nothing really good between us."

"I don't know," he said.

He listened to her; he heard what she was saying. But he did not agree. Now, turning, he saw her lips, dark and full, moving close to his. She was rising toward him.

Maybe it was true, he thought.

Her lips tingled against his own. With her gloved hand, she touched his face, pressing her fingers to him avidly. Her nostrils flared; out of the corner of his eye, he saw the trembling beneath the layers of powder and lipstick, the quivering of her lips and chin. She smelled like raspberries, a hot, sweet smell, a sticky smell. Her veil was up; she had lifted it aside to kiss him.

And the beautiful long legs, he thought. Nothing in this life was permanent. No sensation, not the most vivid nor the most meaningful. Not even this. She was right. The feel of them was gone already, and one day even the sight would be gone. And, he thought, someday, in a few decades, the legs themselves, the superb body, the arms and face and dark hair and waist would perish and vanish and become ashes. And he would not remember them because he would be dead, too. All the intricate working parts would stop working; the joints would dissolve and the fluids would dry up and it would be dust, dust.

He thought: If this could go, then anything could and would go. Nothing could be saved. Nothing survived. Where was all the talk, the music and fun and cars and places? Here went the greatest of the sensibilities, here went civilization itself in its blue suit and veil and heels and matching purse and gloves. Thousands of years had gone into the forming of this object. The hell with the buildings and cities and documents and ideas, the armies and ships and societies. They had persons prepared to lament for them. He lamented this. He thought: I was out to get this as soon as I laid eyes on it. And I did get it, and I did have it, and it was every bit as good as I had imagined.

In the vicinity of Redwood City, he left the freeway and crossed to El Camino Real. Near Menlo Park, at the side of the highway, was a motel.

Why not here? he thought.

Starting, Pat raised her head and looked out. "Are you stopping?"

"This looks like what we want," he said.

"A motel," she said, reading the sign. "The Four Aces Motel."

"It looks clean," he said.

"I've never stayed at a motel. We always had the cabin if we wanted to go somewhere. How far is this from San Francisco?"

"Around twenty miles," Art said.

When he had brought the car up onto the gravel shoulder and had parked, she got out and looked back in the direction they had come.

To the north was San Francisco, too far now to see, but nonetheless there. She felt its closeness. The line of office buildings, like two-dimensional cardboard cutouts, assembled and pasted up against the late-afternoon haze. The air was dry and tasted of cinders. She sniffed; she inhaled the presence of trucks and cars, the sky-borne wastes from factories.

Into San Francisco went concrete ramps, the freeway system over which they had come. The ramps were high off the ground, elevated, remote; the cars whizzed along, and the lines of traffic divided, passed in various directions, passed under the black directional signs with letters as large as the cars themselves. To her this sense of the city, this view of it, was disturbing and at the same time exhilarating. To be here, on the edge of the city . . . to be camped just outside, not in it but beside it, close enough to enter if she wanted, far enough out so that she was away; she was free, on her own, not bound or contained by it.

The trucks rumbled past. The huge diesel trucks. Under her feet the pavement shook.

Ah, she thought, breathing in the air. The freedom, the sense of motion, the trucks, the cars. Everything was on its way somewhere. Transition, she thought; there was nothing stable here. Nothing fixed. She could be anything she wanted. This was the edge.

16

The blue pre-war Plymouth halted by the curb, and Ferde Heinke hopped out and ran up the path and down the stairs and knocked on the door of the basement apartment. A light was on behind the shade of the living room window, and he knew either Rachel or Art was home.

The door opened and Rachael, looking wan and listless, said, "Hi, Heinke."

Always shy in her presence, he scuffed his feet and said, "What say. Is Art around?"

"No," she said.

"I sort of wanted to pick up the dummies." She did not appear to understand, so he explained, "The dummies for *Phantasmagoria*; they're around someplace. Art was working on them."

"Oh," she said, "yes. He asked me to go over the spelling." She held the door open and Ferde Heinke entered. "I'll get them."

Ill at ease, he waited for her. The apartment had a deserted quality, a lack of life. While he was standing around, he realized that a man was sitting in the corner with his legs stuck out, a grown man in a suit. At first he thought the man was asleep, and then he realized that the man was awake and looking at him.

"Hi," Ferde Heinke murmured.

The man said, "Hi, Ferde."

Recognizing Jim Briskin, he said, "How are you?"

"Not so good," Jim Briskin said, and that was all.

Rachael appeared with the dummies. "Here," she said, giving them to Ferde. Her tone was so weighed down that he decided not to stay;

169

he accepted the dummies for his science fiction magazine, thanked her, and went off up the steps to the path.

Behind him Rachael shut the door of the apartment. He continued along the path, past the iron gate, to the car. At the wheel Joe Mantila said, "You didn't stay long, anyhow."

"He wasn't home," Ferde said, getting into the car.

They stopped at the lithograph shop, which was still open. The man behind the counter, fat and wearing suspenders and a colored shirt with the sleeves rolled up, inspected the dummies. His stubby fingers riffled the pages as Ferde Heinke and Joe Mantila stood circumspectly a short distance away.

"You want it folded and stapled, don't you?" The man scratched estimates with a ballpoint pen. "How many copies?"

Ferde Heinke told him around two hundred, and the man wrote that down. He also wrote complicated figures about the number of pages, size of pages, and cryptic letters suggesting the weight of paper, the type of chemical process.

"Can we go look at how it works?" Ferde asked, interested as always in seeing printing processes.

"Sure," the man said, smoking a malacrino cigarette. "Just keep out of the way."

They wandered past the counter and saw the negatives of several dummies from local corporations, and then the actual photographing equipment. Next door was more interesting material; the Rube Goldberg folding-and-cutting machine was clanking away, and hundreds of pamphlets—all alike—were rattling down an inclined belt. The title of the pamphlet was "Tungsten in Time of War," and it was put out by a factory in South San Francisco. The pamphlets hung astraddle the moving belt, and at the bottom they were mechanically collected into a pile. The room banged with the noise of the conveyer; metal arms reached and groped.

"It looks like a Martian," Heinke said. "Or like Abe Merritt's 'The Metal Monster.' I have that in the original edition; it was published in the October 1927 issue of *Science and Invention* under the title 'The Metal Emperor.' "

"Yeah," Joe Mantila said, not listening.

"Nobody hardly knows that," Heinke went on, above the uproar.

"Where was Art?" Joe Mantila said.

"I don't know. He was out."

"If I was married to a girl like her," Joe Mantila said, "I sure wouldn't be out."

"That's no lie," Ferde Heinke said.

They got their estimate and left the bindery. As they walked back to the car, Joe Mantila noticed a flat manila folder under Heinke's arm.

"Didn't you give him that?"

"No," Heinke said.

"What is it?"

"A story," Heinke said, becoming instantly cautious.

"What kind of story?"

"Science fiction, of course. I wrote it all last week. It runs five hundred words." He clutched the folder with both hands. "It's pretty good."

"Let's see it," Joe Mantila said.

An evasiveness crept over Heinke. "No soap."

"What's it for?"

"I'm going to submit it to *Astounding*."

"If they print it, everybody'll read it." Mantila stuck out his hand. "Let's have it, come on."

Heinke stalled. "It stinks."

"What's it called?"

" 'The Peeping Man.' "

"What's that mean?"

Heinke struggled. "That's the lead character. He's a mutant, with psionic powers. He can see into alternate Earths. The whole world is destroyed and in ruins, and he sees Earths in which there was no war. It's not exactly original, but it has a new twist."

Joe Mantila grabbed the folder from Heinke. "I'll give it back to you tomorrow; you can submit it then."

"Give that back, you shit." Heinke snatched it angrily. "Come on, goddamn you." The two of them struggled, during which the folder was dropped, stepped on, picked up, dropped again. Joe Mantila tripped Heinke, and Heinke fell sprawling, still trying to catch hold of his folder.

"You——!" Heinke yelled from the pavement.

"Why don't you want me to see it?" Mantila said, gathering up the

171

crumpled sheets. "What's there that you don't want anybody to find out?"

Sullenly Heinke climbed to his feet. "When you show things to people you know"—he brushed off his jeans—"they always say it's about them."

"Is it about me?"

Heinke plodded along toward the car. "A writer has to gather his materials where he finds them."

Joe Mantila gave him a swift kick in the rump. "If it's about me, I'll de-ball you."

"And I'll sue you for assault and battery, and for theft of my manuscript. How about that?" As he got into the Plymouth, he said, "It's not about you."

"Who then?"

After a long time Heinke muttered, "It's about Rachael."

Joe Mantila snorted. "Goddamn, that's a laugh. You been thinking about her?"

"It's about her and Art."

"No kidding." Seated behind the wheel, Joe Mantila began to read the manuscript:

"THE PEEPING MAN"

A SCIENCE FICTION STORY

BY

FERDE R. HEINKE

Col. Throckmorton's glance turned involuntarily in the direction of the triple-locked chamber around which armed soldiers in uniform with blasters kept a 24 hour vigil. No man had gone into that room. Earth's last hope was in that room. And the door was sealed.

What thoughts went through the Col.'s head? There was no turning back. They had gone too far. The room contained Earth's one hope for salvation from the ruins to which the 3rd world war between Russia and America had brought it.

"It's eerie," the Col. trembled. "Is he demon or a god? Sometimes I don't know which. I tell you, Lt., I haven't

closed my eyes in sleep in days. I hesitate to trust the fate
of mankind to that Being. We know nothing about him,
Lt. How can homo sapiens understand homo superior?
It's beyond comprehension."

"But perhaps he can save us." The Lt.'s voice was quiet
as he spoke. *If he wants to.*

* * * * *

In the room sat a man. Head bowed, the man was thinking. His name—Ronald Manchester. He was 23 years old
and the Psionic power within him had flowered at last to
full bloom. But he was not thinking of that. He was thinking how he was the most powerful human in the world—
yet not a human but an incredibly unique god-like
superman who could save Earth. He was seeing past the
mundane world in which ordinary man lived, he was seeing into an almost unbelievable other universe whose
beauty was hidden to all save him.

What did he see in that other universe? For to him it
was manifest, alternate presents of other possible Earths
that had not been wrecked by man's greed. They were
inside his head. His mind was a space-time continuum that
led from one Earth to the next, and his frontal lobe was
trained on that miraculous salvation which he alone could
see. Beautiful trees he saw and flowers, a great garden very
much similar to the Garden of Eden. It was unspoiled by
greedy man. Animals lay down with other animals. People
walked around in peace and friendship. There was no
strife.

Ron saw all this and he was sad, for he knew that man
had destroyed his own world. Would man destroy this
vertible Garden of Paradise? The heart of the superman
was troubled. He knew the greed of homo sapiens, he was
the beginning of a new race who lacked that selfish greed.
And he had been imprisoned by soldiers because they
hated and didn't understand anything different. He had
been chased by a howling mob of mass men. He had been
stoned and thrown sticks at. Beaten, troubled, he had at
the end crept away from the haunts of man. He could not

173

endure among them because he could not kill. He lacked the ability to destroy. He was like God. He loved everybody. He wanted to be friends.

One day he was sitting alone in his cell and he looked into a different other world of such breathtaking beauty that nobody could imagine it. Nobody could believe it existed, it was so fair and untouched. Even the man of tomorrow was stunned and for a time silent. He trembled and grew cold all over as his eyes made it out. A lovely forest pool rippled in the primevil glade. Animals besported themselves under mountains that rose against the sky. The sky was star-studded and a moon of arresting beauty hung there beaming down.

Suddenly he saw something, a shape moving among the trees. He looked more closely. He saw a woman.

The woman was a goddess. A large cat-like lion whose fur was green instead of the usual was sitting with her at the edge of an untroubled forest pool. The woman stared reflectively down at the water and every now and then dabbled in it sending ripples in ever widening circles. The woman was nude. Her breasts rose in two cones that ended in pink roses that he saw with almost awe. On her face was a sad look as if she was thinking.

Then one day just before they were going to come and shoot him the beautiful woman appeared. A blazing circle of blinding light appeared in the center of the cell and there was the woman.

"Come," she whispered. Her eyes were large and blue and her lips were red. Her hair was a cascade of black down her bare neck and shoulders, her legs shone long and bare in the light of the flaming circle in which she moved. "I will save you," were the words her lovely lips formed. "I will lead you to a world in which you can live."

"Why?" was the other's instant query. Col. Peterson might possibly appear at any instant.

"I have fallen in love with you. I know your plight, superior mutant. But—hurry!" She seemed to glance into the viewscreen attached to her bare wrist. "Soldiers are coming, if I'm to save you I must as soon as possible."

Their telepathic brains met and he saw what he had to do. He shinnied up the wall to the light-globe. From it he took the platinum atomic filiment (an invention of the future that operated without power) and ripping wires from the walls he took his belt buckle and brought out the concealed microscopic tools he carried. He quickly made a machine under her telepathic direction.

"Do you trust me?" her lips whispered.

His rejoinder was, "Yes, my beloved, I trust you entirely. For you are not like the others. You are not like man."

Suddenly there was a blinding flash of light. When the light cleared he was lying on a grassy glade he knew so well. At first he couldn't believe he was there because something in the way the woman talked gave him grave doubts. He wondered if she was not telling him something. Then she appeared.

She wore a simple plain white robe looped at her waist. On her feet she had sandals. The cloth seemed to cling to her breasts which were full and upright. Her body moved as she walked.

"You are here," she said calmly. The strange smile on her face had grown. She led him stumbling from the glade down to the edge of a mountain. The sun blazed down on them and temporarily he was blinded. When he opened his eyes what he saw was impossible. He cried out but there she was beside him. She sensed and knew.

For what he saw was that he was still on Earth. There was the ruined cities all broken and ruined as he remembered them. It was the regular Earth! He was stunned.

"This is your real world," the woman told him. She pointed with her bare arm out over the ruins at the foot of the mountain. "I have brought you back to it. I and you will rebuild together. We will not turn inward and shrink our terrible responsibility. We offer eternal hope to mankind which deserves being rebuilt. With your ability and our money we can help repair the damage bacteria and

Philip K. Dick

H-bombs did. Millions have died horribly. War has taken a ghastly toll. But do not despair of men, it was the military not all men. I am a woman, you a man. We will help man, not turn our backs on them."

He listened to her, and gradually a dawning discovery came to him. The point she was saying was this, that he had been wrong. He had taken the easy road. And the woman had helped him to see what he had to see.

"And all the Col. Peters?" he asked.

"We have triumphed over them," was the answer as she stood beside him on the mountain top. "They are no more. The power of goodness and love finally won out over war."

Already, far below the two of them, the rebuilding had begun. They walked slowly to greet it.

END

Joe Mantila returned the manuscript and folder. "It sure is corny," he said. He started up the Plymouth.

"No good," Ferde Heinke agreed, discouraged. "Is that what you mean? You don't think I ought to submit it?" He knew in his own mind that the story was hopeless.

"Was that Rachael?" Joe Mantila said. "That goddess?"

"Yeah," he said.

"I don't get the ending."

Ferde Heinke said, "The idea is that she was really a human being and not from some other universe."

"You mean like a Martian?"

"A mutant. He thought she was a nonhuman mutant."

"Is that supposed to be Art, that whatever his name is?"

"It's based on Art."

"What's he supposed to be, a mutant like her?"

"That's what he found out," Ferde Heinke said. "He was a human being, too. His duty lay with mankind, not to himself. She showed him that. His duty was to rebuild the world."

After a while Joe Mantila said, "I sure wouldn't mind being married to her."

"You can say that again," Ferde Heinke said.

"And you know, she's real smart."

176

"Yeah," he agreed.

Joe Mantila said, "What do you think the purpose of life is?"

"That's hard to say."

"Well, what do you think?"

"You mean the ultimate purpose?"

"What we're here on Earth for."

Ferde Heinke, pondering, said, "To help mankind evolve up the next step in evolution."

"You think the next step is with us already, but we don't know it?"

"Maybe so," he said.

"I used to think the purpose of life was to do God's will," Joe Mantila said.

"How do you define God?"

"God made the universe."

"Have you ever seen Him?"

"Hey," Joe Mantila said, "I read this story where the military shoots down this angel. You know? And it's wounded or something." He developed the plot for Ferde Heinke's benefit, repeating the details endlessly.

"I read that," Ferde Heinke said.

Joe Mantila said, "It's funny all the different things she knows. Rachael, I mean. Maybe she really is a superior mutant." Gesturing, he went on, "I wouldn't be surprised to discover that she has those powers mutants have. I mean, she's not like anybody else. When she says something, you know it's right. Maybe she has that faculty of—what is it?—reading the future."

"Precognition," Ferde Heinke said.

"You think so?"

"No," he said. "That was the whole point of the story. She's actually a human being, and there's really a lot of human beings not like the military."

"If she was here now," Joe Mantila said, "and she heard us talking, you know what she'd do?"

"She'd laugh."

"Yeah," Joe Mantila said. "You notice that most things like what other people like you and I believe, she don't believe? When you talk to her, she doesn't even hear you. Like all the different things we do, the Organization and the Beings from Earth. I think she really is a superior mutant, and after everybody else is gone she'll take over the world."

Ferde Heinke said, "I think this is the last dying days of our society, the way Rome went out."

"Why did Rome fall?"

"Rome fell because their society became hollow. And then the barbarians swarmed in and that was the end."

"They burned all the libraries and buildings," Joe Mantila said.

"Tough," Ferde Heinke said.

"That was wrong; they killed all the Christians, they walled them up in the catacombs and set animals on them."

"It was the Romans that did that," Ferde Heinke said. "In the gladiator fights. The Romans hated the Christians because they knew that the Christians would pull down their empty society, and they did."

"The Emperor Constantine was a Christian," Joe Mantila disagreed. "It was the barbarians who killed the Christians, not the Romans."

They argued indefinitely.

17

The Four Aces Motel was a series of square stucco cabins, modern in appearance, Californian in style, well located at the edge of the highway entering San Francisco from the south. The neon sign was immense. The interior of each cabin was a dim chamber, and in the center of the chamber was the shower.

After the paying guest had set down his suitcases and closed the door against the fatigue and glare of the drive, he looked about and saw the bed—clean, wide—and the lamp—brass and slender and amazingly tall—and then he saw the shower. And the guest stripped off his sweaty clothes, his slacks and shorts and sport shirt and shoes, and went happily into the shower.

Under his bare toes the floor was a rough and sensuous porous stone, similar to limestone but sprayed a pastel blue-gray. The walls, also porous and stonelike, were green. The shower was a part of the room, not an annex. A foot-high rampart of adobe blocks retained the water. The blocks were irregular, like the foundation of a ruined Spanish fort, and the guest felt as if he—or she—were standing in the center of some ancient, secure, unchanging structure in which he or she was free to do what he liked, be what he wished.

Beneath the shower of cabin C, Patricia Gray stood with her legs apart as she reached to scrub her ankles.

The door of the cabin was partly open, and the late-afternoon sunlight poured in through the slot. And with the sunlight, the image of gravel, a field of gravel, spreading to the square of lawn and deck chairs and beach umbrellas in the shade behind the neon sign. And then El Camino itself. The trucks and the San Francisco commuter

179

traffic went nose to tail, and the noise was a deep, ceaseless drumming. Now they were leaving the city. Now, at this moment at the end of the day, the traffic moved south.

Over the bed a plastic Emerson radio played a dance record. On the bed Art lay spread out in his slacks and shirt, reading a magazine.

"Do me a favor?" Patricia said.

"A towel?"

"No," she said, "turn off the radio, would you? Or get something else." The jukebox tunes reminded her of the station, her job, and Jim Briskin.

Art made no move to get up.

"Come on," she said. He did not stir, so she took the immaculate white bath towel supplied by the motel and padded across the room. Drizzling water from her hair and head and body, she clicked the switch of the radio.

"Okay?" she said. She was afraid enough of him to remain close to the radio as she dried herself.

The silence seemed to oppress him. "Get something on it," he said.

She said, "I don't want anything from the outside." This must be complete, she thought. If it is going to have any chance at all.

From the clothes that she had bought him, she picked up a red-and-gray sport shirt. He had worn it once, on the drive from San Francisco; holding it, she went to the bed and said, "Can I wear this?"

Glancing up, he saw her and the shirt. "Why?"

"I just want to," she said.

"It's too big."

But she put on his shirt. The bottom of it trailed across her thighs. From one of her suitcases she took a pair of jeans and put them on; she unfastened her hair and began to comb it. In the jeans and sport shirt she padded about the room; she carried bottles and jars and tubes and packages to the medicine cabinet in the bathroom and to the top of the dresser. The closet was already full of her clothes. She did not unpack the rest; there was no room.

"You sure have a lot of stuff," Art said.

"No," she said, "not so much."

"All those b-b-bottles."

She went into the tiny kitchen to see if there was cupboard space.

They had brought no cooking utensils. On the drainboard was a package of cookies and four navel oranges and a carton of milk and a loaf of Langendorf bread and a jar of cheese spread. And, by itself, a fifth of Gallo port. She opened the wine and, rinsing out the tumbler supplied by the motel, poured herself a glass.

Through the back window of the motel, she saw a yard of planks and uncompleted concrete foundations. On a clothesline trousers and work shirts hung. A desolate scene, she thought. Returning to the living room, she said, "This is nice here."

At the front door she stood watching the trucks go by. The time was seven o'clock, and the sun was beginning to set. The flow of traffic had dwindled. They were already home, she thought, the commuters in their business suits and neckties.

"When did you want to eat?" she said.

"I don't care."

"There's a coffee shop up the road," she said. "You want to go there?"

He tossed aside the magazine. "Sure."

As they walked along the shoulder of the highway, she said, "What's wrong?"

"I don't know."

"Do you want to drive on? Stop somewhere else? We could drive all night, if you want."

"You got your s-s-stuff unpacked."

"I can repack it," she said.

The door of the coffee shop was propped open. It was a wide, modern coffee shop, with a counter at one side and booths at the other. Cars were pulled up in the gravel lot beside it. Most of the people were from the motel, middle-aged men and women on their vacations. She thought: From the East, from Ohio, coming out here to California for a week, in their Oldsmobiles.

At the counter Art spun a stool and seated himself; he picked up the menu and examined it.

"I'm hungry," she said. "I have an appetite . . . you know what I'd like to do? Let's ask them if they can fix the food to take out. So we can take it back with us."

"What?" he murmured.

"To our cabin. And eat it there."

The waitress was before them. "Are you ready to order?" she said, swabbing the counter with a white cloth.

Pat said, "Can you fix food to go?"

Speaking in the direction of the cook, the waitress said, "Can we fix food to go?"

"Depends on what they want," the cook said, appearing. "Salads, sandwiches, coffee. Not soup."

"What about the dinner?" Pat said. On the menu they listed veal chops and green peas and potatoes.

"If you have a plate," the cook said. "But we don't have any kind of cartons."

"We can eat it here," Art said. He ordered two of the dinners; the waitress went off with the order.

Pat said, "How do you feel?"

"Fine," he said.

The food arrived and they ate. "Is this what you wanted?" she said. "I mean—all of this. Where we are. What we're doing."

He nodded.

After they had eaten, they ordered beer. Nobody questioned him; he was served his bottle and glass. The beer was cold; the bottle was white with frost.

"Let's go back to the cabin," Pat said suddenly.

"Why?"

"I don't know. These places—you can sit in them for hours." All the times, she thought, that she had sat with Jim in a bar and eatery like this, at the edge of the highway. Drinking beer, listening to the jukebox. Fried prawns and beer . . . the smell of the ocean. The hot night air of the Russian River.

On the way back to the cabin Art seemed resentful. She could not tell; now the sun was gone and the sky was dark. Beside her he was a dim shape, plodding over the gravel. Bugs, perhaps moths, flew in their faces, and Art swiped wildly.

"Do they bother you?" she said.

"You darn r-r-right."

She said, "Let's lock ourselves in; let's stay inside and not come out."

"Ever?"

"As long as we can. The rest of the night, until tomorrow. Let's go to bed early."

They entered the cabin and she closed the door; she bolted it and pulled down each of the window shades. The cabin was air-conditioned and she turned on the fan. It roared, and the noise gratified her.

"This is what I want," she said. She felt elated. This was complete; they had everything they needed. Finally they were self-sufficient. Throwing herself down on the bed, she said, "Come and lie with me. Please."

"And do what?"

"Just lie," she said.

Begrudgingly, he sat down on the edge of the bed.

"No," she said, "don't just sit, lie down. Why don't you? Isn't this what we ought to be doing?" Trying to explain to him what she meant, she said, "This just involves the two of us. Lying here like this."

Kicking his shoes off, he put his arms around her. Then he reached up to turn off the lamp above the bed.

"No," she said. "I won't let you turn it off."

"Why not?"

"I want you to see me."

"I know how you look."

"Leave it on," she said.

Arising, he left her. He went over and picked up his magazine and seated himself in a chair.

"You are ashamed," she said. "You really are."

He did not look up.

"I wanted to look at you," she said. "Isn't that all right? Shouldn't I do that? I like the way you look." She waited and then she said, "Could you leave on some light? The light in the bathroom, how about that?"

His magazine under his arm, he went to the bathroom and turned on the lamp by the washbowl. Then he came back, and on his face was the fretful look; he reached past her head for the lamp. When it was off, he returned to the bed. The bed sank under his weight.

At first she saw nothing, and then she was able to make out the texture of his hair, the bridge of his nose, his eyebrows and ears, his shoulders. Lifting her hand, she unbuttoned his shirt. She slipped his shirt from him, and then she raised herself up and clasped her arms

183

around him and pressed her head against his chest. He did not move.

"Take off your clothes," she said. "Please. For my sake."

When he had taken off his clothes, she lay beside him, her arm under his head. But there was no response. She slipped down until her dark hair flowed across his stomach, but still he did not stir. No, she thought. Not at all.

"This is fine," she said. "Just lying here."

"Okay," he said.

She kissed him. His body was cold, hard, without spirit. "Can't we just lie here?" She unfastened her shirt, and then she took off her jeans; she lay against him with her mouth at his neck, her eyes shut. She buried her fists in his armpits, and she thought: Never. Never at all.

"It's only around eight o'clock," he said.

"I love you," she said. "Do you understand what I mean? For god's sake—" She dug her nails into his face and made him look at her. "I want to stay with you. This is exactly what I want, what we have now. This is enough."

He said, "I'm not just going to lie around here."

"What do you want? What do you need?"

"Let's go somewhere."

She held him down; she pressed down his wrists, his loins—she gripped him with her legs; she hugged him until her body ached and her breasts were bruised. "Where?" she said at last.

He said, "I saw this skating rink up the road. We d-d-drove by it."

"No," she said.

"Come on," he said. With his hands he lifted her from him; he set her beside him in the bed.

Getting to her feet, she began putting her clothes back on. "What sort of skating?"

"Ice skating."

"You want to go ice skating?" she said. She went away and put the palms of her hands to her chin; her fingers covered her eyes. "I can't believe it, Art."

"Why not?" he demanded. "What's the matter with that?"

"Nothing," she said.

"Don't you want to?"

"No," she said, "I don't feel like it. I'll stay here."

"Don't you know how? I'll teach you." He arose and rapidly dressed. "I'm pretty good; I taught a couple of people."

She went into the bathroom and locked the door.

"What are you doing in there?" he demanded at the door.

"I don't feel well," she said. She sat down on the clothes hamper.

"You want me to stick around?"

"No, go ahead," she said.

"I'll be back in an hour or so," he said. "H-h-how about that? Okay?"

She stared down at her hands. Presently she heard the front door of the cabin shut. Gravel crunched as he crossed the lot to the shoulder of the highway. Opening the bathroom door, she ran through the cabin and out onto the porch. Far off by the highway, his figure moved. He became smaller.

"Goddamn you," she said.

He went on.

"Goddamn you, Art," she said. She shut the door.

Putting on her shoes, she ran from the cabin, across the gravel to the highway, after him. Ahead of her his figure moved, and then it was swallowed up by the lights of a roadside bar and then a gas station. She slowed down. The neon sign of the skating rink was visible, and she kept her eyes on that; she could not see him, but she saw the sign and she went toward it.

By the skating rink, cars were parked, some of them locked up, some still full of people. Kids, she thought. Boys in sport coats and slacks, girls in dresses. A lunch counter was attached to the rink, and the kids were going in there. At the window of the rink a line of kids waited, and Art was one of them. In front of him was a girl in a checkered skirt and saddle shoes, a red wool sweater over her shoulders. The girl was no more than fifteen. Behind Art a soldier, round-faced, gangling, waited with his girl.

She stood, away from the light, gasping and getting back her wind. The line became longer. Art reached the window, paid for his admission, and then went on inside.

A car full of teenagers pulled up, its exhausts thundering. Boys piled out and ran to the ticket window. Behind them two girls in jeans and sweaters followed. At the window they struggled and swarmed and shoved one another; the kids blended together, the jeans and shirts, the faces, the hair.

When they had gone inside the rink, she turned and walked back to the cabin of the motel. She bolted the door after her. A roaring filled every part of the cabin and at first she did not know what it was; she could not tell if it were inside or outside her head. It was outside. It was the air conditioner, she realized. They had left it on.

With her drink in her hand, she stood before the mirror and declared with certitude that she would have looked absolutely perfect beside him. Together they would have attracted favorable attention; they would have been an outstanding couple.

And then she began to cry. She started to sit down, but her hand struck the arm of the chair; the glass tumbled and the remains of her drink spread in a pool across the rug. She touched the pool with her toe. The rug was wet. The coolness felt nice.

God, she thought.

Walking into the kitchen, she fixed herself another drink. She turned on the radio over the bed, but she could not get KOIF; the transmitter was too far away. On a San Mateo station she picked up classical music; she turned the volume up loud, as loud as it would go.

She brought the wine bottle to the bed. Lying down, she snapped off the light; she lay in darkness, drinking, listening to the music. Outside the cabin, cars and trucks passed along the highway.

In the next cabin laughter and voices shrilled out into the darkness. She listened to that, too. When the voices ceased, she turned her attention to the music.

The music, suddenly, was gone. She sat up. At first she tuned the dial, wondering what had happened to it. And then she realized that the station had gone off the air. The time was midnight.

She made her way to the bathroom, washed her face, and then scrubbed her skin; she pressed her face into the fabric until her face ached.

Then she came back out and seated herself by the phone. She dialed the KOIF number, but of course there was no answer. With a shock she realized what she was doing. Not there, she thought, hanging up the phone. He couldn't possibly be there. Nobody was there. It was after midnight; the station was shut down.

Holding the receiver in her lap, she dialed her own number. The phone rang on and on. Not there, she thought. She hung up. Next she dialed his apartment. Again there was no answer.

Nowhere, she thought.

She hung up the phone and went to refill her glass. The wine was almost gone. She poured it all into the glass.

Once more she telephoned. Using the San Francisco phone book, she looked up and dialed the Emmanuals' number, the apartment on Fillmore Street.

"Hello?" a voice said.

"Jim," she said. She began to cry again; tears spilled down her cheeks, onto her knuckles and the phone.

"Where are you?" he said.

"I'm in a motel," she said. "I don't know the name."

Jim said, "Where is it?"

"I don't know." She sat crying, clutching the phone.

"Is he with you?"

"No." From her pocket she got out her handkerchief and blew her nose. "He went out."

Jim said, "See if there's a match folder. Look by the phone."

She looked. She found a match folder with the name Four Aces Motel on it. "Jim," she said, "I don't know what to do."

"Did you find a match folder?"

"No," she said, "I don't know." She buried the match folder in the phone book, out of sight. "I know where I am, but I don't know what to do. He went out ice-skating. Can you believe that?"

"Tell me where you are," he said, "and I'll come and get you. Are you in San Francisco?"

"No," she said. "It's down on El Camino Real."

"Near what town?"

"Redwood City. He's up at an ice-skating rink with a lot of kids. What's the matter with me, Jim? How did I get mixed up in this?"

"Tell me the address."

"No," she said, shaking her head.

"Tell me," he said. "Pat, come on. Tell me where you are."

"What am I going to do?" she said. "He's up there with those kids. All he is is a kid; he showed me this place they go, this attic. He came over to the apartment and got me to go to dinner with him. We went out to Chinatown; I didn't want to go, but he got me to. I did everything I could, but good god, what can I do if he's going off and ice-skate?"

"Pat," he said, "tell me where you are."

"I'm scared of him," she said.

"Why?"

Holding the handkerchief to her eyes, she said, "I don't want you to come down. How can I get out of here, Jim? I have to get away. This didn't work out . . . you were right."

"Why are you afraid of him?"

"He hit me," she said, crying.

"Are you hurt?"

"I'm okay. He hit me in the eye. And we went on and on that night until there was nothing left of me. He wore me out and now he's ice-skating. There was this girl ahead of him in the line; she—"

"I want to come and get you," Jim said. "So tell me where you are. I can't get you unless I know where you are."

She said, "He's afraid of you, Jim. That's why we're down here. He was afraid you'd show up at the apartment. You're the only one he's afraid of; he isn't even afraid of Rachael. How is Rachael?"

"Fine," he said.

"Is she mad?"

"Look," he said, "tell me where you are."

"I'm at the Four Aces Motel."

"Okay."

"Wait," she said. "Jim, listen. I did everything I could; I bought him enough clothes so he looked like a man and not like a kid dressed up for Saturday night. It's my car we came down in. What else could I do? All I wanted to do was just lie here in bed and not do anything. But he wouldn't do that."

"I'll see you," he said, and hung up. The phone clicked in her ear. For a time she held it, and then she put it on the hook.

"Christ," she said.

Now it had happened. Now it was over. She went unsteadily to the closet and changed from her jeans and sport shirt to a blouse and bolero and long skirt; he liked her long skirts. Then she began braiding her hair.

188

At twelve-thirty the cabin door flew open and Art entered. "Hi," he said.

"Hello," she said.

"What you been doing?" He saw the empty wine bottle by the bed. "What'd you do, drink the whole bottle?"

She said, "I called Jim Briskin."

"Y-y-yeah?" He came around beside her. "No kidding?"

"I had to," she said. "Why did you go off and leave me? I don't understand how you could."

"How long ago'd you call him?"

"I don't know."

"What's he doing? Coming down?"

"Yes," she said.

By degrees his face darkened. "Get your stuff packed; let's go."

"I'm going back," she said.

"Oh y-y-yeah?"

Standing up, she said, "You sneaky little kid, if he ever gets his hands on you, he'll kill you. So you better run as fast as you can and hide."

"What'd you call him for?"

"Ice-skating," she said. "What else do you do? Why don't you go out and get me an ice cream soda?"

He shuffled his feet and stuck his hands away, into his back pockets.

"Did you have fun?" she said. "Did you meet any kids you knew?"

"No," he said.

"Why'd you leave?"

"They closed."

"Did you walk some girl home? Or what did you do, buy a hot dog and a malt?" She felt cold and terrified; she did not dare stop.

Art said, "I tried out this guy's MG."

"Then you go drive his MG," she said. "You just drive it as long as you want."

"Are you really going back?" he said in a plaintive voice. "We j-j-just left."

"Blame yourself," she said.

Fooling with his belt, he said, "I couldn't see sitting around."

"With me," she said, "you couldn't see sitting around with me."

"There's nothing to do," he said.

From the closet she got her suitcases. "Will you help me pack?" She began putting skirts and sweaters and blouses into the suitcase. "Come on, Art. Don't make me do all the work."

Going to her purse, he began rooting.

"What do you want?" She walked over and took the purse from him.

"The car keys," he said, not looking directly at her.

"Why?"

"I can't hang around here."

"You can't take my car. If you want to leave, go ahead. Go catch a bus or something."

In an instant he had yanked the purse from her hands; holding it over the bed, he dumped out the contents. "I'll leave it off someplace," he said. "You'll get it back."

She said, "If you take my car, I'll call the police and tell them you stole it."

"You will?"

"It's my car." She held out her hand. "Give me back the keys."

"Can't I use it?"

"No," she said.

"Suppose I just take it up to San Francisco and leave it off? I don't want to run into Jim Briskin; he's probably sore as hell."

"He'll kill you," she said.

"Did he say so?"

"Yes," she said.

"It was your idea."

She put her hand up to her eye. "See what you did to me?"

After a long, uncertain pause, he said, "You got a couple bucks I could have? I mean, if I have to get a b-b-bus or something."

"Did you spend everything you had?"

"I paid for some gas," he said. "For this guy's MG."

From the contents of her purse, she took her wallet.

"I'll pay you back," he said.

She gave him six or seven dollars, and he put the bills away in his coat. "You better leave," she said. "Before he gets here."

She led him by the arm; his body responded sluggishly, and at the door he hung back, dragging, unwilling to go. "I'm not leaving," he said. "I don't believe you called Jim Briskin; that's a lot of h-h-hot air." Tugging away from her, he walked back and stopped by the kitchen door, his shoulders hunched.

"Suit yourself," she said. She continued packing; she collected the bottles and jars and packages and fitted them into the suitcases.

"Is he really coming?" Art said.

"Yes," she said.

"You're going back with him?"

"Yes," she said, "I hope so."

"Are you going to marry him?"

"Yes," she said.

His chin sank down. His body hunched until he looked like a little old man, a gnarled old gnomish fellow, near-sighted, hard of hearing; he strained to hear her, to gather his faculties. The youthfulness was gone. The purity. "What's so good about him?" he said.

"He's a very fine person."

"And you're a skinny old bag."

Lifting a suitcase from the bed, she carried it to the door and set it down. That was one of them, and she began on a second. But it did not seem worth it. She sat down on the bed.

"Just an old bag," Art said. "Why don't you get a cat or a parrot or one of those birds the old maids have? So you can have something to mother."

"Art," she said, "would you go outside and leave me alone? Please leave me alone."

"You're not a girl at all," he said. "You're dried up. You're all worn out."

"Stop it," she said.

"Tough," he said, immobile.

She got up and went outside, onto the porch of the cabin. Headlights of cars flashed by. She walked toward the highway, closer and closer until under her feet the gravel was gone and she had come onto the pavement. A car honked. Behind it a second car slowed and swerved; the distorted features of the driver were visible, and then the car vanished. Its taillight glowed red. The taillight became smaller, and then at last it was gone.

After a while a car left the highway and bumped across the shoulder. Its headlights fastened on her and she was blinded; the car grew and she put up her hands. She smelled the hot engine as the hood of the car passed in front of her. The door opened; the car stopped rolling.

"Is that you, Pat?" Jim Briskin's voice came.

"Yes," she said. She lifted her head. Inside his car, behind the wheel, he sat with the door open, peering at her. When he had recognized her, he got out.

"How are you?" he said, as they walked toward cabin C. He patted her on the back.

"I'm pretty good," she said.

"You look run-down." Halting her, he scrutinized her. "He really hit you, didn't he?"

"Yes," she said.

Ahead of her, he stepped up and into the cabin. "Hello, Art," he said.

"Hi," Art said, flushed and nervous.

Jim said, "What'd you do, hit her in the eye?"

"Yeah," Art said. "But she's okay."

Turning to Pat he said, "Let's have your car key." He looked all around the room as she got the keys from the heap of things on the bed. "Thanks," he said. He seemed preoccupied. "Here, Art." He tossed the keys to the boy.

"What's this?" Art said. The keys fell to the floor, and he stooped to pick them up. The keys slipped away from him, and he stooped again.

"Your stuff isn't packed, is it?" Jim said to her. "I see it all around."

"No," she said. "I have one suitcase packed."

Going over to Art, he said, "You finish packing her stuff. Put it in the Dodge and then come on up."

"Up where?" Art said.

"Leave the car in front of her place." He led Pat from the cabin.

"You want me to unpack it," Art said, following after them to the door, "w-w-when I get it up there?"

"No," Jim said, "leave everything in the car."

"What about the keys?"

"Put them in the mailbox." Holding Pat by the hand, he took her to his car.

As they drove out onto the highway, she said, "Will he do it?"

"Do you care?" Jim said.

She said, "Thanks for coming."

"I think that ends it." Behind them the Four Aces Motel was already lost among the neon signs. "How are you otherwise?"

"I'll live," she said.

"It was certainly hard getting the name out of you. The motel name."

After that neither of them said anything. They watched the road, the cars and signs, the headlights that flashed by. Leaning back against the seat, Pat slept a little. When she woke up, they were on the freeway. To their right was the Bay. Now there were fewer lights.

"That dirty little squirt of a kid," she said.

"Okay," he said.

"He socked me right in the eye; he knocked me out."

"Now you have something to talk about," he said. "Something you can point to."

"And he pulled a knife on Bob Posin."

Jim said, "Who cares?"

She shrank away. She found her handkerchief in her pocket and began to cry into it, her head turned away from him; she cried as quietly as possible.

"Don't listen to me," he said.

"No," she said, "you're right."

He reached over and caressed her arm. "Why don't you shut up? Nobody feels sorry for you. When we get into town, we'll stop and buy something for your eye."

"I don't want anything," she said. "You know what he called me? He called me a lot of terrible things—I haven't heard words like that since I was a child. And he wanted me to borrow on my car; he wanted—" Again she was crying. She could not help it. She cried on and on, and Jim Briskin paid no attention.

The freeway joined with other freeways leading into San Francisco. In due time they were driving above houses. Most of the houses were dark; their lights were off.

18

His apartment was cold and dark. Patricia remained by the door while he lit lamps and pulled down the window shades.

"Haven't you been here?" she asked.

"Not for a while." In the light he saw how really tired she was, how lined and unhappy her face had become. A careworn face, he thought. "Better sit down," he said.

Pat said, "You know, at first he drove me wild; he was always after me."

"You said that first night was terrific," he said.

"Yes." She nodded, sitting with her hands folded, her feet close together. "But the next night, after he hit me . . . it went on and on—my god, I thought I'd die. He kept coming back. I'd think he was asleep—maybe he was, for a little—and then there he'd be, wanting to start again." She glanced up timidly. "So we kept at it. And in the morning when I woke up, I was sore all over. I could hardly get out of bed."

"Get a good long rest," he said.

"It's awful to say," she said. "To tell you."

He gestured. "Why not?"

"Can I have a cup of coffee? I—drank a bottle of wine. I feel sick." She did look sick. But he had seen her a lot sicker. All in all she was lucky.

"Sweet wine?" he said.

"Port."

"You kind of dropped your guard. Did you want it to break up?"

"Yes," she said, "it had run its course."

He knelt down so that he was facing her; taking hold of her hands, he said, "Is that the slogan?"

Her lips moved. "I don't know. What do you mean, Jim?"

"What now?" he said.

"Now," she echoed, "I realize my mistake."

He left her and went into the kitchen to fix the coffee.

When he came back, she was still sitting with her feet tucked under her and her hands folded in her lap. How forlorn, he thought. How glad he was to get her back. The difference it made . . . the importance.

Giving her the coffee cup, he said, "You think I don't love you as much as that kid loves you or said he loves you?"

"I know you do."

"Will you marry me?" he said. "Again?" Now, he thought; if ever she could be persuaded, it would have to be now. "You're through with that. And you don't give a damn about Bob Posin—do you?"

"All right," she said, holding her coffee cup. "I'll marry you. Remarry you. Whatever they call it."

The cup tilted; he took it away and set it on the floor. The giving-in, he thought. The surrendering on the part of the woman, the woman he completely loved. There was nothing like it on earth, nothing until the sky rolled up like a scroll and the graves opened and the dead walked. Until, he thought, the corruptible man put on incorruption.

"You won't change your mind, will you?" he said.

"Do you want me to?"

"I don't want you to change your mind."

"All right," she said, "I won't." Looking at him steadily, she said, "You don't consider me used up, then?"

"Are you?"

The tears rose up in her eyes and spilled out. "I—don't know."

"It's unlikely."

"You don't want me," she said, tears pouring down her cheeks onto her collar.

"You mean I shouldn't? Is that what you're trying to say?" He lifted her up out of the chair. "Or you mean I should plead and beg? Which is it?"

She tried to speak. Helplessly clutching at him, she said, "I don't feel well. Take me into the bathroom. Please."

Half carrying her, he got her there. She refused to let go of him;

holding on to her, he let her be sick. For a minute or so she passed out. But almost at once she recovered.

"Thanks," she whispered. "God." He lowered her until she was sitting on the rim of the tub. Wan and shivering, she rubbed his hand with her palm; she seemed feverish, and he wondered if she were really sick. "No," she said, "I'm feeling better. It's psychological."

"Let's hope so."

She smiled brokenly. "My conscience. I told him we would have to pay. This is it, maybe."

When she was stronger, he washed her face and led her back to the living room. Removing her shoes, he wrapped her in a blankct and propped her up on the couch.

"It was the coffee," she said.

"You didn't drink any."

She wanted a cigarette.

As he lit it for her, he said, "You want me to go see if he brought your stuff up?"

"I'm not staying here," she said. "I want to be in my own place. I don't want to be anywhere but there."

"Suppose he shows up?"

"He won't," she said.

"No," he agreed, "I guess not."

"I'll stay with you," she decided. "I can't go back to that, the evasion, the way we were. I'll stay here, and then when we're married we can stay here or there, whichever you want. Or we can get a new place. That might be better."

"I think so," he said.

As he put his coat on, she said, "I'll go with you. So I can see it and get what I need. We could go get the Dodge and bring it here . . . we could unload the stuff here."

They sat around until she felt well enough, and then they drove to her apartment.

The Dodge was parked at the entrance. Inside the back her stuff was piled helter-skelter; Art had dumped it in and the hell with it. Bottles, clothes, shoes, even the carton of milk and the oranges and the loaf of Langendorf bread. And, on the floor, the empty wine bottle.

"Anyhow," Pat said, "it's probably all here."

He parked his car, and then he drove the Dodge, with Pat beside him, back to his own place.

To bed she wore a pair of red-and-white polka-dot pajamas. "I feel new," she said, "in these."

In his shorts he brushed his teeth at the washbowl in the bathroom. The time was three-thirty. Except for the bedroom and bathroom, the apartment was dark. The door was locked and the lights were off. In the bed Patricia lay smoking, an ashtray on the covers.

"You finished in there?" Jim said, coming out of the bathroom.

"Yes," she said, feeling content.

How lean he was, she thought, in his shorts. To her the sparse torso and arms and legs were a relief; for three days she had been held fast by a thick-limbed boy whose body dwindled from the loins down, a rubbery, boneless body, made up of muscles and fat, supported on legs too short. A boy's body, she thought, not at all like this.

Switching off the light, Jim removed his shorts and got into the bed. In the darkness he put his arms around her.

"Isn't it strange," she said. "Now we're back again. After two years. Nothing separating us, nothing holding us apart." She was very happy. It was all for some purpose, she thought. It had ended in this. So it made sense. Not merely wasted motion . . . fatigue and injury for nothing.

Beside her Jim said, "You want to hear about Rachael?"

"Is there something?" She was almost asleep. But now, in her peace, she felt a coldness. Seeping into her, the coldness grew. "What do you mean?"

"Well," he said, "you knew I was there. You called me there."

She said, "I called you everywhere. I called you at the station and at your place here and at my place. And then I called you there."

"I was there."

"Does it mean anything?" She was wide awake, staring up into the darkness.

"She asked me to stay with her. Until Art showed up. So I did."

She waited, but that was all; he was silent. "Did you live there?" she asked finally. "Is that what you mean?"

"Not exactly. She's peculiar."

197

"How?"

"It was mostly meals. She wanted me to be there when she came home, so she could cook for me."

"Peasant," Pat said. "Dinner table. The farm."

"I hung around in the evening until she went to bed, and then I left."

"What about in the morning?" Two mornings, she thought.

"Nothing."

"Are you telling me the truth?" she said.

"Of course I am."

She said, "I'm scared of Rachael."

"I know you are."

"Will she do anything?"

"She has Art back."

"Yes," she said, encouraged. "That's right." She rose to put out her cigarette. "What do you think of her?"

"I don't know."

Lying back, Pat said, "Maybe she'll stab him."

Jim laughed. "Maybe. Maybe he'll beat her up."

"What would you do if he beat her up?"

"It's not my business."

"How would you feel?"

He did not answer. She waited; she listened. Had he gone to sleep?

To herself she said: I paid for what I did; I was sick in the bathtub. Isn't that enough? Doesn't that do it?

On the bedroom floor was her package of cigarettes, and she reached to pick them up. She lit another cigarette and lay on her back smoking. The man beside her did not stir. He was asleep, she thought; he was.

This is perfect, she thought. I see that. I understand that. Don't I deserve it?

Her cigarette glowed and she studied it; she tapped it against the ashtray which she held, and she thought: This is where I make my stand. This is where I put up my fight. For this. For what I have here.

In the morning she got up early, at seven o'clock, to telephone the station. Jim slept on. Without awakening him, she put on her robe, closed the door to the bedroom, and seated herself in the living room by the phone.

"Hello," she said. "Mr. Haynes?"

"How have you been, Patricia?" Haynes said in his formal voice. "We've been concerned about you. Not a word from you in what is it, two days?"

"I'm better," she said. "Could I come in late?"

"You don't have to come in at all today," he said. "Don't come in until it's completely gone."

At first she could not imagine what he meant, and then she realized that he was talking about the flu. "Thanks," she said. "Maybe I'll wait until tomorrow. I don't want to give it to anybody."

"Is it that intestinal kind?"

"Yes," she said. "I was sick . . . at my stomach."

"Cramps? That's the kind that's going around. Don't drink any fruit juices, just toast and eggs and custard. Mild foods. No acids, tomatoes or pears or orange juice."

She thanked him and hung up.

Returning to the bedroom, she tiptoed to the bed and saw that Jim was awake. "Hi," she said, kissing him.

"Hi." He blinked owlishly. "You up?"

"Stay in bed," she said. "I want to take some of my things back to my apartment and get some things that are still there."

"How do you feel?" he said.

"Much better."

"Your eye looks better."

While she was in the bathroom, she examined her eye. The swelling was gone, but it was black; the color, the deep smudge, remained. Maybe, she thought, forever.

"I won't be gone long," she said to him. "You look so luxurious in bed . . . stay there until I get back. Okay?"

Again she kissed him.

As she drove along the early-morning streets, she thought to herself that in some respects this was the best time of day. The air was cold, but it was bright; it smelled good and it seemed to her to be healthier. The night fog was gone and the haze had not yet arrived.

Parking the Dodge before her old apartment building, she carried a suitcase upstairs. As rapidly as possible she hung the clothes up in the closet, took what she needed, and with the first armload returned to the car.

By the car waited a girl in a brown coat. Her legs were bare and she had on flat slippers. In the morning sunlight she frowned as she started toward Pat, her hands in the pockets of her coat. She squinted and, raising her hand, shielded her eyes.

I know her, Pat thought. Who is she? I've seen her before.

The girl said, "Where's Jim?"

"He's at his place," she said. Her head buzzed and she felt giddy. She did not feel frightened, only a little shocked to recognize her. "I've only seen you once in my life," she said.

Rachael opened the car door for her. "Are you taking your things over to his place?"

"Some," she said. "One more armload. I just saw you that time we came by, that one night."

Behind her Rachael remained by the car. Patricia ascended the stairs, gathered up the rest of her things, and started back down. On the stairs she halted to get her breath. Light streamed through the front door of the building, into the lobby; she saw Rachael still at the car, still waiting for her.

When she emerged, Rachael said to her, "Are you going over there now?"

"Yes," she said, putting her armload into the back seat.

"I'd like to come along."

Protest was impossible. "Why not?" she said. "Get in." She switched on the ignition, and as she put the car in gear Rachael got in beside her.

At eight-thirty she was back at Jim Briskin's apartment building. She and Rachael stepped out onto the sidewalk; she carried one armload and Rachael carried the other. Together they went upstairs to the apartment. She let herself and Rachael in with the key he had given her.

He was out of bed, sitting at the kitchen table. In his blue bathrobe, his hair uncombed, he regarded her and Rachael with a mixture of expressions.

"Hi," Rachael said.

His head inclined. And then he said to Pat, "Did you get your things?"

"What I needed," she said. "Most of it's here. Have you had breakfast?"

"No," he said.

"Are you just sitting?"

Rachael had gone to the living room window. Her coat over her arm, she stood, specterlike, off to one side. Jim said to her, "What'd you do about Art?"

"When he showed up I told him, and he went off," Rachael said.

"You told him what?"

"That he couldn't come back."

Jim said, "Where'd he go?"

"Over to the loft, I guess. I haven't seen him today. That was last night, real late."

"Did you get any sleep?"

"A couple of hours." Her words were pinched off.

"Did you talk to him at all? Did he tell you anything about it?"

Rachael said, "He had a lot he wanted to say."

"But you didn't listen."

"I listened to some of it."

Pat said, "He beat me up."

"No," Rachael said to her, "he didn't beat you up; he hit you once and that was all. Is that what you call getting beat up? His father used to beat up his mother, and sometimes he beat up Nat, his older brother. They were always fighting. Italians fight like that. Where we live people all fight like that."

Getting up from the kitchen table, Jim walked into the living room. He lit a cigarette and offered Rachael the pack. She shook her head. "Did you expect me to come back last night?" he said.

"No," Rachael said, "I knew you would stay with her."

"You never forgive people," Pat said.

"You, you mean? What do I care about you?" Her tough little face glowed. "You know what the first thing you said to me was, the first thing when you came in the door and saw me?"

"I know," Pat said.

"If I had been in the kitchen instead of Art, you would have taken me down to the store, not him."

"Not exactly," she said. She began to unpack the things she had brought. Jim returned to the kitchen; he put bread into the toaster and laid out dishes and silverware.

"I'm going to eat," he said.

Patricia said, "I brought over my oils. How do you feel about that?" She unfolded the small easel and unwrapped the tubes of paint and the turpentine and linseed oil and the palette. "I thought maybe I'd do some painting. Will the smell drive you out of the apartment?"

"No," he said from the kitchen.

"What about the mess?"

"It's okay."

"Excuse me," she said to Rachael. In the bedroom, with the shades down, she changed to a pair of blue cotton trousers, Chinese trousers, and then she picked out a plaid sport shirt and buttoned it up, thinking how loose it was, how comfortable to work in. And then she identified the shirt as one of Art's; she had bought it for him to wear. A little hysterically she shed the sport shirt and pushed it away in a suitcase; instead she put on a T-shirt, paint-smeared, from her college days.

In the living room Rachael ignored the paints. She had not even taken off her coat.

"Can I play some records?" Patricia asked.

"Go ahead," Jim said. At the stove he was frying himself ham and eggs.

Sinking down before the record cabinet, she examined the albums. At last she pulled out an album of Bach *Brandenburg Concertos*—the album held four of them, one after another—and with the records playing on the phonograph she proceeded to mix the paints.

"Bach at nine in the morning?" Jim said.

"Shall I take it off?"

"It's eccentric," he said.

"I always liked it," she said, "the *Brandenburg Concertos*. You played them for me . . . we played them all the time."

Rachael said, "What are you going to paint?"

"I don't know," she said levelly. "I haven't decided."

"You're not going to paint me."

"I don't want to paint you." On the easel she arranged a square of fiber paper. Her brushes, gummy and stiff, had to be soaked; she placed them upright in a glass of turpentine. The smell of paint and turpentine filled the room, and she opened two of the windows. Jim disappeared into the bathroom. The whirr of his electric razor startled her, and she thought how long it had been since she had heard an electric razor in the morning.

"Did you stay here last night?" Rachael said to her.

"Of course she did," Jim said from the bathroom. "What do you think I did, leave her for Art to knock around? I'm keeping her with me, where she belongs. When she feels better and this thing isn't hanging over us, we're going to remarry."

Rachael said, "And I can go to hell."

"No," he said. He finished shaving and put on a white shirt and tie. His chin was smooth; his hair was combed. Now he unclipped a pair of pressed slacks from a hanger in the closet.

"What then?" Rachael said.

"You have a husband."

"What about you?"

He said, "I'm not your husband."

"You are," Rachael said. She continued to look at him, but she said nothing more.

"I feel so goddamn sorry for you," he said. "But this is just a long shot. It's too much of a long shot for me, Rachael."

"You thought about it. The first night you stayed with me."

Cold morning air blew into the room from the open windows, and Patricia shivered. On her arms goose pimples formed; she stopped to rub them. She felt dizzy. From the paint fumes, she decided. And from not having eaten any breakfast. A drop of paint fell on the rug, and she realized, stricken, that she had forgotten to put down newspapers.

Papers, in piles, were in the cupboard under the sink. She got a stack of them and spread them over the rug. Maybe, she thought, she should roll back the rug. How long it had been. She had forgotten how to go about it.

When Jim came out of the bathroom, she said, "I better get the rug out of the way."

"You going to dance?"

"No, I don't want to get paint on it."

"Paint in the kitchen," he said. He put on his coat.

"Where are you going?" she said.

"I'm taking Rachael home. She shouldn't be here. I'll be back; you go ahead and paint."

Patricia said, "You don't know how long you'll be gone, I suppose."

"If I get tied up," he said, "I'll call you."

"Good luck," she said, studying her paints.

"Same to you." He kissed her on the temple and then nodded Rachael toward the door.

"Goodbye," Rachael said.

The door shut after the two of them. She was alone in the apartment, with her paints.

On the phonograph the stack of records had come to an end. She lifted them up onto the spindle and restarted them. The same music, she realized, but she did not care. She increased the volume, and then she kicked off her shoes and returned to painting. For an hour she worked; she involved herself in the picture. It was nonobjective, an exercise to bring back to her the sense of the brushes and colors. But her touch remained clumsy, and at ten o'clock she gave up and wandered into the kitchen for something to eat.

How still the apartment was.

After she had eaten, she returned to her painting. By now the picture was a failure, and she tossed the square of fiber paper aside.

On a fresh square she started over. She sketched a face, the spotty circle of a man's face. Jim Briskin, she decided. The picture was of him. But it did not look like him. The image had a muddied quality, as if the flesh were running together, slipping and sliding. The image, the face on the fiber paper, deteriorated until it was a grotesque, masklike thing, feeble and infantile. She gave up and put the brushes into the glass of turpentine.

Now the time was twelve noon and he had not come back. She washed her hands. The records on the phonograph had long ago finished and been put back in the album. She got them out again and restarted them. With the music playing she entered the bedroom and began searching through the dresser drawers.

In a manila folder were letters and pictures that he had kept. After a minute she located the photograph she wanted; it was a picture taken during a camping trip to Mount Diablo and it showed him full-face, smiling. In this picture he did not look worried, and she liked him that way. He wore a canvas shirt, and behind him was the car they had owned, and their tent, and the rocks and brush of the mountainside. She herself had taken the picture; her shadow fell across him.

Propping a fresh square of fiber paper on the easel, she tacked the photograph beside it and began again. But still the picture did not come. At one o'clock she tossed the brush down, wiped her hands, and went into the kitchen for something to drink.

On the tile drainboard she spread out the makings of the drink: the ice cube tray, the gin, the lemon, the tumbler and spoon, and the jigger glass. Holding the tray under the hot water, she smacked the metal with her hand; ice cubes slid into the sink, and she put two of them in the tumbler. Onto the ice cubes she poured gin, and then she added an inch or two of lemonade.

Carrying the drink, she strolled about the apartment, humming with the music. Now she did not feel so lonely. She set the drink down on the arm of the couch and resumed painting.

The smell of the paint blended with the smell of her drink. Her head began to ache, and she wondered if she wanted to paint after all.

When her drink was gone, she returned to the kitchen for another. The ice cubes were still on the drainboard, and she dumped them into the sink; they were half-melted. Into the glass she poured gin and then water from the tap. Swirling the mixture she seated herself at the kitchen table.

For the first time in her life the idea of suicide entered her mind. Once it was there, she could not get rid of it.

She went about the kitchen, examining the knives in the drawers. Then she gave serious thought to the electricity, the wiring and out-lets. What an awful thing, she thought. But the idea continued to revolve; it built itself up. She went back and forth through the apart-ment, seeking something to break into her mind. Hammer, chisel, drill such as a dentist's drill cutting through bone . . . splinters of bone flying.

Enough, she thought. But it was not enough. She picked up her brush and tried to paint. The colors dazzled her; she pulled down the shades and painted in the half-light. Now the colors ran together, browns and grays and somber clouds like soot.

205

She continued painting. The square became dark and at last it was blotted out. All colors, she thought. In her mind the schemes and ideas of suicide grew and became more elaborate, more extravagant, until she had considered everything.

Putting down her brush, she went out of the apartment into the hall. The hall was deserted. She stood by the door and after a long time a middle-aged woman passed by with rubbish for the disposal chute.

"Good afternoon," Pat said.

The middle-aged woman glanced at the open apartment door and then at the glass in her hand. Without answering her, the middle-aged woman went on.

Enough, she thought. She put her glass down inside the apartment, and then she walked steadily down the hall to the stairs, down to the ground floor, down the front steps to the sidewalk, down the sidewalk, down the hill to the corner, to the liquor store. The polished tile floor sloped, and she walked gingerly to the counter.

"You have any Rhine wine?" she asked. The first thing that came into her mind, something new in her mind.

"Lots of it," the clerk said. He went to a shelf. While he was looking, she walked back out, onto the sidewalk, up the hill. On the hill she halted, getting her breath. Then she walked back to the apartment.

The phonograph was on, but the records had ceased playing. She lifted them up onto the spindle and started them over.

Where are you? she said to herself.

Nobody answered.

Are you coming back? she said. You're not, she said, and I know why not. I know where you are. I know who you're with.

I don't blame you, she said. You're right.

She picked up her brush and put the tip of it into the paint. In the darkness of the apartment, she painted; she put more darkness around her. She lifted darkness and carried it about the living room and the bedroom and into the bathroom and the kitchen. She took it everywhere. She brought it to each thing in the apartment, and after that she turned it to herself.

19

Beside him in the car Rachael said, "You don't have to go through any legal thing. Just stay with me, especially after I have the baby."

"They'd send me to prison for life," Jim Briskin said. They were parked before her house, and he looked down the walk to the basement steps; he gazed out at the house, at the stores and people along Fillmore Street.

"Is that why?" Rachael said. "Is that the reason?"

"I can't marry a seventeen-year-old girl," he said. "No matter how I feel about her."

"Just tell me if that's the reason."

He gave it serious thought. While he thought, Rachael kept her eyes fixed on him; she studied his face, his body, the way he sat, the clothes he was wearing. She was taking each part of him in. Gathering and collecting him, every bit of him. Tucking him away.

"Yes," he said finally.

"Let's leave, then. Let's go down into Mexico."

"Why?" he said. "Do they do that down there? Is that something you read in a magazine or saw in a movie?"

Rachael said, "You know more than I do. Find out where we can go where we can do it."

"Oh, Rachael," he said.

"What?"

I'll do it, he wanted to say. He almost said it. He almost told her. "You're too logical," he said. "You're too rational. I can't."

"Suppose I talk with Pat."

"Keep away from Pat. Don't go near her. She has enough troubles."

207

"Do you think I'll hurt her?"

"Yes." he said. "If you can. If you can figure out how."

"I know how," Rachael said.

"Do you want to?"

Rachael said, "I don't care about her. I care about you."

"I'd be lying," he said, "if I said I don't care about you. But she's the one who can't live by herself. You have an economic problem, but eventually you'll solve it; you'll be older and you'll earn more money. One of these days you'll have it worked out. We'll still be in the middle of our problems. It's a question of time, nothing else."

Rachael said, "That's just a lot of words."

"You don't want to hear it. That's why you say that."

"I want to hear the truth; I don't want to hear what you think would be nice. I never knew you before, but now I know you and I'm going to know you for the rest of your life. Isn't that so?" She pushed the car door open. "Usually I work in the morning; you didn't even ask me why I'm not working."

"Why aren't you?" he said. "What did you do, quit your job? I'm off for a month; Pat's off indefinitely; I suppose you're through completely."

"I switched with a girl," Rachael said. "I'm working tonight instead of this morning."

"When do you start?"

"At eight o'clock tonight."

"Then you have time to sit here."

"I have all these errands. I have to get started on them; I have a lot to do." She reached into her coat pocket. "Here's a note." She passed him a folded slip of paper. "Take it and don't read it until you're driving home. Promise?"

"Notes," he said.

"I'll see you." She started off down the path toward the house. As soon as her back was to him, he unfolded the note and read it. On the paper were no words, no writing, only a drawing she had made. Probably she had gotten the idea from Pat and her painting. It was the drawing of a heart, and he understood from it that Rachael wanted to tell him that she loved him.

Putting the note in his pocket, he got out of the car and followed after her, gaining on her, until he was beside her.

"I'll go in with you," he said.

"Don't you want to go home?"

"Not right away."

Rachael said, "You opened my note."

"Yes," he said.

"These are just ordinary errands. I have to shop and get some medicine at the drugstore and take the clothes over to the launderette. And I have to clean and sweep." She glanced apprehensively up at him. "Do you think you would want to have lunch with me? You didn't have much breakfast."

"Okay," he said.

She walked ahead of him, down the steps to the basement door. "First I have to clean," she said, opening the door. It was not locked, he saw. "I have to vacuum the floor. We got this old vacuum cleaner. I was going to clean yesterday, but I didn't want to while you were around."

She opened all the windows and doors in the apartment. And then she dragged an obsolete upright vacuum cleaner from the closet. While the machine rattled and shuddered, he stood outdoors, on the cement path.

"You want to move the couch for me?" she said, shutting off the vacuum cleaner.

"Be glad to." He lifted the couch away from the wall.

"You sound so mournful," she said.

"No, I'm just thinking."

"Does this bother you, this cleaning?"

"No." Again he went outside.

"I don't have to do this," Rachael said. "I just wanted something to do; I can't stand sitting around like we were, just talking. It's so—it's a waste of time."

After she had vacuumed the floor and rugs and curtains and cushions of the couch, she put the vacuum cleaner away and began to wash the dishes in the sink.

"Your note was eloquent," he said to her.

"Well," she said, her arms in soapsuds, "I thought you were leaving and I had that to give to you the last minute or so. Just before you took off. Otherwise you wouldn't know . . . you'd think I was just after some arrangement so I could be sure of a place to stay. You know?"

"I know," he said.

"And I mean it," she said. "The way I feel."

"It's too bad," he said.

"Why?"

"I was afraid that was behind it."

"It shouldn't make you afraid. You ought to be glad. Don't you feel very strongly about me?"

"Yes," he said.

"Maybe something will come of this," she said, rinsing out the sink and then drying her hands and arms. With a rag and a can of Dutch Cleanser, she began scouring the bowl and faucets in the bathroom.

"After everything you said," he said, "you still believe what you see in the movies."

"What's that?"

"True love wins out."

"Sometimes it does."

"Very seldom."

"But it can," she said.

"Why? Does it shove everything else out of the way?"

Rachael said, "If I was married to you, I'd have a lot of children. That's something she's never done."

"You're wrong," he said.

"I know I would." She put her hand on her stomach. "You can see."

"Not my children," he said. "I'm sterile."

She straightened up. "Really?"

"So what you said is just a little silly."

"I thought it was her," Rachael said. "But it doesn't matter. I have a baby already. It would be the same as yours." She went back to her methodical scrubbing.

"That's why Pat and I broke up," he said.

"Yes," Rachael said, "I believe it. She needs children she can take care of, so she won't have time to sit around and feel sorry for herself. I don't see how you can talk about going back to her; if you can't have children, it'll never work out. She'll be sitting around drinking and brooding, and she'll start crying and wishing she had kids, and then she'll leave again. But you know I wouldn't do that."

"I know," he said, and it was true; it probably was.

"We'd have a child," Rachael said, "one at least. Maybe I'll have twins. Art has a brother. My mother has a twin brother." Putting away the can of Dutch Cleanser and the rag, she said, "The hospital would charge more if it were twins. But I'd like to have more than one child if I could."

"How much do the hospitals charge for a delivery?" he said.

"Do you mean a normal delivery? Without complications? Usually from one hundred and fifty dollars to three hundred. It depends on whether you want a private room."

"A private room is more," he said. "I know that."

"If they have to use instruments," Rachael said, "even forceps to force delivery, then they call it an operation and charge for an operation. So that could cost anything, depending on the circumstances."

"How long would you be in the hospital?"

"Not very long." She looked in the refrigerator to see what she needed to buy. "Three days or four. It depends on how quick my delivery is and how I stand up under it. I haven't had any children before, so I'll probably have a hard delivery. And I'm small. I'll probably have a lot of false labor, maybe a couple of days of it."

"How long before you have the baby will you have to quit your job?"

"It depends on how I feel. But the problem is when I get back. I can't go to work after I have the baby. I'm going to stay home." She had made out her shopping list; now she wheeled a shopping cart from the corner of the kitchen. "You want to walk down to the store with me?"

As they walked slowly along the sidewalk, he said, "Do you feel different about me?"

"Because you can't have children? Yes, I guess so. You didn't know before you and she were married, did you?"

"No," he said.

"But I know," Rachael said. "So it wouldn't be the same. Like you know about me, you know about Art, you know I liked him enough to marry him. And the baby is his. But that's not so bad, is it? You can have a child this way. It would be the only way."

"I thought of that," he said.

"When?"

"The first night I stayed with you."

211

"Yes," she said, "I knew you were thinking about something, and it had to do with the baby. "You want to, then?" She turned toward him. "You want to marry me as soon as we can get it fixed up? It would be a year or so, and the baby would already be born. But we could be together most of that time."

"We could," he agreed.

To their right was a fruit and vegetable market; she pushed her shopping cart through the doorway and he followed. At the bin of lettuce, she examined the heads. She weighed them and stripped off the outer leaves. After she had found the lettuce she wanted, she began filling a paper bag with squash.

"Morning, young lady," the old man at the counter said as she brought up what she wanted to buy.

"Hello," she said. At the counter were tomatoes. She took two of them and put them with the green onions and celery. To Jim she said, "I want to make a salad for you."

"Is that something you're good at?"

"I'm not too bad," she said, paying for what she had bought. "I have to get some Italian cottage cheese . . . have you ever had any? It's called ricotta."

At the delicatessen she stood at the glass counter, scrutinizing the sausages and cheeses. The clerk recognized her and greeted her. They all recognized her, the old Italian grocery-store owners, the people behind the meat and fish counters. This was her route; with her shopping cart she went from store to store, looking into everything, finding out what was good.

"Here," the clerk said to her, giving her a wedge of the white Monterey jack cheese. "See what you think."

She tried it. "No," she said, "it's too mild."

"You want it for a salad?" The clerk found her some cheddar.

"That's fine," she said. "And the ricotta." She paid the clerk, put the packages in her shopping cart, and then they went outside.

"They let you try stuff?" Jim said.

"If you don't ask them," she said. "If you just stand looking. Do you like how it smells in there? It's the garbanzo beans and the olive oil and spices, and the different sausages. I can't usually afford to buy any of the sausages."

"They know you," he said.

"I spend a lot of time in there."

At the supermarket she bought brown rice and a pound of butter, which was on sale, and a quart of mayonnaise, which was also on sale.

"They don't have eggs on sale," she said. "Look, they want sixty cents a dozen. We'll have to go over to the Safeway and see." Pushing her cart to the checker's stand, she joined the line. He remained beyond the railing. Behind her was a large, elderly woman in a silk dress, and ahead of her were two colored women. Among the housewives and shoppers she was confident; she smiled at him.

"You know how to shop," he said as they left the store.

"I enjoy it."

"Do they get in front of you?" he asked. "In the line?" It did not seem likely.

"They try. But you can tell before they do it. They get a certain kind of look."

At the Safeway she bought eggs and coffee.

"Now," she said, "I want to go to the drugstore. Then we can go home and I'll fix lunch."

With a prescription in her hand she waited by the magazines and chewing gum and display of razor blades. This was her element. The routine of shopping. The measuring, the judgment, the comparing of prices, one store with another. The cautious proceeding from one store to the next.

On the trip back to the apartment the shopping cart was weighed down with packages.

"Where'd you get it?" he said, meaning the cart.

"Art made it."

In the front room of the apartment she unloaded the packages one by one onto the heavy oak table; she was careful with each, making sure that the eggs and tomatoes were undamaged. She had bought a package of berries, and now she carried them to the kitchen to wash them. Filling a pan with water, she lit the burner under it and put in two of the eggs. She took out a large bowl and began fixing the tomatoes and lettuce and green onions for the salad. Seated at the kitchen table, with the bowl in her lap, she cut bits of celery and hard-boiled egg.

"There's nothing they can do about your sterility?" she asked.

"No."

213

"It won't change?"

"It won't go away," he said.

Rachael said, "Do you think about it?"

"Sometimes. When I have nothing else to do."

"It must make a man feel awful. What do they do, do they find out by—I guess they can't use a rabbit."

"They make counts on a slide. Number of sperm per cubic centimeter. There has to be sixty million."

"Were there?"

"Yes," he said, "but too many of them were irregular. So they weren't fertile."

"But there were some that were okay, weren't there?"

"If," he said, "I had intercourse day and night, over a period of years, I might conceivably impregnate some woman. Pat and I went to find out why we hadn't had any success, and that was the reason; it was my fault."

"Sixty million sounds like a lot."

"But statistically," he said, "there just isn't enough of a chance."

With the salad she fixed cheese sandwiches. "I made the bread," she told him.

The bread was excellent.

"Do you like the salad?" she said.

"Fine." He ate as much as he could. Across from him she watched; she kept her eyes on him.

"Do you think she went after Art because she knew he had had a child?" she said.

"Maybe. That's part of it."

"It was to make up for you?" She did not seem embarrassed.

"I think she didn't know what to do," he said. "She wanted to do something, and she felt she couldn't have anything to do with me. And then she ran into Art."

Rachael said, "Don't you see how no good she is?"

"Let me decide that," he said.

She nodded.

"It's up to me," he said.

"Then decide." Her eyes ignited; she gazed at him menacingly. "She's no good. She isn't; why do you pretend she is? I don't see how somebody like you can get mixed up with her."

"You have no charity," he said.

"What's that? What do you mean?" She was suspicious.

He said, "You're too much of a Puritan, Rachael. You're too righteous."

"Are you marrying her to get away from me?"

"No," he said.

"Why then?"

"Because I love her."

"You don't feel she's sort of—public property by now?"

"No," he said.

"Do you know what I meant by the note I gave you?"

"Yes," he said, "I know. That's why I followed after you."

"How do you feel about it?"

He had no answer for that.

Rachael said, "I think you ought to forget about her and marry me. Will you? I'd make you a good wife; don't you think I would? Don't you think I'd do everything in the world to make you happy?"

In his mouth the words fell into bits. "I can't say yes," he said finally.

"What, then? You mean you won't?"

He knew that this was the last time she was going to ask. And, he thought, when he said no to her this time, it was finished. How much of a temptation it was; how close he was to saying yes. The hell with everything else, he thought. Surely this was worth more than all the rest of it.

"Wait," Rachael said. She put her hands up over her ears. "Don't say anything to me right now. Walk with me to this store . . . I want to look at some maternity clothes."

She collected the dishes and put them in the sink. Then, with her brown coat trailing, she went out of the apartment. He followed along, willing to go with her, wanting to be with her as long as he could. They both felt the same way; they loitered and moved reluctantly past the stores, across the streets. They looked at the window displays and people. Rachael entered stores and talked to the clerks; she poked into everything. By the time they reached the clothing store, the time was three o'clock.

On the trip back, she said, "Let's stop and have a Coke." Ahead of them was a hot dog counter; a radio played jump tunes.

"What do you want?" he said, getting out change.

"Just a Coke."

With her Coke she leaned against the side of the stand, her coat over her arm, her package of clothes by her feet. She did not say anything to him; she appeared to be mulling over the things he had said.

"Are you sorry for her?" she said. "Is that it?"

"No," he said.

"Then I don't understand."

He said, "How do you feel when somebody is helpless? Do you take advantage of them?"

With her straw between her lips, she studied him; she was listening and she said nothing.

"Some people do," he said. "Most people do."

"It's their own fault if they're weak," she said.

"Christ," he said.

"If they're weak, then they disappear. Isn't that evolution? Isn't that the survival of the fit or something?"

"Sure it is," he said futilely.

"What's wrong with that?"

"Nothing."

"But you don't feel that way," she said.

"I don't feel that way when I love somebody; if they're helpless and need help, I want to help them. You feel the same way. You said so."

"No," she said. "Did I?"

"You said I should want to take care of her."

"But," Rachael said, "she doesn't deserve it."

"Let it go," he said.

"Can't you tell me?"

"No," he said, "I guess not."

"Do you love her because she is weak; is that it? You can't have children, so you want somebody you can take care of."

"That's not it," he said.

"You can—look out for her." Finishing her Coke, she put the empty cup down on the ledge of the window; she picked up her package and started off.

"That's some of it," he said. "The rest of it is that she and I understand each other in a way I can't explain. You're trying to make this into a rational thing, and it isn't. I don't love her because she's helpless, any more than I might love you because you aren't helpless. I love her first, before anything else, and if she's helpless I want to take care of her. If I were helpless, you would want to take care of me, wouldn't you? You'd be glad. It would make you happy."

She nodded.

"You can see it in yourself," he said. "That feeling is one of the strongest elements in you. You'll have a baby pretty soon, and maybe you can turn some of them onto him. And you have Art; god knows he can use some help."

In the front yard of a house, in a fenced yard, a vast dahlia plant with shaggy cactus blossoms caught Rachael's eye. The blossoms were as large as plates. She went to the fence, and before he could stop her, she had reached over the fence and had broken one of the dahlias from its stalk.

"That's a mortal sin," he said.

"It's for you," Rachael said.

"Put it back."

"It won't go back." She held out the dahlia, but he refused to accept it.

An elderly heavy-set woman was sweeping the walk by the house, and when she saw the flower she hurried toward them. "What is this?" she demanded, wheezing with outrage. The wattles of her neck lifted and fell. "You people have no right to steal flowers out of other people's yards. I think I'm going to call the police and have you arrested!"

Rachael handed the dahlia to the old woman. Without a word the old woman snatched the flower, picked up her broom, and went inside the house. The screen door slammed shut after her.

As he and Rachael walked on, Rachael said, "Who am I supposed to look out for?" Suddenly she stood up on tiptoe and kissed him; her lips were dry and chapped. "I don't have anybody." Again she kissed him, and then she let him go. "That's all I can do," she said. "Isn't it?"

He said, "Take the poor kid back."

"No," she said.

"Relent just a little."

On her face emotions appeared and were suppressed. She struggled inside herself; she fought it out inside.

"Give him this feeling you have," he said. "That's where it belongs. He's your husband and the baby is his."

"It's yours," she said.

"No," he said. "I wish it was, but it isn't. It isn't mine and you aren't mine."

"I am," she said.

He said, "I can't marry you, Rachael. I'll pay for your baby, if you'll let me. You want me to do that? And if you don't want to keep the baby, if you're by yourself and you feel you can't keep it, maybe we can adopt it."

"You and Pat?"

"Maybe. If you decide you don't want it."

"I want it," she said. "It belongs to me."

"That's good," he said.

"You can't have it," she said, "without me. You have to take both of us."

"Then it's out," he said.

For the rest of the walk back, she did not look at him or say a word. At the door of her apartment, as she fitted her key into the lock, she said, "Would she take care of you?"

"I hope so."

"Tell her to go on the wagon."

"I will," he said.

"Maybe if she didn't drink she'd be okay. I can't see how a woman can drink like that." She started into the apartment. "I have to get ready for work. I have to say goodbye."

"Goodbye," he said. He touched her hair, and then he went off, up the steps, to the path.

Still at the door, she said, "If you're going to marry her, I want to give you a present."

"Just go find your husband," he said. But she was already coming up the stairs.

"What would she like?" she asked. Her face was grim and intense. "Maybe I can get her some kitchen thing; I wouldn't want to get her any clothes. She knows more about clothes than I do."

"Just wish us luck."

Rachael took hold of his hand. "Can I hold onto you? Just for a while. You don't mind, do you?"

THE BROKEN BUBBLE

Together, holding hands, they walked until they came to a Wool-worth's dime store.

"No," she said, stopping. "This isn't any good."

After a time they came to a jewelry store, and she started in.

"You can't afford any of these things," he said, halting her. "If you're serious about this, buy one of those cards."

"Are you going to have a party?"

"I don't know. Maybe."

She went into the jewelry store, to the front counter. "I only have three or four dollars," she said to him.

In the front counter were a number of silver and silver-plated articles, and she had the clerk bring them out one by one for her inspection. After much consideration she bought a cake server and had the clerk wrap it as a gift.

"She'll like that," she said, as they left the jewelry store. "Won't she?"

"Sure," he said.

"Did you look at it?" Rachael said. "It was made in Holland. It isn't big and ornate like most of them."

At her place she unwrapped the cake server and rewrapped it with her own wrapping paper and ribbon and seals.

"This is better," she said, curling the ribbon with the blade of the scissors. "I worked a couple of Christmases at this department store downtown . . . I wrapped packages."

Into the ribbon she put a stalk of gladiola and some green leaves; she used Scotch tape to hold them in place.

"Very pretty," he said.

She put the package into a paper bag. "This is for both of you," she said.

"Thank you," he said, accepting it.

"I better not come along," she said.

"Maybe not."

Following him to the door, she said, "Can we come over and visit you?"

"Any time," he said.

At the door she lingered, speaking slowly, not facing him. "Can I ask you something?"

"Whatever you want."

"Maybe this is a favor. I wondered if you had decided to go back on your program."

"You want me to?"

"If you do," she said, "then we can listen to you again."

"I'll go back."

"Fine." She nodded. "I'd like to hear you. I always felt better listening to you. It always seemed to me you really cared about us."

"I did," he said. "I do."

"Even now? Right now?"

He said, "Certainly."

"Goodbye," she said. She put out her hand, and he took hold of it.

"Thanks for the lunch," he said. "Thanks for cooking for me."

"I cook pretty good," she said, "don't I?"

"Very good."

She walked away. After a moment he went on outside the apartment and up the stairs.

"Wait," Rachael said. "You forgot to take this." In her hand was the present, the brown paper package.

Going back, he took it from her. This time she watched him as he left; behind him she came out into the doorway and stood until he had gotten into his car and started the motor. As he drove away, he saw her. She did not cry; she showed no emotion in the least. She had accepted things and now she was planning; she was deciding what to do. She was working out the problems and difficulties, considering herself and her husband, her job, the future of her family. Even before he was out of sight, she was busy at work.

The time was four o'clock in the afternoon when he parked in front of his apartment house and started up the steps. The door of his own apartment was unlocked; he opened it and found the apartment dark, the shades pulled down, the room silent.

"Pat?" he said.

By the record cabinet the phonograph hummed, and on the turntable the stack of records revolved on and on. He shut the machine off and put up the window shades.

The room was smeared with paint. On the furniture, the walls and drapes, the paint shone. The paint had been smeared by hand; her prints were everywhere, the childish outline of her thumbs and palms. She had gone about pressing her hands against everything she touched; the easel and brushes and tubes lay in a chaotic heap on the floor, by an overturned glass. Red paint trailed across the rug, and he thought suddenly that it was not paint but blood. He bent down and touched it; the paint was sticky and hot. It was both paint and blood, mixed together and spread throughout the apartment.

She was not in the bedroom. But the paint and blood were there, too, on the bedcovers and walls.

"Pat," he said. He felt alert and rational. He went into the kitchen.

In the corner of the kitchen, crouched against the cupboards, she stared up at him. She was covered with blood and paint; her clothes dripped shiny, sticky red, the warm mixture from the tubes and from her body. As he approached, she lifted her hand up at him. Her hand shook.

"What is it?" he said, kneeling down.

"I—cut myself," she whispered.

By her was a kitchen knife. She had cut almost through the flesh of her hand, to the bone itself. A handkerchief, soaked with blood, was tied around her wrist. At the cut the blood was thick and drying; the bleeding had slowed to an ooze. She gazed at him piteously, her lips apart; she wanted to say something.

"When did it happen?"

"I don't know," she said.

"How?"

"I don't know."

"Does it hurt?" he said.

"Yes," she said. Her face was stained with tears that had caked and dried. "It hurts a lot."

"Did you do it on purpose?"

"I—don't know."

On the drainboard of the sink were melted ice cubes, a lemon, the remains of the gin. He said, "I should have come back sooner."

"What'll I do?" she said.

"You'll recover," he said, stroking her hair back from her face. Blood and paint sparkled in her hair; red drops stuck to the hair. Paint streaked her face and neck, her arms; she had paint on her shirt and jeans, on her feet. And on her forehead was a dark bruise.

221

"I fell," she said.

"Is that when you cut yourself?"

"Yes," she said.

"You were carrying the knife?"

"I was taking it into the living room."

"I'll drive you over to some doctor's," he said.

"No," she said, "please."

"You want me to get him to come here?"

"No." She shook her head. "Just stay here."

"I'll have to bandage it," he said.

"Okay."

From the medicine cabinet in the bathroom he got gauze and tape and Mercurochrome. The cut was clean; it had bled enough, certainly. As he washed her hand and put on the Mercurochrome, she did not seem to feel pain; she seemed numbed.

"You're damn lucky," he said.

Pat said, "It hurt a lot."

"Be careful. Don't carry knives around."

"Are you back for good?"

"Yes," he said. He helped her up, and with his arm around her led her into the living room. She clung to him.

"I thought I was going to die," she said. "It kept on bleeding."

"You couldn't have died."

"Really?"

"Not from that. Kids do that all the time. Kids fall out of trees and cut their hands and skin their knees." When she was stretched out on the couch, he dipped a handkerchief in turpentine and started cleaning the paint from her hair.

"I thought I was going to bleed to death," she said.

When he had finished with her hair, he found her a clean shirt and helped her put it on. "Here," he said when she was finished. "Here's a present." He gave her the package with its wrappings and gladiola and leaves and curled ribbon.

"For me?" Pat said, unwrapping it. He had to help her. "Who from?"

"Rachael," he said.

She lay with the cake turner on her lap, the wrappings in a wad beside the couch. "It's nice of her."

"You sure got paint everywhere."

"Will it come off?"

"Probably so," he said.

"I guess you're mad."

"I'm just glad you're alive," he said, gathering up the wrappings from the package.

"I'll never do it again."

He put his arms around her and held her against him. She smelled of paint and turpentine; her hair was damp and her throat, close to his face, was mottled with blue and orange paint, a stain from her ear to her collarbone. He held her tightly, but she was solid and her body did not give. Fastening the top button of her blouse, he said, "The next time I'll stay here."

"Will you? You promise?"

"Yes," he said. He sat on the couch, holding her, until the room became dim. The warmth of the room dissipated, but he remained where he was. At last the room was totally dark. Beyond the window the traffic sounds diminished. Streetlights came on. A neon sign flashed.

In his arms she was asleep.

20

Sunday was the final day of the optometrists' convention at the St. Francis Hotel in San Francisco, California. By ten o'clock that night many of the optometrists were beginning to say goodbye and trickle out of town by car, bus, train, however they had arrived at the start of the week. Their hall in the hotel was littered with paper and cigarette butts and along the wall were empty bottles. Here and there small groups of optometrists shook hands and exchanged addresses.

The inner circle that had gathered around Hugh Collins met for their secret and expensive last fling of entertainment, at Ed Guffy's hotel room in a less publicized and less strict hotel in the Negro slum business section near Fillmore and Eddy Streets. In all there were eleven men in the inner circle, and every one of them was damp with eagerness.

Hugh Collins cornered Tony Vacuhhi, who was already in Guffy's hotel room when the group arrived.

"Where is she?"

Vacuhhi said, "She's coming. Keep your pants on."

All week he had been nosing near Thisbe, but this night, this concluding interlude, promised to be the one. Louise, to his relief and delight, had obligingly remained in Los Angeles. Everything was set. He could scarcely contain himself.

"All set?" Guffy said, smoking on his cigar.

"She's supposed to be coming," Collins said, rubbing his upper lip with the back of his hand. This beat anything, the gewgaws from Mexico that he had distributed among the boys, the art films he and

Guffy had got from the amusement park people, his own scrapbooks of models and sun-worshipping nudists.

"Is it going to be worth all the loot?" Guffy demanded.

"It sure is," he said. "You bet your bottom dollar." He began to pace restlessly, wishing she would show up; the optometrists were murmuring, exchanging wisecracks and jokes, punching one another. Some of them had their gewgaws with them and were putting the plastic figures through their paces. But the boys were tiring, seeking the genuine article. One of them cupped his hands and catcalled at Collins, "What say, fella? About ready?"

"About," he said, perspiring.

Another yelled, "Where is this pig?"

"Hey, hey," they chanted, "bring on the greased pig."

"Keep it down," Guffy warned.

The optometrists, squatted in a circle on the floor of the hotel room, chanted in unison: "Bring it on—bring it on." One of them got up and began to shimmy in his nylon shirt and pinstripe trousers; his tie flopped foolishly as he placed his hands behind his head and wiggled his fleshy hips.

And then they were silent. The optometrists ceased their horseplay. The jokes stopped. Nobody moved.

Thisbe Holt, in her transparent plastic bubble, rolled into the room. An audible gasp went up from the optometrists. Vacuhhi, in the hall, had booted her in through the open door. He now shut the door and locked it. The bubble came to a stop in the middle of the room. Thisbe filled the bubble completely. Her knees were drawn up, hugged to her stomach; her arms were wrapped around them, clutching them tight. Her head was bent forward. Below her chin and above her knees, her bloated breasts jutted up and were flattened at the inner surface of the bubble.

The bubble rolled a little more. Thisbe was now face-down, her buttocks visible, the two bare, divided hemispheres. A distortion of the plastic made them seem to spread out against the bubble surface. Again the audible gasp went up. One of the optometrists pushed the bubble with his shoe; it rolled and the forward side of Thisbe returned. Her nipples, enlarged by the transparent surface, were blood-red splotches, smeared and caught.

She was smiling.

Oh god in Heaven, Hugh Collins thought, and his avidity made him shiver. All of them, all in the circle, were twitching and grimacing; a St. Vitus dance moved through the room.

"Look at those tits," an optometrist said.

"Wow."

"Get the size of them."

"Turn her," an optometrist said, "so her ass is up."

The bubble was shoved. It revolved, and again the underside of Thisbe was visible.

"Look at that flesh," a voice said.

"Can you get the bottom up?" one of the optometrists said. "You know, from down under. So we can look up."

Several of them delicately tapped the bubble. It rolled too far and again they were staring at Thisbe's knees and breasts.

"Try again," Guffy said, down on his hands and knees.

They tried again. This time they were able to get the bubble just right.

"Wowie," an optometrist breathed.

"Look at that."

It was unbelievable. They nudged the bubble from one side of the ring to the other. Thisbe, magnified and distorted, rolled toward them and away from them; as the bubble turned, her leering face, breasts, knees, feet, buttocks came and went, a procession of steaming pale yellow flesh. The waxy surface rotated, and the inside of the bubble became transluscent with her perspiration. Now her mouth was pressed to the breathing holes of the bubble's surface; she was taking in deep gasps of air.

"Say," an optometrist said, "can we get her around in that different, so the hole is—you know, at a different place."

But when they tried to turn the bubble, Thisbe turned with it.

Hugh Collins, sitting on the floor, stuck out his foot as the bubble rolled toward him. He had taken off his shoes—most of the optometrists had—and now he booted the bubble with his bare foot. The bubble was warm, heated up by the woman inside. It was like kicking her bare flesh. He giggled.

On the far side Ed Guffy kicked the bubble back.

"Over here!" an optometrist yelled, his feet up and ready. The bubble started in his direction.

"Mine," another yelled, sticking his hand in the path; the bubble rolled over it, and he squawked.

Faster and faster rolled the bubble. Thisbe, her mouth to the holes, wheezed and struggled for air. The mists, rising from her flesh, rose up and obscured her. A glimpse now and then: they saw the blood-red nipples, the spheres of her behind, the soles of her feet pressed to the inner surface.

"Oh boy!" an optometrist shouted, lying full-length on the floor. "Roll it over me! Go ahead!"

The orgy mounted. It came to an end abruptly when one of the optometrists conceived the idea of pouring a Dixie cup of water through Thisbe's breathing holes.

"Okay," Tony Vacuhhi said, stepping forward to take charge. "That's enough. It's over."

Spluttering, flushed, Thisbe climbed from the bubble. "Goddamn beasts," she said, standing up and flexing her legs. Tony threw her a robe, which she buttoned around her.

"Is that all?" Guffy demanded, chewing angrily on his cigar.

"For two hundred bucks," another optometrist said, "we ought to at least get to goose her."

Tony herded the girl out of the room, keeping the optometrists off with his shoulders. The door to the hall slammed; he and Thisbe were gone.

"What a robbery," Guffy said.

In the center of the room the empty bubble remained.

Hugh Collins scrambled out into the hall and after Thisbe and Vacuhhi. "Wait a minute," he panted, catching up with them.

"What is it?" Tony said unsympathetically. Thisbe, beside him, was muttering an uninterrupted flow of abuse. "You had your fun; you got what you paid for."

"Wait," Collins said. "I mean—let me talk to her alone for a second."

"What do you want to say?" Vacuhhi said. "You can say it in front of me; come on, we don't have all night. I gotta rub her down."

"I had the impression," Collins said, glancing at her prayerfully. "You know, the motel room. This is the last night."

"Get him," Thisbe grated, and she and Vacuhhi disappeared out onto the street.

227

Collins, humiliated, slunk back to Guffy's room.

When he entered, the optometrists were in an uproar. Some wanted to go out on the streets looking for fun; others wanted to give up and go home. One was on the phone calling for a cab. He had a cab company which he claimed would transport them *en masse* to a halfway decent house of prostitution.

Guffy was examining the empty bubble.

"Look at the size of this thing," he said to Collins. "You could get a couple hundred pounds of stuff into this."

"Like what?" Collins said, uninterested.

"Anything. Say, I think I've got an idea for some fun—" He drew Collins over to the bubble. "Look, you can seal it up; maybe it'll leak a little, but not much." He fitted the section back into place, closing the slot through which Thisbe had entered and left.

The optometrists gathered to see what was up.

"Like the old water bomb," Guffy said, making a pow motion with his fist in his palm. "Smack, right off the roof, and then we get the hell out of there."

"By god," Collins said, struggling to salvage something from the collapse of his schemes.

"Right—one big grand slam. Something they'll all sit up and notice. Hell, we'll be out of here in a couple of hours or tomorrow at the latest. What do you say, for old times' sake!"

They experienced the sentimental tug; they were bound together in this parting hour of their comradely union. Not for another year, not until 1957. Who knew the changes in a year? Ah, the bonds of the old pals.

"Go out with a bang," Guffy said. "Right? So they'll know us. 'That was back in '56 when the boys dropped the bubble from the roof— remember that night in 1956?' That's tonight, boys; we're having that great old night right now."

This was optometrist history. This was a milestone in convention roguery.

"How are you going to fill it?" Collins demanded. "Where're we going to get two hundred pounds of crap this time of night?"

Guffy laughed. "Let's get started; it's a cinch. That's the trouble with you guys, no imagination."

They collected ashtrays, a couple of small table lamps, toilet paper from the bathroom, a pair of old shoes, beer cans, and bottles, and dropped them into the bubble. It was only a beginning.

"Here's what we do," Guffy said. "You fellows get outside and pick up stuff, whatever'll fit in. Tin cans, anything you see. Get back here in twenty minutes." He set his watch. "Right?"

In twenty minutes the optometrists straggled in, some with nothing, some more soused than when they had left, a few with armloads.

At a supermarket, still open, they had bought dozens of eggs, aging vegetables, quarts of milk. At a drugstore they had picked up tin wastebaskets, a set of cheap dishes, some empty cardboard cartons. One optometrist had picked up a trash dispenser from a street corner. Another had lugged back in his car a garbage pail from the doorway of a locked-up restaurant.

They dumped everything into the bubble. Space remained.

"Water," Guffy said, "from the bathroom."

They rolled the bubble to the bathroom and managed to get it near enough to a faucet to fill the remaining space with water. Gushing and dribbling, the bubble rolled about the bathroom; water spurted from Thisbe's breathing holes.

"Hurry!" Guffy ordered.

The optometrists, perspiring and grunting, rolled the bubble from the room, to the stairs. There they hoisted it up and lugged it, step by step, to the top floor of the hotel. The door to the roof was unlocked and they rolled the bubble out onto the asphalt surface and to the edge.

Below them was the street, the cars and neon signs and pedestrians.

His hands slippery with water and egg and milk, Guffy said, "Here we go, boys!"

They lifted the ponderous, rubbish-filled bubble over the railing and let it go.

"Scatter!" Guffy shouted, and the optometrists, without waiting for the results, ran back down the stairs. In a moment they were scrambling from the back door of the hotel, to the parking lot and their cars.

Ludwig Grimmelman, within his third-floor loft, felt the stir of the night and knew that he could not evade the elements around him. He could not escape reality.

In his heart he knew that they got everyone sooner or later and they would get him; they would have him and there was nothing he could do to save himself. He put his eye to the slot and saw out onto the dark evening street; he saw the shapes and shadows, the objects in motion. He saw the figure across the street, and he knew that Mr. Brown of the FBI had him; Mr. Brown was there, in the obscurity, waiting. Mr. Brown had caught him and he was going to destroy him. There was no mercy for the Ludwig Grimmelmans.

He thought to himself that his mistake had been to believe that by putting it off a short while, by delaying and protracting, he had got away with something. But he had got away with nothing, because now they had him even more completely than ever. They would not settle for anything less than the disposition of Grimmelman and his hopes and fears. And he was not prepared to give that; he had withheld himself, and he would not now give up; he would not surrender merely because his situation was hopeless.

The people who had met him and watched him thought that he was a kind of nut, but he was not a nut and Mr. Brown knew that. Mr. Brown had looked for him and found him, and he had spent a great deal of time in this job. There was not that much time to waste on nuts. But, he thought, Mr. Brown was not going to tell anyone, and that was part of the situation.

He put on his black wool overcoat and his paratrooper's boots, and then he activated the emergency alarm hidden under the corner of his work desk. An Army Signal Corps transmitter, bought from a surplus supply store, put out a coded message in response to his act; Joe Mantila, in his room at the back of his family's house, received the message and knew that the time had arrived.

Now nothing remained but the escape itself. He had already destroyed the vital papers, documents, maps, and clippings. Leaving the loft light on—so as not to tip off Mr. Brown—he opened a side window and tossed out a descent cable. A moment later he was going down hand over hand. His feet touched the ground and he released the cable; it was drawn back up into the loft by a spring.

The night was dark, and he felt the invisible motion; he was aware of the comings and goings, the messages alive in the air.

Climbing a fence, he dropped into a yard. He went up a driveway, hunched over and running, looking back to see if Mr. Brown had followed.

Nobody had seen him. He sneaked over fences; he ran by houses, across lawns, in and out of yards, creeping and hurrying and climbing and gradually making his way across town toward the flat industrial section. Pausing for breath, he looked back; he studied the darkness behind him. Then he went on, his black coat billowing and his boots slapping the pavement. A car rolled by, its headlights blinding him, and he hid behind a parked truck. Was it them? Had they seen him? He ran on, down a driveway and over a fence.

When he reached the corrugated iron shack, the motor of the Horch was already on. Noise and fumes filled the shack as he slid the door open. Joe Mantila stepped out and said, "All ready."

"You have the transmission disconnected from the relay?" Grimmelman said, snorting.

"It's all finished. Ferde's out in the Plymouth. Who goes with you in the Horch?"

Grimmelman said, "Take the Plymouth and go on back." He got into the Horch, behind the wheel. "This is a negative situation. If I manage to break through the police apparatus, I'll contact you. Otherwise assume that the Organization has ceased to exist."

Joe Mantila stared at him.

"Did you think we had a chance?" Grimmelman said.

"Sure," Mantila said, nodding.

Shifting into gear, he drove the Horch from the shed and out onto the street. Joe Mantila raced past him and across to the Plymouth. The Horch turned right, and he was going in the direction of the freeway leading out of San Francisco.

Wind rushed at him as he drove. From his coat pocket he took out his goggles and fitted them over his eyes.

On Van Ness Avenue he made a right turn.

Two blocks later a San Francisco police car fell in behind him.

Grimmelman saw the police car, and he realized that he was not going to get away. But he had realized that already. He put his foot down on the gas, and the Horch moved ahead; he got down in the seat as low as possible and gave the engine more and more gas. The police car continued to follow.

The siren, softly at first, began to wail. The red light behind him blinked on; he saw it blinking, blinking. The light peered at him.

Along Van Ness the other cars pulled to a stop, and he was the only object in motion. He drove faster.

How cold the night air was. He tugged his coat around him and held onto the wheel with one hand. Wind whipped at him, and for a moment he could not see; he put his hand up to straighten his goggles. Ahead of him a second police car appeared from a side street, and Grimmelman drove across the double line to avoid hitting it. The police car disappeared behind him, and he drove back into his own lane.

In that instant the Horch sideswiped a car that had halted for the siren. A fender tore away, and Grimmelman spun the wheel. Again the Horch veered to the left. A shape, its headlights white and immense, grew directly in the path of the Horch. Grimmelman threw up his hands and the massive Horch crashed into the lights.

Behind him the police sirens whined to silence. The two police cars appeared to his right.

Grimmelman clambered from the wrecked Horch. His coat was torn, and a gash across his neck dripped blood. He ran a few steps and stumbled on the curb. Then he was up on the sidewalk, and one of the police cars had started after him. Still he ran. He did not slow down or stop.

The signs along Van Ness Avenue were off, and he hid in the darkness of a used car lot. Before him was a tower, and he crept past it; he slid behind a car as two policemen hurried by with flashlights. As soon as they were gone, he crawled to the front of the car. From his coat he took a jumble of wires and keys; he fiddled with the lock of the car door. The door opened, and he crept inside the car. Closing the door after him, he lay on the seat with his head down beneath the dashboard; he opened a knife and sawed through the insulation of the ignition cable.

Down the street at Hermann's Garage, Nat Emmanual and Hermann were working together, pulling the head off a 1947 Dodge that belonged to Nat's Auto Sales.

"Hey," Nat said, "what's the racket?"

He walked to the entrance of the garage, peering to see.

At first he saw only the two police cars, and then he saw one of them move on farther along the street. He saw the wrecked cars, the Horch and the car it had struck.

"Jesus," he said.

"What's going on?" Hermann said, coming out beside him.

Peering, Nat saw the two policemen hurrying along the sidewalk with flashlights. The policemen passed Looney Luke's lot, and Nat, still watching, saw the shape creep from behind the tower, to the row of cars, and then into one of the cars. He saw the door open and shut. He saw Grimmelman inside Looney Luke's car, fiddling with the ignition.

"He's stealing one of Luke's cars," Nat said.

"Yeah?" Hermann said. "Where?"

"See?" Nat said, "he's in the car; look at him, he's trying to jump the ignition cable."

"He sure is," Hermann said.

Nat said, "I'm going to call the cops."

"Why?" Hermann said.

"He's stealing one of Luke's cars."

Hermann said, "Don't call the cops."

"Why not?" Nat ran back toward the phone.

"So he steals one of Luke's cars," Hermann said. "You damn fool, Luke's the biggest thief in San Francisco. Every car in that lot he stole in the first place, you know that."

"It's against the law," Nat said. He disappeared into the garage, and Hermann heard him dialing excitedly.

"What's one car," Hermann said, "to Luke?" He watched the figure within the car trying to get the engine started. What kind of a man, he wondered, was Nat Emmanual? What a strange idea he had of what was right. How little Nat had learned. "Let him steal it," he said, but he was talking to himself.

Parked off Van Ness Avenue in the Plymouth, Joe Mantila and Ferde Heinke witnessed the wrecking of the Horch and the capture of Grimmelman by the police.

"It's gone," Ferde said.

They drove with their headlights off, away from Van Ness Avenue. When they were safely on a side street, they switched on the lights and speeded up.

"He sure didn't have a chance," Joe Mantila said. "He never even got that car off the lot."

233

For a half hour they parked at Dodo's, trying to decide what to do. If they stopped by the loft, they ran a risk. Neither of them said it, but the Organization had ceased to exist. Now they hoped only to stay out of the hands of the police.

"We better tell Art," Ferde Heinke said.

"The hell with it," Joe Mantila said. "I'm going home. We better not be seen together for a while."

"Suppose he goes over to the loft?"

"He stopped going there," Joe Mantila said. "He's gone back home." But he backed the Plymouth onto Fillmore and made a left-hand turn. "I'll keep the motor going while you run and tell him."

In front of the house, Ferde leaped from the car and ran up the walk to the basement steps. The lights in the living room were on, and he knocked on the door.

Art opened the door. "What's going on?" he said, surprised to see Ferde Heinke.

"They got Grimmelman," Ferde said. "Don't go near the loft."

"How about the Horch?"

"They got that too. Better lie low for a while." He started back toward the Plymouth. "There's nothing we can do."

Art waited until the Plymouth shot off, and then he went back inside the apartment.

At the kitchen table Rachael was writing a letter. "What was it?" she asked, putting down her pen.

"Nothing," he said.

"Did they get Grimmelman? I knew they would." She continued writing. "It's too bad. But you knew it was going to happen. I think it's a good thing as far as we're concerned, but I'm sorry for him."

He seated himself across from her and leaned back until his chair was resting against the wall. "That's the finish," he said, "of the Organization."

"Good," she said.

"Why?"

"Because it was a mistake. What was Grimmelman trying to do? Fight them the way they fight. So naturally they won. If you fight them that way, they have to win; they have all the power. The thing we have to do is keep quiet and not let them notice us."

"It's too late," he said. "I'm already down on the draft list."

Rachael said, "But maybe they'll get tired and give up. They may decide it isn't worth it. If every time you're called we go down there and argue with them and keep stringing it out . . ."

"Sometimes I feel like giving up," Art said. "And just saying, w-w-what the hell. Go ahead and draft me."

"If they draft you, we won't make it."

"Will we anyhow?" he said.

"If we want to."

"I sure want to," he said vigorously.

Rachael said, "Did she buy you the clothes you were wearing when you came back? I never saw them before, and you didn't have any money."

"She bought them for me," he said.

"Even the suit?" She put down her pen. "Did she pick them out?"

"Yes," he said.

"It's a nice suit. I was looking at it. I guess she really liked you, and she wanted you to look nice." She beckoned him toward her. "See if there's anything you want me to change."

Going over he found that she was writing to Patricia. In the letter she was wishing them luck in their marriage and saying that she hoped the four of them could get together some day soon.

He read the letter, and it seemed okay to him. Below his wife's signature he signed his own name. Rachael folded the letter and put it in an envelope.

"How do you feel?" she asked. Since his return, both of them had been under the weather; they were still hesitant in each other's presence.

"Better," he said.

"How would you feel," Rachael said, "if I worked full time for a while? So we'd have more money."

"I don't think you have to."

"It might be a good idea. Then there wouldn't be any chance that we'd have to ask somebody for help." She picked up her coat and put it over her shoulders. "You want to come with me?"

"I'll mail it," he said, taking the letter.

"Do you want to see them again?"

"Sure," he said, "I don't care."

"But we have to be careful," Rachael said. "Anything from outside could hurt us. Isn't that so? Anything that might come in and get between us again. There's so much danger that something that isn't real might come along, and they'd convince us it was important. You know? Something they made up, a bunch of words. They never stop. There's always something they're saying."

Her face showed worry, a tight little face, lined with concern. He kissed her, and then he walked to the door. "I'll be right back," he said. "Anything you want?"

"Maybe you could pick up something," she said. "Maybe at Dodo's. Some ice cream." Following him, she said, "You know what I'd like? One of those pizzas."

"Okay," he said, "I'll bring one back."

He walked up the steps to the path, and then, his hands in the back pockets of his jeans, he turned in the direction of Dodo's. Against the pavement his heels scuffed and clacked. In the cold evening wind, his black leather jacket flapped back, lifted up, and held.

At the corner he mailed the letter. Then he went on toward Dodo's. The drive-in was several blocks away, and he walked slowly, gazing at the bars, the closed-up shops, studying the cars that passed. He nodded to a couple of friends. At a corner four guys he knew were lounging at the side of a drugstore, and he stopped to say a few words to them.

Going on, he crossed the street and continued past a closed-up clothing store. Ahead of him was a group of people, and now that he looked, he noticed a parked police car. A police ambulance drew up to the curb, and he realized that something had happened.

The group of people had collected at the entrance of the old Pleasanton Hotel. Bits of debris were littered across the sidewalk: egg shells, pools of liquid, lettuce leaves and stalks of vegetables and trash and broken dishes and crumpled paper. The ambulance attendants were carrying the stretcher onto the sidewalk and the group of people were being moved back by a San Francisco cop.

"What happened?" he said to a couple of kids standing at the edge of the group.

"Some joker dropped a lot of crap off the roof," the taller of the kids said.

"Yeah?" he said. They all watched, hands in their back pockets.

"Every damn kind of thing." The kid bent down and picked up a fragment of glass. "Some sort of plastic."

"Anybody get hurt?" Art asked.

"This lady, she was walking along. It must of landed on her. I don't know; I just heard the noise."

Art pushed up closer until he could see. The junk was heaped up on the sidewalk, and the remains of some globe-shaped transparent shell rested in the center of the debris and rubbish. A policeman was taking down information from an elderly gentleman with a cane.

Stepping from the pavement, Art walked on past the ambulance and away from the group. As he reached the corner, a police car slid in front of him and a light was flashed in his eyes.

"Let's see your ID, kid," a cop said.

While he was searching through his wallet, two cops stepped from the car and up to him. "How come you're out after eleven o'clock? Don't you know there's a curfew?"

"I was mailing a letter," he said.

"Where's the letter?"

"I mailed it." He was still fumbling in his wallet; he started to reach inside his jacket to see if his packet of ID cards was there. Suddenly one of the cops grabbed his hand. The other cop shoved him back against the wall.

"What do you know about that stuff off the roof?" the first cop said.

"What stuff?"

"Off the hotel roof. Were you up there?"

"No," he said, and his voice was thin, weak. "I was just coming by—" He pointed back in the direction he had come. "I was out mailing this letter—"

"There's a mailbox back there."

"I know," he said, "I mailed it."

Another cop appeared with three more kids. Each of the kids was trembling and scared. "These were back of the hotel." He gave them a shove, and they stumbled forward.

"They must have run out the back," a cop said.

"Take them down," another cop said, already starting off. At the curb the radio in the police car bellowed out calls and numbers.

"They're out after the curfew; book them on that until we get some kind of story from them."

He was yanked away from the wall and shoved, with the other kids, into the police car. As the car pulled away and into traffic, he saw that the police were picking up more kids. More police cars were entering the block, and he thought to himself: If I hadn't come out to mail the letter . . .

"Honest," one of the kids was saying, "we don't know nothing about it; we were just walking along." He was a Negro. "We were just going up to the drive-in, you know?"

None of the cops answered.

Art, looking through the window, held onto his wallet and identification cards. The cops had not examined them; they had loaded him into the police car in too much of a hurry. He wondered if they would still want to see the cards. He wondered if they were going to ask him his name, or if they really cared.

21

During the weekend the paint was scrubbed from the furniture and walls of Jim Briskin's apartment. The apartment, cleaned up, looked as it had before. Patricia put the easel and brushes and paints away in the closet, and neither of them said anything more about it. He let her do most of the cleaning and washing and scrubbing; in jeans and cotton shirt, her hair tied up in a turban, she sat on the floor, working with soap and water, a bucket, a heavy brush. She did not seem to mind. All day Saturday and Sunday they kept at it. On Sunday evening they invited Frank Hubble over. The three of them drank wine and talked.

"What happened to your hand?" Hubble said.

"I cut it," she said, hiding her hand away.

"Can you type like that?" Hubble said.

"I'll do as well as I can," she said.

Hubble said, "Are you two married again?"

"Not quite," Jim said. "We have the blood tests. We'll pick up the license in a couple of days and then get married. There's no rush."

"You're coming back to work tomorrow?"

"Yes," Pat said. "On Monday."

"How about you?" he said to Jim.

"I'll be back," Jim said. "At the end of the month."

"What happens when they give you a Looney Luke plug to read?"

"I'll read it," he said.

"Why?"

"Because I want to stay on the air."

Beside him Pat shifted about; she drew her legs up and tucked them

239

under her. "Jim is going to expand 'Club 17,' " she said, "so it runs in the evening. He's going to bring it back at eight and keep it going until sign-off."

"If I can," Jim said. "If Haynes can see it."

"You going to spin a lot of rock and roll?" Hubble said. "The networks are starting to clamp down . . . you seen the latest list of banned discs? Mostly the small labels, the race and blues labels. Somebody showed me a BBC statement; they say they don't have a list of banned records, just a list of music they don't play."

"Restricted," Jim said.

"Yes, it's their restricted list. You better be careful on that stuff. You'll get the old ladies writing in. Better stick to the regular bands and tunes."

"Guy Lombardo?" Jim said.

Hubble laughed. "Why not? A lot of people like that sweet stuff; look at Liberace. You'll draw a bigger audience with that. Rock and roll is on its way out. They've got Presley's number; in another six months, nobody'll remember him."

Jim got up and walked across the room to the phonograph. An LP of Bessie Smith had come to an end; he turned the record over. The old ladies, he thought, the same old ladies who had supported his classical music. They would be writing in; they would start the pressure.

By the door of the apartment the bell rang.

"Who's that?" Pat said. "Did you ask anybody else over?" She was still in her jeans and cotton shirt.

Opening the door, Jim looked down the hall. Two shapes appeared. They were Ferde Heinke and Joe Mantila.

"Hey, Mr. Briskin," Ferde said, "the police picked up Art Emmanual."

"What?" he said. The words did not make sense; he tried to get at their meaning.

Ferde said, "They got Grimmelman—you don't know him—and they picked up Art because of this crap somebody threw off a hotel roof on Fillmore Street, and they claim it was some kind of plot the Organization had."

"A gang," Joe Mantila said. "But we don't know nothing about this junk off the roof."

Jim said, "What are they holding him on?"

"I don't know," Ferde said. "Rachael's down there trying to see him. They say he isn't of age, he's a minor, and his parents have to get him out. And his parents don't care. So he's in juvenile hall or something. And they won't let her put up bail because she's a minor too, but she says she's his guardian because they're married."

"It's all fouled up," Joe Mantila said.

"So maybe if you could lend us some dough," Ferde said, "we could take it down and give it to her. And maybe she can get a lawyer or something and get him out. Because they're married, so she ought to be able to get him out, don't you think?"

He gave them the money he had in the apartment. Joe counted it while Pat searched her purses for more.

"Forty bucks," Joe said. "I don't know if that's enough."

Going to the phone, Jim called the station. Bob Posin answered from his office. "If I send two kids around," he said to Posin, "do me a favor and give them some money. It's an emergency."

"How much?" Posin said. "I don't see why I should—"

"Fifty or sixty bucks. I'm good for it."

"You're sure it's an emergency?" Posin said.

"It is," he said. He hung up. "Go over to the station," he said to Ferde and Joe. "She can get a lawyer with a hundred-dollar retainer. I'll get out and try to cash a check."

They thanked him and hurried off.

In the bedroom Pat was changing her clothes. "I want to go with you," she said.

Hubble, his wine glass in his hand, said, "What's this all about?"

"Friends," Jim said. "I'm not going yet," he said to Pat. "What's the name of that lawyer that handled the divorce for us?"

"Toreckey," she said. "I have his number. Here."

He picked up the phone and called Toreckey.

"It might be they could keep him there," Toreckey said. Pat, coming out of the bedroom, stood beside him with her ear to the receiver, listening. "If there's some gang he's been running with, they'll really throw it at him; Chief Ahern is cracking down on those juvenile gangs. This sort of vandalism is exactly what the San Francisco police department is trying to stamp out. Of course, I'm not much involved with these things."

241

Jim said, "This is out of your line?"

"I don't usually handle cases of this sort. But I can give you—"
He thanked Toreckey and hung up.

"We can get somebody else," Pat said.

"No," he said. His head ached, but he was able to think; his thoughts were lucid enough. "She should be doing this, not us. Let's scare up the money."

"Maybe so," Pat said.

The time was eleven-thirty. The streets were deserted. The good people, he thought to himself, were in bed where they belonged.

They have him, he thought, but I can get him away because I have enough money. Or at least I can raise enough money. I can sell my car. I can borrow. Pat can borrow. I can go out and beg if I have to. Sooner or later I'll have enough. So eventually he'll be out.

"I'll go down there," he said to Pat. "To the Kearny Street jail."

"Can't I come?" She followed after him as he got his coat. She had on a blue skirt and bolero, and her face was dark with concern. "Isn't there something I can do?"

He said, "It might be better if I went alone."

"Whatever you say," Pat said. "But—I feel it's my fault."

"Why?" he said, pausing at the door to the hall.

"I don't know."

"It's not your fault," he said.

"This time," she said, "it isn't my fault this time."

"What's this about?" Hubble said. "Some kids steal a car or something?"

Jim left the apartment and went downstairs to his car. While he was warming the engine, Pat appeared beside the window.

"If you won't take me," she said, "I'll drive along after you in my own car."

"Get in," he said, with rage.

She got in next to him, and without waiting for the engine to warm or the windshield to clear, he drove the car forward into traffic.

"Can you see?" Pat said. "Maybe you should wipe off the windows."

A car, a nebulous shape, honked at him. Lights flashed and dazzled; he brought out his handkerchief and scoured the windshield before him. Cold water dripped onto his fingers and wrist.

"Be careful," Pat said.

"Yes," he said, still angry, still shaking. A car materialized in front of him; he tramped down on the brake, and his tires screeched. For an instant the side of the other car rose in the windshield and confronted him, and then it disappeared; the car had got out of his path. Somebody yelled. He had driven through a red light. Slowing down, he pulled over to the side of the street. For a time neither of them spoke.

"If you want," Pat said, "I can drive."

"Maybe I can just sit," he said, "for a second."

"The wind's cold," she said presently. She pressed her coat around her ankles. "It's amazing that in July the weather could be so cold. It must be the fog."

"Okay," he said, "you drive." He got out of the car and came around. Pat slid behind the wheel, and she drove the rest of the trip to Kearny Street.

"Thanks," he said as she parked across the street from the jail.

At the corner, several cars away, a blue pre-war Plymouth was parked. Inside were three figures, one of them a girl.

"I'll stay here," Pat said.

He walked down the sidewalk, and the door of the Plymouth was opened for him. Joe Mantila and Ferde Heinke sat on each side of Rachael.

"Hi," Ferde said.

"You went over to the station?" Jim said, getting into the car.

"Yeah," Joe Mantila said.

"We're waiting for her lawyer," Ferde Heinke said. "He's supposed to be on his way here; she called him."

Rachael said, "Thanks for the money."

"Was it enough?"

"Yes," she said.

"How do you feel?" he said.

"She'll be okay," Joe Mantila said.

Rachael said, "We'll be able to get him out. The police say they won't hold him. I was with him during the evening, and he didn't go outside. So he couldn't have had anything to do with the junk from the hotel roof. But I know they'll get us sooner or later. If not now, then some other time."

"They're going to put Grimmelman in prison," Joe Mantila said. "A felony. Draft evasion. The FBI was after him."

"Did you know that?" Jim asked them.

"No," Ferde Heinke said, "he didn't tell us. But we knew he was scared of something; he had the Horch all ready to go, so he could get away. But he didn't get away."

"That sure was a cool car," Joe Mantila said.

Jim said to her, "What do you think? Was that a good idea?"

"No," she said. "You mean Grimmelman? No, it was a mistake. Because they did get him."

"But if they hadn't."

She said, "They did." Her face was colorless and thin with worry. Her hair hung unevenly against her cheeks and ears. What a little hungry-looking creature, he thought. And the lovely eyes. Black-violet and immense, and the long lashes. He thought: She was afraid, and now I've lived to see that.

I will put whatever I have into this, he thought. I will do the best I can. When they come in and get at this family, then I will fight them. I am upright and full of anger.

Rachael said, "It may be that they're going to say we're not married. We lied about our ages, so maybe they can say it's void. I thought about that. They always have that there, hanging over our heads. When they feel like it, they can use it."

"But you are married," he said.

"Are we?"

"Yes," he said. "You are. You and Art are."

Her face, violently alive, filled out and lost its hollowness. He saw the colors and lines blur; he saw the warmth from inside her. The tremendous warmth. "You think we can get through this?" she said. "You do, don't you?"

He thought: They know you will win. They know they are doomed. You have repudiated their words, their culture and customs and refinement and taste. Their precious things.

And, he thought, I have been forced to take sides. You are our enemy, they said to the kids. We will kill you. We will demolish you. And he said to them: If you are going to fight the kids, you are going to have to take me on, too. Because I am going to stand by them. I am going to see the kids survive you.

***

In January, at two o'clock one morning, Jim Briskin woke with the telephone ringing. Beside him in the bed, Pat stirred and sat up as he reached for the receiver.

"H-h-hey!" Art shouted as he put the receiver to his ear. "Hey, Jim?"

"Is it time?" he muttered. The apartment was pitch-dark and cold. Pat snapped on the lamp. "Now?" he said, rubbing his eyes.

"Yeah, I think so," Art said. "Can you come around?"

He dressed, got in the car, and drove to the house on Fillmore Street.

At the door Art met him. "Yeah," he said desperately, "it's every five minutes."

Entering the apartment, he said, "Rachael?"

She had put on a long, pink-wool robe; she was sitting on the edge of the bed, pushing at her hard pale temples with her hands.

"Yes," she said in a grating voice.

"She's in a lot of pain," Art said, hurrying past him to his wife. "Let's go."

Jim picked her up, robe and all, and carried her out to the car. A few minutes later they were driving in the direction of the hospital.

Later, as he and Art sat in the hospital waiting room, he thought to himself that this was the only time. He had never waited for this; he had never waited while a woman gave birth to a child. From the pay phone he called Pat to tell her how it was going.

"I guess they give them something so they won't feel it," he said to Art, walking back to him.

"Y-y-yeah," Art said.

"But that doesn't help us," he said. It did not take away his own concern. So this, he thought, was how it felt. After a while he said, "That's a sweet wife you have."

Art nodded.

"You're lucky," he said. "I've never seen anybody like her."

Beyond the doors of the hospital a few cars moved in the early-morning darkness. To ease his tension, Jim Briskin walked over and stood with his hands in his pockets.

One of the cars towed behind it a huge white papier-mâché floatlike sign. The car moved inflexibly and the sign followed. On the sign were words, vast words for everyone to read.

Words, he thought. Here, at four o'clock in the morning, with no one up to read, the words were still being towed by. Even here. Still circulating the streets.

For a moment it seemed to him that the sign was a Looney Luke sign. But he was wrong. It was not. Even so, he thought, it might as well have been.

He watched the sign. The words hovered; they remained as long as possible. No, he thought. You can't come in here.

The words began to leave.

Leave, he said.

Slowly the words were gone. He stood at the doors to be sure. And they did not come back. He watched and waited, and they did not come back.